Was he watching?

Yes—Karina could see Alex sitting near his window.

She let her hand drift along her thigh. She could only imagine how sensitive she'd be if it was Alex's hands on her. The pure pleasure would be stupendous.

Several hours had passed since she'd eaten the chocolate and she was still aroused. The effects should have worn off by now, but she remained hot and primed for action. She could think only of getting satisfaction.

She slipped a hand beneath her silk robe, stroking over her ribs, up to one breast. She peeped out between the curtains. Alex was still there, standing with his nose practically pressed to the glass. Trying for a better view, she assumed, gritting her teeth against the impulse to give it to him.

Damn Alex anyway! *He* was supposed to be the one who couldn't control himself. Eventually, though, he would eat one of the chocolates and know the hunger and longing.

Then *she* would be the one in control.

Dear Reader,

I'm a fan of *Chocolat,* both the book and movie versions, so the SEX & CANDY miniseries wouldn't be complete without a chocolate-shop setting...especially one that sells some very special truffles. Those who eat them become extremely amorous!

Shop owner Karina Sutter resists enhancing her love life with the aphrodisiac truffles—until she sets eyes on an alluring mystery man living across the street. Alex Anderson is on the run, his life in danger. But he can't say no to the sweet blonde who shows up on his doorstep with a gift box of truffles....

Happy holidays! May you all get *Unwrapped.*

Carrie Alexander

P.S. Next up, look for the Harlequin Blaze LOCK & KEY trilogy I'm writing with Jamie Denton and Shannon Hollis, coming to you in the first three months of 2005. Check out my book, *Slow Rule,* available in March.

Books by Carrie Alexander

HARLEQUIN BLAZE

20—PLAYING WITH FIRE
114—STROKE OF MIDNIGHT
"Enticing"
147—TASTE ME*

HARLEQUIN TEMPTATION

925—THE CHOCOLATE SEDUCTION*
929—SINFULLY SWEET*

*Sex & Candy

UNWRAPPED

Carrie Alexander

HARLEQUIN®

TORONTO • NEW YORK • LONDON
AMSTERDAM • PARIS • SYDNEY • HAMBURG
STOCKHOLM • ATHENS • TOKYO • MILAN • MADRID
PRAGUE • WARSAW • BUDAPEST • AUCKLAND

ISBN 0-373-79167-4

UNWRAPPED

This edition published by arrangement with Harlequin Books S.A.

www.eHarlequin.com

Printed in U.S.A.

1

"WHAT'S YOUR FAVORITE DIP?" Debby Caruso asked, her brown curls bobbing as she bounded from the kitchen of Sutter Chocolat carrying a tray of triple-dipped strawberries. Each plump berry had been enrobed in layers of white and milk chocolate, then finished off with a sinfully rich coating of the shop's signature brand of dark Swiss chocolate. "I can't quite decide between strawberries and cherries, though I used to favor apricots, for some ungodly reason."

As Karina Sutter opened the display case, she smiled at the telltale juice that had trickled down Debby's round chin. The head confectioner was prone to sampling. "What about banana?"

"Too mushy. I like the squirt of juice in my mouth." Debby slid the tray inside, then set her hands on her ample hips. Her tongue swiped up the trickle. "You'd think I'd have more dates, huh?"

"Especially since you swallow," Karina teased, then reached into the glass-fronted case to straighten the decorative paper lace edging at the front of the tray. She rearranged the back row to cover the gap made by the missing strawberry.

A bemused Debby watched her fuss before closing the door on the display of decadent fruits in their pleated gold paper cups. "Not even tempted to try one? I'll never understand you."

"I may have one for dessert after lunch."

"Me, too, if there are any left by then," said Debby. The triple-dipped strawberries were a fast seller. "That's the difference between us. I'm a double helpings girl and you—you're disciplined." Debby screwed up her face in disgust, betrayed by the generous grin she couldn't contain for long. "You realize that your perfection is very aggravating to the rest of us."

Karina was only half listening, toying with the heavy gold chain at her neck as her gaze shifted outside. "I'll try to do better at being bad."

Debby watched her employer gaze at the upper stories of the apartment building across the street. "Oh, really? He's home? Is today the day?"

Karina backed off. "Maybe not *today*..."

She turned to smile at a customer ogling the marbled chocolate scallop shells, offering the woman a sample. The store handed out a lot of samples. One bite of any of the array of fine chocolates and assorted sweets and most people were hooked. Karina had been accused of being personally responsible for a mass neighborhood weight gain, although the accompanying improvement in her customers' sex lives more than made up for the calories.

"Why not today?" Debby asked. "It's been three weeks."

"I don't want to rush into creating a situation I'll regret."

"What's to regret?" Debby put a hand on Karina's arm and nudged her toward the window, away from the twin cash registers and the workers busily filling orders from the walk-in traffic. The December cold snap hadn't slowed business at all. Nothing went so well with a frosty winter day as sex and chocolate.

"You feed him the chocolates," Debby continued, "you show up at his door naked beneath a trench coat, you have a weekend of fabulous sex."

"Shh." Karina darted a look at the customers, even though it was likely that none of them would be shocked at the titillating talk. In fact, sex was probably foremost on their minds, second only to their chocolate cravings.

Debby lowered her voice. "We're not talking *relationship* here. You want him only for a fling, right? One torrid fling to give you memories that'll keep your bones warm when you're a little old lady married to a little old man who can't get it up without a crane."

Yes, that was what she'd convinced herself that she wanted after her first glimpse of the mystery man, though she'd never put it as colorfully as Debby.

Karina had followed the rules all of her life, aside from one major exception when she'd tossed out her degree and the offer to teach at a prestigious small college to open a chocolate shop instead. Her parents had been dubious, especially as she was taking advantage of the family recipe handed down through the generations. But the shop had become a rousing success as word of mouth spread about the amazing amorous side effect of the chocolate. Before long her supplies and staff could barely keep up with demand.

She was devoted to the shop, as well as making a home from the bi-level apartment above it, newly renovated now that she owned the building. But she was also careful to make time for a proper social life. She took advantage of New York's cultural and sporting amenities. Connections to family and friends were duly maintained. And she'd dated a selection of fine, upstanding young men. Eventually she'd choose one to marry, now that she was approaching thirty, the ideal age to get serious about a husband and children.

However...

Karina pinched the tip of her nose, but there was no distracting her from the plan.

Often, especially during the past several weeks, she'd wished she could be as natural and spontaneous as Debby—and many of her customers, thanks to the cocoa beans that stimulated sexual arousal. But she doubted that it was possible to change her true nature.

Even with the help of the chocolate, even when she was halfway gone with lust for the man who'd recently moved into the building across the street....

Debby, Karina's closest confidante, had been pushing the idea that for once she should take advantage of the secret Sutter family recipe for personal gain. A *very* personal gain.

She was reluctant. Manufacturing an interest from her intended partner seemed cheap. Almost like cheating. Then again...how many opportunities presented themselves so perfectly? She couldn't use the chocolate on any of her male acquaintances, the prospective groom pool. That might lead to a false romance it would be awkward to remove herself from. She didn't want complications. She only wanted...

Hot sex.

Just this one time. Sure, she was naturally a controlled person, but she could be spontaneous. After some thought and planning, granted.

Karina's eyes strayed to the city street outside her shop's window. The mystery stud should be walking by any minute now. He didn't keep to a schedule, but after watching him for three weeks she'd picked up on his tendencies. At some point during the day he went for a walk, frequently returning with a newspaper, a coffee or take-out food, but rarely staying away for more than an hour.

He always returned alone.

She glanced at her watch. Fifty-two minutes and counting since he'd exited the street door of his building.

"It's too complicated," she said to Debby, knowing that she'd get an argument—and probably wanting one. "With him living so close and all. What if the plan goes wrong? I'd still have to see him every day."

"Only from behind a window," Debby replied. "It's not like he ever comes in."

That point had been nagging at Karina. What kind of man could walk by a chocolate shop filled with women exuding obvious carnal appetites and never even hesitate?

Only once had he so much as broken stride—the day that a frequent customer, an adorable blonde, had been away for two weeks without her usual rations. She'd run headlong out of the shop with her mouth full of fudge, practically orgasming with relief right there on the sidewalk. The aphrodisiac effect packed more of a wallop after deprivation. The customer had swooned into the stranger's arms, all feverish and dewy-eyed, babbling about how hot she was. He'd merely set her back on her feet and continued on his way.

"We don't know that it would even work," Karina said. "He seems to have no interest in my chocolate."

Or me. As humiliating as it was to remember, a week ago she'd undone the third button on her blouse and provocatively positioned herself as she rearranged the front window display during his coffee run. Mystery man's eyes had skimmed right over her.

"True, men don't tend to be as susceptible to the secret recipe." Debby wasn't about to let that stop the plan, bless her. "Luckily, I've got a double-strength batch of Black Magic truffles cooling in the kitchen. I'll make you up a gift box. He won't know what hit him, but he'll be grateful forever."

Karina glanced at her fervid patrons. Bright eyes and flushed cheeks prevailed. Those who were new to the shop looked a bit startled at the jittery excitement in the air. "What if this goes the other way, and he becomes addicted?"

"Hmm." Debby pooched out her lips. "What if? You'd end up with a gorgeous guy who wants you day and night. I don't see the problem."

"You know I don't want a romance founded on a trick of chocolate. Besides, this one has no long-term potential. He's a loner and he's unemployed."

"You don't know that for sure."

Karina shrugged. "I've never seen him with another person. He doesn't seem to own a suit or be interested in finding a job. Most of the time, he's home all day." And all night, but she wasn't ready to tell Debby about *that*.

"Maybe he works out of his house, on the computer or something."

"Maybe..." Except that she could see into his apartment from hers, and she'd never noticed him spending much time at the computer. Of course he kept his blinds closed an awful lot, even during the day.

"Doesn't matter anyway. When you've had your fill of his Christmas package, you cut off his supply of chocolate and be done with him."

Karina shook her head. "That's too calculating." Besides, the chocolate was only a stimulant. It couldn't control libidos quite so neatly.

"But that's the point! I can't imagine that he'd have any problem with the plan. Even a grouchy loner won't say no to a blonde who wants to use him as a boy toy."

"I suppose." Karina smoothed her hair, although it didn't need smoothing. She kept it in a tight bun or braided knot at work. "I'll think about it."

Debby rolled her eyes. "Uh-huh. I knew you'd chicken out again."

"I'm not chickening out. I'm—" Karina tilted her nose into the air, trying to suppress a grin. "I'm being careful."

"Yeah, well, be careful you don't wind up delaying so long he gets snagged by one of our customers on an afternoon sugar high."

Karina watched a trio of women rush into the store, along with a draft of cold air from the open door. They stamped their boots and pulled off gloves, hungrily examining the display cases. The avaricious gleam in their eyes said that no man nor truffle was safe from their potent hungers.

Karina was taken aback. "You do have a point."

Debby knew when to let Karina ferment in her own juices. She returned to the original topic—dipping fruit. "Since strawberries are out of season, I'm planning to switch to pears for the holidays. Strictly fresh. Dipped in dark or milk chocolate and topped with a dollop of custard. Except that wouldn't be very portable. Caramel, you think? That might work."

Karina let Debby's musings slide over her. She didn't need to respond except to offer an encouraging murmur now and then. The head confections chef was worth double her weight in cocoa beans.

While Sutter Chocolat had been prosperous from the start, business had tripled in the past three years under the combination of Debby's brilliance in the kitchen and Karina's painstaking management. They now had two full-time workers behind the counter, another to answer phones and handle shipping and deliveries, a handful of part-timers who filled in as needed, plus the kitchen staff. Each employee had been selected with utmost care, as they had to be entrusted to handle the secret supplies and knowledge of a recipe that would be worth a fortune to the big candy makers.

With the steady flow of revenue, Karina could have easily expanded into a chain of stores or a mail-order business, but that would have gone too far against the family's preference for moderation. The secret recipe was not meant for mass consumption on a grand scale. Nor were there enough of the rare, ultra-expensive cocoa beans—grown only on a western-facing slope in the shadow of a remote Brazilian mountain—to handle such volume.

"I'll experiment with the different varieties," Debby rambled on. "Anjou might do. I'm not so sure how well pear slices will keep and I can't bring myself to go the dehydrated route...."

"No worries. We'll sell them fresh every day, like the strawberries." A pedestrian caught Karina's eye—a head of dark brown hair moving above the rest of the crowd. She leaned toward the front window, bracing herself on the display counter. *Yes. It was him.*

Oh, yes.

He was striding along the opposite side of the street,

oblivious to the wintry weather with a gray scarf dangling around his neck and a long brown leather coat flapping open in the breeze. Tall, tanned, fit—by the looks of him, no one would ever guess he was a mole who spent most of his days huddled in a closed-up apartment.

Not for the first time, Karina mulled over where he'd come from. A tropical climate would be her first guess, though he didn't look like an island bum except on the surface, with the deep tan, the ruff of overgrown mahogany hair that sported natural highlights, and the way he usually managed to have a five o'clock shadow by noon.

Otherwise, there was a restlessness about him. His gaze roved, rarely lighting, always sharp as flint. He never smiled. The somber mouth and hollow cheeks spoke of an intriguing air of experience. A city vibe, not an island one.

Merely the sight of him gave Karina interesting tingles, and she'd had only one nibble of a new employee's molded ganache medallions that morning, so she certainly couldn't blame her arousal on the chocolate.

"There he is," she murmured to Debby. She sighed. "*That's* my favorite dip."

Debby chuckled. "How would you know until you've sampled him?"

"I just know. He's delicious."

Surprisingly, the man didn't return directly to his building, but veered off to cross the street, nimbly dodging traffic with one hand raised to stave off a cabbie blaring his horn.

"He's coming this way," Debby said.

A hot self-awareness flushed through Karina, especially as she realized that she'd walked out from behind the counter toward the windows without realizing it. She wadded her apron in stricken hands. "Oh, no. He can't. I'm not ready."

They scrambled to get her out of the linen apron with eyelet trim. "Knot's too tight," Debby said, working on it.

"Over the head." Karina pulled the apron up past her face, but the tie had been crisscrossed twice around her waist and it caught beneath her breasts. She tugged. Her blouse pulled out of the waistband of her skirt. "Help."

"I'll get scissors." Debby bustled away to search the supply shelves hidden below the display cabinet.

Karina gave another yank and the apron popped past her breasts. She ripped it off over her head, only to discover that the man was directly outside the shop window, looking inside as he walked by. More than looking. Staring wide-eyed.

She was so startled by his unusual interest that she stood stock still. Strands of loosened hair floated around her face, her clothes were in disarray and the crumpled apron hung off her left shoulder and arm.

For once, his gaze didn't skim her. He didn't halt either, but he continued to stare directly at her, his stride slowing as his eyes ignited her with their intense, lingering appreciation.

Karina went hot, then cold, then even hotter as her skin was shot with prickling needles of arousal. She blinked once and the man was gone.

And there was Debby, wincing. She waggled a finger. "Uh, your blouse..."

What about it? Karina's head floated like a helium balloon until she put a hand up and touched skin. *Pop.* Her blouse—

Was hanging open.

Wide open, in an inverted *V*. All but the top button had come undone when she was struggling to get the apron off over her head. The mystery man hadn't been looking at *her*; he'd been leering over her breasts, almost fully exposed by the lace-trimmed cups of a dainty demilune bra.

Stunned, Karina looked down. Her nipples were as hard as bullets. Worse, they peeped over the lace edging, winking naughtily at the passersby.

She grabbed both sides of the blouse and wrapped them across her torso. "Oh, God."

Debby chortled. "You sure have his attention now."

"This is terrible." Karina tossed a weak grin at the gawking customers and quickly slipped behind the counter, heading for the swinging doors that led to the back of the store and the kitchen and office areas. On the way through the first short corridor, she shook free of the apron, clutching it to her chest, needing the extra covering.

"He saw *everything*," she said to Debby, who followed her into her private office, past a startled Janine Gardner, the young woman who'd been recently hired as their receptionist and shipping clerk.

Debby shut the door on Janine's inquisitive stare. "Aw, hell, Kare. Maybe not." She gave her employer's shoulder a comforting rub. "I mean, your blouse was sort of draped open across your breasts, so…"

"But my arms were raised." Karina dropped the apron on her desk, then lifted her arms, letting the blouse hang open again from its lone button. Hard to tell how much of her had been exposed, except that when she'd looked down the first time, it had seemed like plenty. More than enough to attract the attention of even a detached, brusque loner.

She collapsed into the chair behind her desk. "This is just *terrible.*"

Debby eased into the visitor's chair. "Not really."

"I flashed him!"

"And he enjoyed it."

Karina nudged her breasts deeper into the bra cups where they belonged. She didn't normally go around with her nipples out. The struggle with the apron must have lifted them an inch or two, just enough to poke out of the skimpy bra.

At the most inopportune moment. She mentally cringed while rebuttoning her blouse.

"You know what?" Debby said. "Putting aside your embarrassment, this might be the best thing that could have happened." She waved off Karina's flustered denial. "Look at it this way—he's *got* to be thinking about you now. Probably even fantasizing." Debby smirked. "You have great tits."

Karina groaned.

"They're so perky. Mine are, you know—" Debby stretched the scoop neck of her neon-pink top and peered into her deep cleavage "—pendulous."

"I'm pretty sure men prefer pendulous."

"Sometimes." Debby smiled. Regardless of the contemporary preference for skinny, she was not neurotic about her voluptuous figure. She frequently said that being thin wasn't worth giving up chocolate.

Karina envied her friend's confidence in herself. She diligently worked to maintain her weight through diet and exercise, which was also a good thing. Just not very freeing. "I don't care if he liked them. I never intended to—"

"Put 'em on display?"

"I'm humiliated." Karina squeezed her eyes shut. "I can't face him now."

"You have to. As soon as possible."

She shook her head. "Oh, no. No. Absolutely not."

"But he's thinking about you. Wanting you."

"Probably thinking I must be desperate. Wanting me to leave him alone."

"I really doubt that. And I'm sure he realized that you didn't mean to flash him. He had to have seen you trying to get the apron off."

Karina cracked an eye. "You think?"

"Yep. And I *know* you, Kare. You're gonna use this as an excuse to retreat for another month." Debby stood and slapped her palms on the desk. "I won't allow it. I'm going to the kitchen right now and putting together that assortment of truffles. Get your coat on. You're delivering them personally."

Karina pressed a couple of fingers to her mouth. "I can't."

"Sure you can."

"No, I mean—" She searched for an obstacle that Debby would accept. Other than her personal humiliation. "I don't know his name. Even if I can get in, there's no way I'm knocking on the door of every apartment in his building. That would be so obvious there'd be no doubt remaining about how desperate I am."

"Like I said, I never met the man who cared, but you do have a point." Calmly, Debby walked behind the desk and flicked on Karina's computer. "Take me to the store's customer list please."

Karina typed in a password to access the protected files and called up the database. "He's not a customer."

"But Annie Rittenouer is, and she lives in the same

building. I bet she'll know who our mystery man is and what apartment he lives in."

"Oh." Karina frowned. "Um, wait. Do we really want to ask Annie? She's the chatty middle-aged woman with short bleached hair, right? The one who sends her husband over for a new supply of peanut clusters every Friday morning."

"That's Annie." Debby scrolled to the *R*s and read out the customer's number as she lifted the desk phone and dialed. Karina made frantic motions and grabbed the phone away as a woman's voice said, "Hello, hello?"

"Good day, Mrs. Rittenouer. This is Karina from Sutter Chocolat, calling to tell you that we're running a holiday sale for our regular customers. Twenty-five percent off peanut clusters, today only."

Karina hushed Debby while the customer made ecstatic noises. "Oh, really? Your favorite? Shall we have a box delivered on account? My pleasure, ma'am. Thank you."

"But you didn't get any information," Debby said when Karina hung up.

"I'm into the building. That's enough. I'd rather keep the rest of it quiet."

"Then you're actually going?" Debby was clearly surprised by Karina's initiative.

"I'm going." An intoxicating flutter in the pit of her stomach made Karina pinch the end of her nose to sober herself. *Toughen up. It's only a sexual attraction, not a peace treaty at Versailles.* "Because you're right. It's now or never."

"Now. Absolutely." Debby clapped her hands and squeaked a *yippee* sound before she swung around in the small office, reaching for the knob. "Give me five minutes."

"No hurry."

"Yes, hurry. There will be no backing out." Debby threw open the door, catching Janine hovering. "Back to your desk, missy," she said, sailing by with the tails of her apron flapping.

Janine's nose twitched. "Can I help you with anything, Ms. Sutter?"

"Thank you, no. Oh, wait—how about getting me a receipt slip from one of the girls at the front? I have a special delivery to make to Mrs. Rittenouer across the street."

"Right away, Ms. Sutter."

Karina watched Janine hustle away. The new employee had come with impeccable letters of recommendation from the sweets division of Royal Foods. The connection to big business had made Karina hesitate, but Janine had professed a wish to learn candy-making at a more intimate scale, where quality was most important. She was always eager to please and had exhibited a strong curiosity about every aspect of the business. One day, she might make a good assistant manager.

Karina brushed the thought aside, for a time when she would want to spend less hours at work, like when she had a husband and children to keep her occupied. That was suddenly a more distant prospect than it had been.

There was room for only one man in her head. And it was a shock to remember that she didn't even know his name. She really was crazy for doing this.

But, wow, the risk was giving her quite a rush. Maybe she should have jumped out of the box years ago.

Debby and Janine both arrived at once, bumping into

each other at the office door. "Got your truffles," Debby said, holding the signature copper-metallic box high.

Janine gave her shoulders a twist. "Here's the receipt." She surveyed the box with skepticism. "Doesn't Mrs. Rittenouer always buy peanut clusters?"

Debby's smile was acid. She thought Janine was a suck-up and had no compunction about telling Karina so. "Thanks, but you can go now. I've got this handled. The girls are preparing an order of peanut clusters as we speak."

"Of course." Janine returned to her desk, properly chastised even though the tic near her eyes said otherwise. She'd sworn the twitch came from her new contact lenses, but it only showed up when she was irritated or nervous.

Debby shut the door with an emphatic clap.

"You have to stop the squabbling with Janine," Karina said absently, busy filling out the receipt. "It doesn't make for a happy work environment."

"Never mind that. This is for you."

A dark chocolate espresso truffle appeared on the desk blotter. Karina looked up at Debby with surprise. "I don't need that…yet."

"I think you do. For courage."

Karina poked at the luscious candy with her pen. "It's not courage I'll be feeling after a double-strength Black Magic truffle." The sinfully rich treats were another of Debby's inventions. The dense chocolate centers were infused with a variety of flavors from champagne to mandarin orange, but it was the unique cocoa beans that gave the hefty tidbit its incredible *oomph.* Word was, one truffle could result in an entire evening of passion.

Or several hours of intense frustration.

"Eat it," Debby said.

Karina took a deep breath. "I don't want to waste the effect. We have to give mystery man time to eat a few of the truffles I deliver. Once he's good and worked up, then I'll—" She swallowed reflexively. "I'll take my medicine."

A hoot of laughter came from Debby. "Medicine! Gawd, Kare—I know women who'd kill for these truffles."

Karina caught her lower lip between her teeth, hesitating. She shook her head. "I realize that, but I'm afraid of what will happen if I go over there all hyped up. I might become too aggressive and that's not me."

"You keep forgetting, that's the whole idea." Debby pushed the truffle closer, leaving a trail of cocoa powder on the blotter. "You have this great power at your disposal. Use it, woman."

"It's too soon. I could end up, you know, jumping his bones."

"Exactly. But I don't think so. If it was me, yeah. But you're resistant to the effects because of your inhib—um, your discipline. One truffle should give you just the right amount of daring to see this plan through."

"That makes sense," admitted Karina. She didn't consider herself inhibited. Particularly not in light of the past several weeks and the provocative game she'd been playing with her new neighbor. There were just some things that should be private, a concept Debby didn't always understand.

At the same time, she needed every impetus she could get if she really, truly wanted to go through with this crazy ploy.

And *that* was the real question. *Did she?*

Something inside her answered without hesitation. A newly brazen part of herself that she'd always contained.

I do.

"Go on," Debby urged. "Call it chocolate courage."

In what seemed like slow motion, Karina reached for the round truffle. Temptation exemplified. Beneath the liberal dusting of cocoa powder and cinnamon, the glossy chocolate was so dark it was almost black, swirled into a curlicue on top. Her mouth watered with anticipation.

The generous mound was weighty as she lifted it to her lips. She parted them, her tongue seeking the first silken taste. The heady aroma filled her nostrils as she gave the truffle a lick, then bit into it. Her teeth pierced the shell, sinking into the dense espresso filling that was so rich and flavorful she almost swooned as it coated her taste buds.

"'S goooood," she said through the sweet mouthful. Her eyes closed as she savored the candy to the fullest before swallowing and taking another bite. The Black Magic truffle was the shop's most intense treat and was sold for a hefty price, singly or in various sized boxes. Not to gouge the customers, but to keep them from overindulging.

Karina popped the last bite into her mouth. Already, she was dizzy with a chocolate buzz. Soon, magnified by the secret recipe, the wondrous side effects would begin—the rush of euphoria, the flush of warmth, the growing, spreading hunger that would seep beneath her skin until she was itchy with the desire to rub herself against a hard male body, her supersensitized nerve endings producing a rosy glow that would signal an open invitation to her chosen mate.

Under normal circumstances, Debby would have been correct about Karina's resistance to the chocolate aphrodisiac. But this time, when she was already ripe with teasing and flirtation, Karina knew that the truffle would take her to an unexplored fever pitch of longing.

She licked the last smears of chocolate and cocoa powder from her fingers.

Get ready, stranger. I'm coming over to screw your brains out.

Yikes. That simply wasn't like her. Had to be the cocoa beans talking.

2

MUFFLED IN A WOOLEN COAT, gloves and a knit hat with ear flaps, Karina went to the corner to cross the street at the traffic light. Obeying the jaywalking rules gave her a few extra minutes to pull herself together, but the rolling warmth inside said that wasn't going to happen, no matter how much time she took. Her stomach felt like a dryer on high, going round and round and getting hotter and hotter.

Nervousness. But also the hunger. The *lust.*

She shouldn't have eaten that truffle.

The pedestrian light switched on and the small group surged off the snowy curb, carrying Karina in their momentum. She kept her gaze fixed on the fur trim on the hat of a squat woman in front of her, avoiding eye contact with nearby males, should she become attracted to one of them, or vice versa. Maybe she was overreacting. The Sutter recipe wasn't supposed to be *that* potent. Their chocolate was a sexual booster, not a skyrocket.

Even so, Karina wasn't taking any chances.

Except this one, she silently added, stopping in front of the mystery man's narrow stone-block building. Stamping her boots, she looked it over. A men's clothing store occupied the ground floor, but above it were six stories of residential units. She knew that her guy lived in a third-floor apartment that overlooked the street, so that would narrow the search a lot. Going to him was risk enough; it would be disaster to end up at the wrong place.

She glanced at the Sutter Chocolat storefront, decorated for the winter with a garland of cedar entwined with a string of red lights. Debby stood watch at the window, poised behind the holiday display in her white apron, urging Karina on.

She shooed Debby away. This was getting too much like school, when she and her girlfriends had schemed over how to attract boys' attention but rarely followed through with their plans. She hoped mystery man wasn't looking out his windows again and observing the entire procedure.

The door to the lobby was open. Karina peered through the iron grate over the glass before entering. The space was no more than eight feet square—just big enough for two bodies, a bank of mailboxes and an intercom system. She studied the name labels, looking for ones that appeared newly applied. Apartment 302B had no label at all. Right floor. Had to be him.

Karina juggled the two small Sutter gift bags she'd brought along, then reached up to press the buzzer for apartment 206D. Annie Rittenouer answered with a "Yeah?"

"Karina Sutter, with your delivery."

"Hot damn. C'mon up."

The inner door buzzed. Karina grabbed it with a gloved hand and quickly jogged up the steps, concentrating on breathing evenly despite the tumbling excitement inside her.

Mrs. Rittenouer lived on the backside of the second

floor. She was waiting with the door open and eagerly snatched the bag Karina offered. "Thank God you had a sale because I'm addicted to these darn things and I've already run out of my week's supply," the peroxide blonde said in a gravelly smoker's voice, looking as if she'd be shoving the candy in her mouth before the door was closed. She signed the receipt without double-checking the total. "My Jackie complains about the cost, but I know how to shut him up." Tittering, she backed into the apartment and swung the door shut.

"Enjoy your chocolates," Karina said.

The door opened and Mrs. Rittenouer stuck her head out. "I don't know what you put in these, but don't ever stop."

Karina nodded. "Thank you for your business, ma'am. Happy holidays."

The woman had her nose stuck in the gift bag, inhaling the chocolate fumes. "They will be now."

Certain that Mrs. Rittenouer would run out of the peanut clusters long before Christmas arrived in several weeks, Karina turned and headed for the stairs. Music blasted from one of the second-floor apartments, but no one appeared to ask about her business in the building. She climbed to the next floor, growing moist inside her winter coat. Her skin felt feverish. The truffle packed quite a punch.

At the third-floor landing, she stopped to unbutton the coat and remove her gloves. Merely the chance that she'd get to touch the object of her desire with a bare fingertip set off a new round of tingling excitement.

"These truffles had better work on *him,*" she muttered, searching the doors for 302B, "or I'll be hurting for sure."

The hall cricked to the left, forming a nook where she found the correctly numbered door. She put her ear near it, hoping for a clue about the occupant.

Nothing. Mr. Anonymous *would* be the silent type.

Karina aimed a finger at the doorbell. *I can't do this,* her mind said, but her thrumming body had another idea. When she closed her eyes to summon her daring, an image of the mystery man rose up, accompanied by a fresh surge of lust. She remembered the one scorching instant when the attractive stranger's eyes had connected with hers, the very moment when his interest had seemed reciprocated.

She blinked. Of course, that had been before she knew that her blouse was open, before she'd consumed the intoxicating truffle.

Even so, she wanted to feel that way again.

Do it.

A RUSH OF FEAR streaked through Alex Anderson when the doorbell rang, simultaneous with a shot of adrenaline that had him out of his chair and on his feet before the *dong* after the *ding* had died. He despised the fear, as familiar as it was. The adrenaline was okay. He'd learned how to channel it for his benefit. Self-defense and split-second reactions were all about adrenaline.

He stood in the middle of the living room, waiting, telling himself that he wasn't overreacting. The excessive caution could one day save his life, just as a moment of inattention had almost lost it.

Several seconds later, the bell rang again. He hadn't buzzed anyone up, so he had no intentions of answering.

He went to the window, sliding a finger between the tattered blind and the window casing so he could see the street below. Nothing suspicious at first glance, but he searched the faces carefully while keeping himself hidden. Even the most innocuous pedestrian could be lethal.

His gaze went to the buildings across the street, looking for a sniper, a lookout, anything out of the ordinary at all. There was no sign of trouble, but that meant nothing. It was too soon after the attempt on his life in the Florida Keys to allow himself to believe that he was safe.

Briefly, his glance landed on the row of windows that had been his worst distraction of late. The woman who lived there…

He shook his head, dislodging the alluring images. He couldn't afford to let his guard down.

The doorbell rang a third time, followed by a sharp *knock, knock, knock.* His visitor wasn't giving up.

Alex moved silently into the small foyer. When the knocking started again he put his eye to the peephole.

What the hell? It was *her.*

The woman from the windows, from the sweetshop. The untouchable blonde princess who'd become, with one inadvertent flash of her breasts, the woman he most wanted to touch.

She was harmless, but a very wicked distraction. He'd have to get rid of her, fast. And irrevocably.

He slipped off the chain and flicked the dead bolt, throwing the door open with a snarl that could have peeled paint. "What do you want?"

Surprise flashed across her face. She stepped back. "I'm sorry to bother you."

Alex scaled back the attitude. What had he become? A miserable heel who frightened pretty women with roses in their cheeks.

"Sorry," he said. "I wasn't expecting company."

She gave him a wary look, hesitating for a couple of seconds before she responded. He almost caved when she licked her lips, leaving them shiny pink and looking impossibly tender. "Uh, I was making a delivery in the building, so I thought it would be neighborly to—give you—" She faltered, couldn't seem to find any words, and held out a small gift bag instead of explaining.

He stared as if a rattlesnake dangled from her fingers. "What is it?"

"Chocolates."

"I don't eat chocolates."

"You'll like these."

He peered into the bag. A fluff of green tissue paper concealed the contents. He wasn't all that suspicious of the offering. He'd been observing Sutter Chocolat since he'd moved in and had no doubts about its legitimacy, but the defenses he'd developed in the past couple of years weren't easily cracked. Even by a spun-sugar confection of a woman who couldn't possibly be any danger to him, except as an attractive nuisance.

Which could be as big a mistake as any other, considering the death threat hanging over his head.

"Truffles," she said. Ignoring his scowl, she smiled. "The best you'll ever taste."

He studied her face, rattled by the experience of seeing her up close. She was a classic beauty with large toffee-colored eyes that tilted up at the corners, a long, narrow nose and those incredible edible lips.

On the other hand, one of her eyebrows arched higher than the other, unbalancing the perfect face. She wore a goofy striped hat that covered the hair he knew to be blond. Two fuzzy pom-poms dangled at the end of yarn strings tied in a bow at the top of her head.

The pom-poms brushed her flushed cheek when she tilted her head and shoved the bag at him. "You have to try them."

He pulled back. Why did she sound so urgent?

She blinked. "Excuse me. I didn't introduce myself. I'm Karina Sutter. I own the chocolate shop across the—"

"I know who you are." His gaze went to her breasts. He forced it back up.

The becoming pink glow turned into ruddy splotches of embarrassment. She gave an awkward laugh, clearly appalled by the incident regardless of her surprise appearance on his doorstep. "Yes. Ahem. About that—"

Alex shrugged. "It was nothing."

Her eyes narrowed. "Nothing?"

"I mean—I didn't see..." Of their own volition, his eyes dropped again to the front of the blouse that showed beneath her open coat. The same blue blouse that he'd last seen gaping open over a tantalizingly sheer bra. Until the moment when she'd mistakenly flashed him, he hadn't understood why women spent ridiculous amounts on sexy undergarments, but one look at the pink tips of her breasts set off by lace and, well, he'd suddenly become a believer.

"I didn't see much," he said. Only enough to make him want to worship at her feet.

Her smile wavered. "My buttons got stuck on my apron and as I was pulling it off—" She stopped, seeing that his face remained impassive, as if he didn't care one way or the other. She'd never know the effort that took.

She let out a little sigh. "Let's pretend that didn't happen, okay? We can start again." She switched the bag to her left hand and held out the other for a shake. "Karina Sutter. And you?"

"Alex." The lie came easily, so similar to Lex, the nickname he'd grown up with, that he could react without having to stop and think *Oh, yeah, that's my false name.* Then again, he'd gone by Chris in Big Pine Key and that hadn't stopped them from finding him.

Karina's hand hung in the air. Her left eyebrow inched even higher.

"Anderson," he said, reluctantly taking her hand. "Alex Anderson."

He would have let go immediately, but she clung, her slender fingers curling toward his palm, moving in a subtle, sensuous dance that made him prickle with awareness.

His jaw clenched. *Sonovabitch.* The princess wasn't so untouchable after all. She was coming on to him.

He stared, trying to read her again because apparently his first impressions had been way off if she was really asking for what he thought she wanted with those flirtatious fingers of hers.

After three weeks of observation, he'd believed that she was a rather normal single woman who put in long hours at her store and kept her personal life in neat order. She was prettier than average, but possibly lonely nevertheless, considering the restless way she moved around her apartment at night. There was a unique aura about her—serene, gentle, gracious—but she'd also seemed distant, like the golden-haired angel atop a Christmas tree. Now and then he'd wondered if she knew he was watching since she seemed to lurk near the windows almost as often as he did, yearningly alone, waiting for something to happen.

Looked like her idea of *something* was far different than his. He prided himself on his ability to read people and would have bet a thousand bucks of his dwindling life savings that she wasn't the type to arrive on his doorstep with a come-on. The error in judgment bothered him.

The contact of their handshake had lingered too long. Her eyes flickered uncertainly before her lids dropped, veiling her thoughts as she withdrew her hand from his grasp. "You don't have a label on the board downstairs," she said in a husky voice. She looked at him through her lashes, resuming the flirtation with a provocative curve of her lips. "For your name."

"I'm a private person." *Hunted like a dog.*

She held out the bag again, squirming a little as she rubbed her thighs together. He wondered if she had to go to the bathroom. "A gift, to welcome you to the neighborhood," she said.

This time he took the offering. "Yeah. Thanks."

Suddenly she swept off her knit hat, straightening up and throwing her head back. "Black Magic truffles," she said with an air of command, leaning toward him with an intense focus. "One of my shop's specialties. I *insist* you try one."

He reached into the bag and pulled out a small copper box, the lid embossed with a complicated design centered around an ornate letter *S*. "I'll be sure to do that."

She pressed forward to lift the lid, forcing him to back up a step into his apartment. "Delicious," she said. But her eyes weren't on the contents of the box, an assortment of a half dozen round truffles nestled in pleated cups.

She was looking at *him*—with a noticeable hunger showing in luminous eyes framed by dark gold lashes.

She even licked her lips, sliding the tip of her tongue between them in a deliberately sexual way.

He had the distinct feeling that if he invited her inside, they'd be tumbling naked onto his bed within minutes. For one fantasy-filled moment, he considered letting that happen. It was months since he'd been with a woman. The last time had been unsatisfying—a brief, meaningless relationship in Florida that he'd known from the start could never go anywhere even though he'd been trying to build a regular life. He'd pegged Karina as the serious-relationship type.

Evidently his impression had been wrong. She wasn't so distant after all.

"Invite me in and I'll share them with you," she said, her color deepening again. She brushed a restless hand over the front of her blouse, slipping her fingers into her open collar and caressing the hollow of her throat.

No mistaking that body language.

"Uh..." Alex stood his ground, even when she advanced to within a couple of inches of him. He was *not* letting her into his apartment.

But he wanted her. With a swift, strong passion that was matched only by his instinct for self-preservation.

He'd let go of so much that he'd mistakenly believed there was nothing left to lose. This woman, though...she was offering him the world. Contact, closeness, comfort. He ached for all of that. And the prospect of an hour or two of hot lovin' with a needy blonde wasn't bad, either.

Maybe *too* needy?

She'd lifted her gold chain necklace to her mouth and

was absently running the chunky links against her teeth. With a rising temperature, he watched the links disappear between her lips, then slip out from the side of her mouth. When she saw his interest, she dropped the chain and purred, "I need something to nibble on. Are you willing…"

Ready, willing and able. More than she'd ever know.

"…to share?" She plucked a truffle from the box and bit into it, closing her eyes in ecstasy. "Mmm. Raspberry vodka. You don't know what you're missing."

Oh, yes, I do.

He stood silently, watching with a melting resistance while she finished the chocolate, making little moaning sounds of enjoyment that could easily have been mistaken for sexual pleasure. She was close enough that he could feel her body heat. The warmth mingled with the scents of rich chocolate and her light perfume to further weaken his resolve.

He couldn't take much more of this. He had to get her out of here.

She popped her thumb into her mouth to lick it clean, then looked up at him again. "Take just one taste," she coaxed. Her lips puckered. "I brought them over for you, special."

She reached for the box to select another candy and he pulled it away. "I can't—"

"Why not?"

He could have explained that he was mildly allergic to chocolate. The last time he'd had some his lips had swelled like a blowfish and he'd been hit with a short but fierce headache. Except that getting into a real conversation, especially one that revealed personal information, would only encourage her. And, of course, prolong his torment.

He had to get rid of her *now.* Being rude was the only way to do it.

"Thanks for the candy," he said, clapping the lid back on the box and nudging her over the threshold, "but I'm not buying the rest of it." He laid a hand on her shoulder to turn her, then dropped it to her behind and boosted her away from the door.

"Hey." She whirled, resisting. "What do you—"

He shut the door in her face.

A sound of outrage came from the other side, followed by a thud. Then nothing.

Alex put his eye to the peephole. A microscopic Karina was standing where he'd left her, staring dumbly at his door. She pressed both hands to her cheeks, briefly covering her eyes, then gave the end of her nose a hard pinch.

"Well, that was embarrassing," she said in a conversational tone, then jammed her hat on her head and stomped off.

He let out a breath of relief that she'd given up so easily. Safe again.

Lonely, too, he realized as he returned to the sparse living room of the sublet apartment. He tossed the box of truffles on a scratched desk, one of the few furnishings the leaseholder had left behind, and went to the window. With a snap of the blind, he had a clear view of Karina as she emerged from the building a minute later, moving briskly along the street, the silly little pom-poms swinging at the back of her head.

Regret gnawed at him. If he'd been another man…

Hell, he'd be getting on her if he'd been the man he

once was—Mark Lexmond, firebrand defense attorney at an up-and-coming firm, known as Lex to most acquaintances and all his friends, an idealistic fighter for justice who drove a red convertible with a surfboard sticking out the back, "owned" a corner booth at La Caridad and played drums in a weekend band called The Curl.

But Mark Lexmond was dead.

So were his other identities—Pete Rogers and Chris McGraw—assigned by California's Witness Protection Program as administered by the U.S. Marshals.

Pete had been a stopgap identity while he waited for the justice system to investigate the tangled mess of threats and murder instigated by a notorious crime kingpin named Rafael Norris. A year earlier, Norris's son had been killed in a drug deal gone bad. Lex had been assigned as the defendant's lawyer. He'd helped broker a deal with the federal authorities to reduce his client's charge from second-degree murder to manslaughter. The deal and the reduced charge had enraged Norris, who had sworn vengeance in the name of his son. Soon afterwards, the defendant had turned up dead. Since Lex was next on the list, the Marshals swooped in.

Chris McGraw was supposed to be his permanent name. Strange at first, but after a while he'd settled into his new identity in Florida as a loner with no family ties. He'd found a job as a bartender at a waterfront dive that reminded him of home, rented a bungalow hidden by palmettos. He'd begun to lead a seminormal life. Eventually he'd let his guard down, allowed a few simple pleasures back into his life. And then…

His mind skipped over those last bloody, terrifying hours in Florida.

Maybe it was only paranoia, but the attempt on his life in Big Pine Key had led him to suspect corruption in the Witness Protection Program. Unwilling to trust the system, he'd dumped all contact with the U.S. Marshals and had gone out on his own.

Even so, there was no telling how long Alex Anderson would survive. The huge population of New York City made him feel anonymous and safe, but all it would take to have him moving on was one slipup, one small sign that he'd been tracked down. A loitering pedestrian, an unexpected knock at the door, a stranger showing too much interest in his past…

A stranger showing too much interest, period.

Not that he suspected Karina Sutter of devious intent. Still, welcoming her into his bed would be a monumental mistake.

Lex—*Alex*, he reminded himself—jammed his hands into his jeans pockets, too aware of the thickening at his groin. She'd invade his dreams tonight, as she had most other nights, all golden and pink and cream and heated whispers of enticement, but that was good. Frustrating, but good. Anything was better than the nightmare images he usually suffered.

Cold comfort, he thought, following Karina's progress as a scattering of snowflakes drifted from the sky. At the door to Sutter Chocolat, she turned to glance up at his building before going inside.

He couldn't see the expression in her eyes, but he knew that she'd glimpsed him at the window. Her stance stiffened, as if she were taking a deep breath to control her emotions. Longing clutched at his gut.

He yanked the blind back over the window before she could sense his reaction and decide to try again. Saying no the first time had been extremely difficult. Turning down a second offer might be impossible.

And deadly.

"WHAT HAPPENED?" Debby said.

Karina walked by, jerking her gloves off finger by finger. She looked at her bare hands for a moment—they were shaking—and wished that she could wrap them around Alex Anderson's neck…or cock.

His *cock?* Another surge of hot blood rose toward her face. What was going on with her? She did *not* think that way!

Blame the truffles, she decided. But a voice inside her head said, *That man. His fault.*

She moaned. "I'm in trouble."

"What? How?" Debby was flustered. "Did you meet the mystery man? Did you make a date?"

They went into Karina's office and closed the door. Karina ripped off her coat, hoping to satisfy herself by removing only one layer. Her clothing felt unbearably heavy and itchy on her skin.

She took a deep breath to quiet her drumming heart, but the air caught in her chest. She was all out-of-sorts inside. Nothing working right. "His name is Alex Anderson and he shut his door in my face."

"No," Debby breathed.

"Yes."

"What did he say?"

"Almost nothing. I gave him the chocolates, he gave me his name, we shook hands. Then I threw myself at him—"

"No."

In spite of Karina's own disbelief over her rash actions, she was annoyed. Did Debby have to sound so totally shocked? Sure, she wasn't a femme fatale, but she wasn't a vanilla pudding, either. She had sex appeal. Just not the *obvious* kind.

Hah. That was ironic when she remembered how she'd stroked Alex's hand, her orgasmic consumption of the truffle....

"I ate one of his truffles."

Debby's mouth squared into a visual *uh-oh.* "Why did you do that?"

"He wasn't responsive. I was trying to get him to take a bite, and before I knew it I'd eaten an entire truffle by myself." Karina ran her hands over her hips and thighs. Her skin felt so aroused, as if she were a cat and Alex had caused all her hackles to rise.

"You shouldn't have done that. They were double strength."

"I know." *I can feel it.*

Although part of her wondered if her reaction to Alex was due to more than just the chocolate.

Debby arched a wary look at Karina as she fretfully undid another button on her blouse and opened the collar wide, sliding her fingers beneath a bra strap and pushing it over her shoulder. "What are you doing?"

"Nothing. I'm just so...constricted."

Debby grimaced. "Do you have a vibrator?"

"A what?"

"A vi-ber-ate-her."

"Debby!" Karina fanned her hot face. "No, I don't."

"Cripes. Why not? Do you have an electric toothbrush?"

"Oh please."

"Well, it's either that or get kinky with a clothes washer."

"I'm not interested in dating my appliances. I'll just—" Karina slumped into her desk chair, but she couldn't sit still for long before she had to squirm again. "I'll ride it out. The effects can't last that long."

"Uh," Debby said.

"What?"

"Do you remember Rog Horowitz?"

"No."

"The one who dumped me because he was embarrassed about the broken nose."

"Oh, yeah." Karina's eyes widened. "You're telling me you used the chocolate on him?"

"Rog didn't have much staying power. I fed him a double dose of the Black Magic truffles after dinner one night. We were at my place, so I thought we'd be safe. Well, Rog was so impressed with the surge of energy that he wanted to try a gymnastic maneuver, which was not a good idea for a man of two hundred and fifty pounds with no discernible athletic ability. You know those shelves I used to have behind the futon? Imagine Rog, naked, sweaty and red-faced, humping away—"

"He banged the shelves instead of you? Ouch."

"Sort of. We were doing this odd position and I lost my balance. Rog fell off me, nose first."

"Why did that make him dump you? Wouldn't he want more?" More, Karina thought. God, yes, *more.*

"The doctors assumed Rog had taken Viagra without a prescription, and they warned him that the strenuous activity could be too much for his heart. Since he was a bit of a hypochondriac anyway…" Debby flipped a hand. "Whatever. There are more fish in the sea and I'd rather hook a swordfish than a flounder."

Karina shot her employee a suspicious look. "Why *did* you have that batch of truffles ready to go?" She had a loose agreement with the staff that because the business had to be careful with the limited supply of the unique cocoa beans, personal consumption was to be kept to a minimum. She didn't need a store full of randy workers inventing new uses for the kitchen appliances. Traditionally, her family had always used the precious beans sparingly. In fact, if her Swiss grandmother had been alive, Karina would never have been allowed to go commercial.

"I saw how interested you were in the guy across the street," Debby said. "Figured you'd be needing the truffles sooner or later."

"You thought I couldn't interest him on my own?"

"Of course you could. But a little extra help never hurts. That's what keeps Victoria's Secret in business, and us, too."

"Whatever." Karina sighed, thinking of her new matching underwear. "Looks like I won't be launching myself at any headboards." *No thanks to Alex Anderson.*

Debby shrugged. "I'm just saying…"

"It's not that bad. I'll survive." Karina squirmed.

"I don't get it. How could mystery man turn you down?"

"He was *very* unfriendly."

"Wait till he eats the truffles. He'll be sorry he got rid of you so fast."

Bingo. Karina's head snapped up. "You're right. Except he said that he doesn't like chocolate."

"But he still has them?"

"Yes."

"No one resists my chocolates for long. He'll eat one. Be ready for when he does."

Karina shook her head. "I told you. He was not nice. The chocolate's not strong enough to overcome that. I didn't even get inside his apartment. From what little I could see, the place was nice enough, but practically empty."

"But he just moved in."

"Three weeks ago. Most people get a couch, or at least a futon. They keep food, they smile at neighbors."

"As long as he has condoms, what do you care?"

"No, I won't be back there. Something wasn't right with him." Karina wanted to say more about how uneasy he made her, watching her from a dark, empty apartment, but she bit her tongue. After all, she was partly to blame. She'd been trying to attract his attention, which was vaguely hurtful to her pride now that she knew he had no real interest in her.

"How did he look up close?"

Karina swallowed. "Wary. Hard. Haunted. Sexy."

"Still a mystery then," Debby mused, looking as if she wanted to come up with another plan.

"Don't even," Karina said.

"You'd rather suffer?"

"I'll buy a damned vibrator if it gets too bad."

Debby laughed. "I hear The Pink Pussycat delivers."

3

KARINA DIDN'T LAST LONG at work. Debby claimed that even the double-strength effects would wane after several hours, but by midafternoon Karina was still unable to settle down, what with the cravings and the pictures in her head and the empty, aching heat between her thighs. After snapping at Janine for failing to keep the carafe of ice water filled, she knew she had to either go home or go pound down Alex's door.

Janine's head picked up when Karina sailed through the outer office with her coat over her arm. She blinked beneath the razor-cut spikes of her dishwater-blond bangs. "You're leaving again?"

"Going home early."

"All right. What should I do for the rest of the day?"

"Just, you know—" Karina couldn't focus. "The usual."

"I finished the shipments. I'll organize files."

Karina made an agreeable sound, even though her files were already organized, alphabetized and cross-referenced, both hard and soft copies.

Hard and soft...ooh.

She put her head down and squeezed the end of her nose all the way out of the store, determined not to linger over the displays of Bellini truffles or the mocha-mint mousse cups or the tins of hot-chocolate mix that would taste so good on the kind of long, lonely night she had in front of her....

The trip from the front door of Sutter Chocolat to the vestibule of the apartments upstairs was ten steps long. She counted each one, exerting tremendous willpower to keep herself from looking up at Alex's windows. Perhaps she should have been equally concerned with random male pedestrians—in case the chocolate aphrodisiac was indiscriminate—but the possibility of other men didn't really enter her mind. Alex filled her thoughts, all on his own.

Fill me.

"Stop it," Karina said as she unlocked the door and just about threw herself inside.

Fill me. Hard and deep and fast.

Frederick Alonzo, who lived in the second-floor apartment across from her own, was getting his mail. "Miss Sutter," he said, bobbing his head. He was in his early fifties with salt-and-pepper hair and a shy smile. As her tenant for less than a year, he'd proved to be clean and quiet, always a gentleman. "Good day."

Karina closed her eyes, feeling for the wall so she wouldn't lose her balance. "Hi, Mr. Alonzo."

There was a moment's silence while he shuffled through his mail. Karina cracked a lid and saw that he was looking at her with concern. "Dizzy, Miss Sutter?" He took a step closer. "Are you ill?"

She held up a hand to stop him, then waved it at her face. "I'm, er, a little hot."

"Fever. *Tch, tch.* You ought to get upstairs and crawl into bed. Take care of yourself."

Karina almost choked at the image that brought to

mind. Did she have The Pink Pussycat's number? Did they really deliver? Of course they did. One of the benefits of living in New York was having all your needs met via telephone and courier service. Even *this* kind.

"Yes, thanks," she said to the tenant. "I will be sure to do that."

"You don't want the flu."

"No."

Mr. Alonzo offered his arm. "I'll help you up."

"Thank you, but no." Although she had only neighborly feelings for the guy, she wasn't taking any chances. He wore tweed jackets, wrote bad poetry and wasn't altogether unattractive. She'd always thought that his kind nature gave his mild blue eyes, lop ears and round tummy a certain cuddly stuffed-animal appeal—

Karina slammed her eyes shut again. Alex Anderson had unadulterated animal appeal. *Rrrowr.* She'd stick with him for the time being.

Mr. Alonzo edged toward the stairs. "If you're sure, then."

"I've got to pick up my mail," she said brightly, wiping her forehead with the back of a hand. "I'll be along in a minute."

"Take care, Miss Sutter. Give me a ring if you need anything."

She'd flag an SOS at Alex if it got to that. No doubt he would be sneaking peeks at her again, especially after the fool she'd made of herself.

Karina's whirring mind snapped to a stop. If Debby was right and Alex *did* eat one of the truffles—well, there was still a chance of there being a seduction tonight. Or at least of getting some of her own back.

Resolutely, she climbed the stairs, each step an escalating degree in torment as her thighs swished back and forth, rubbing until she was so sensitive she swore she'd go off at a touch. If she'd lived any higher than the second floor, she'd have had to stop for a cigarette.

Finally home. She let herself inside with a relieved exhale and locked the door behind her. The apartment was her haven, even on days when she wasn't desperate for privacy. After the business had proved such a success, she had consulted with her accountants and bought the entire building as an investment instead of continuing to pay exorbitant rent. She'd indulged herself by combining two small apartments into one, taking down a section of the ceiling and having a spiral metal staircase installed to give herself access to the loft and bedrooms above. The rooms were now generously sized, the decor simple, modern and elegant. There were blond wood floors and shelves, lots of cream and ivory, with clean-lined furnishings upholstered in ice blue and palest green. Tasteful was the word, except for a few funky touches from her carnival collection. There was even a fortune-telling machine near the archway to the living room.

Esmeralda the Gypsy Queen. She was a gaudy creature boxed in Plexiglas, the top half of the life-size mannequin done up in a glitzy costume with fringe and hoop earrings. Karina kept a bowl of quarters on top of the case for the guests who invariably wanted their fortunes read.

She reached for the coins. "I need answers, Esme," she said, feeding fifty cents into the slot. "Will I be lonesome tonight?"

The colored lightbulbs outlining Esme's booth flickered on and off in an alternating pattern of red and purple and gold. A crystal ball had been affixed to a platform draped in velvet to disguise Esme's missing lower half. The fortune-telling prop lit up with a twinkle of lights concealed inside the frosted globe. Next, the mannequin whirred to life. Her eyes opened and one arm came up, raising an open palm near the glass. "Give me your hand," the automated voice said. "I will tell your fortune."

Karina placed her palm on the touch pad, which shone green, warming her skin. For fun, she told her friends that Esme was never wrong, but of course that was pure bunk.

After a few tinkling bars of carnival music, Esme's black marble eyes blinked and a card dropped into the receptacle near the coin slot. "Fortune foretold."

That was what Esme always said—she was a very limited conversationalist. Only the cards differed. Karina had entertained the thought it would be amusing to refill the machine with more unique hand-printed cards, but she'd never gotten around to it. With little expectation, she reached for her fortune.

"A dark stranger will enter your life," she read.

Wow. What were the odds?

With a short laugh, she gave Esme's cubicle a pat. Maybe one in twenty. Karina had never kept track of how often the cards were repeated. She couldn't actually remember a specific instance of a person getting the "dark stranger" card, but she was almost certain that it had happened.

"Pure coincidence," she said, thinking of the man who was no longer a complete stranger as she crossed to the windows. The afternoon light was already beginning to fade. These December days were so short. But she didn't turn on the lamps. Not yet.

The sheer curtains were open and the linen shades up. She clung to the exposed brick framing the tall windows that overlooked the street, the fortune card clasped between her fingers. One peek. Just to see if he was there.

The dark stranger.

"Nonsense." Karina tilted her head to look out the window, quickly scanning for Alex's window. His tattered blind was down. If he was watching for her, she couldn't tell.

She withdrew and pressed her forehead to the brick. The fortune, meaningless though it was, had only served to ratchet up her tension. Her body was strung taut, vibrating even at the marrow. She needed relief so badly that every fiber of her being was screaming for it. And there were a lot of them. She ate her muesli religiously, to combat the high fat content of the shop's sweets.

Another peep out the window. *Go for the truffles, Alex. Please. I need you to want me as badly as I want you.*

Still clinging to the brick, she put the card between her lips, then brushed her palm across her front. Yes, her nipples were hard and rubbing against the lace edges of the bra. She slipped a couple of fingers inside her blouse to free them, stopping to flick the sensitive nubs a couple of times as the heat inside leapt higher, making her soften and swell with wanting. She rocked her hips, chafed her thighs. *I could call someone else.* Bradley or Quinn, any of the men she'd dated in the past. They might be willing to engage in a quickie without expecting more.

But…that wouldn't be the same. For some reason, she was obsessed with Alex.

Some reason? She laughed silently. *You* know the *reason.*

The game had begun a week after he'd moved in, when she'd first begun to notice him on the street. Having no previous interest in exhibitionism, she hadn't consciously decided to tease him. That had crept up on her.

First she'd seen him a couple of times standing near his window during the day, looking out. Nothing strange about that, except that he'd always ducked out of view whenever a pedestrian glanced up. She'd even waved to him once while she was washing her windows on a Saturday morning. He'd seen her, but he'd turned away without returning the friendly gesture. She'd shrugged that off.

Next she'd become aware of him in the evening, when his blind was halfway up more frequently. That had seemed odd, so she'd paid attention and eventually realized that he rarely turned the lights on in his apartment. He sat in the dark, a shadowed figure near the window. Barely visible. Just watching.

Watching what? Who? *Her?*

Karina's initial response had been outrage at the violation of her privacy. She'd been more scrupulous about keeping her windows covered. But the dark stranger had become a part of her life, even her dreams, and she'd found herself thinking about him all the time. Wondering, imagining, supposing.

Supposing she was the kind of woman who liked to be watched.

She'd begun leaving her windows uncovered a while longer than usual. When the lights were on, she knew he'd have a perfect view into her place from his third-floor apartment. The living and dining room, the master suite upstairs—all faced the street with eight-foot-tall windows that offered an equally good view inside as out. She wasn't ready to go as far as a true exhibitionist, but she was always aware that he might be watching, so she began to move with more grace, almost posing herself when she lay on her couch, swinging her hips as she walked about the rooms, lingering near the window while she took her hair down and brushed it out, or buttoned her shirt.

Her modesty had prevailed and drawn the line at nudity. But that line had become smudged after she'd taken to wearing a robe with only underwear—occasionally nothing—on underneath. He might have caught glimpses if he was a dedicated watcher: the curve of a breast, the flash of a thigh. Nothing more explicit. Harmless titillation, she'd assured herself.

"Until today," she whispered, mortified all over again. After the show she'd been giving him for the past two weeks, Alex had reason to believe that she'd flashed him on purpose, regardless of his denial. Her only saving grace might be that he still believed she was an innocent player in their voyeuristic little game.

In all of her previous posturing, she'd tried not to be obvious about staring his way, even though she *knew* he was watching. The angle of his head in the darkness, the prickling tension of her reaction. Some evenings she swore she could feel his gaze roving across her body. And she knew that he wanted her.

Hah. Delusional.

But was she? Hadn't there been a hint of desire in his eyes when he'd watched her moan over the truffle? His jaw had clenched so hard he might have cracked a tooth. If it hadn't been desire, he'd been withholding a strong emotion of some sort.

Maybe disgust. She slipped the fortune card from her

mouth, letting the edge drag across her lower lip. But then why did he watch her?

Karina took a breath and pushed away from the brick wall. Let him stare all he wanted!

Tonight, she was reckless. Tonight, she'd really give him something to see.

ALEX SAT DRUMMING his fingers on his knee. There wasn't much for a man to do, isolated in a small apartment, night after night. Television didn't interest him, though occasionally he turned on the small portable set for the company. He liked movies, but had no DVD player and not much desire to get one when it was only another item to leave behind the next time he moved. His laptop computer sat on the desk and he amused himself there at times. An hour or two of inaction was all he could take before he was pacing the studio space like a cat in a cage.

Mark Lexmond had been a get-up-and-go kind of guy. Running, surfing, playing in a volleyball league, meeting up with friends at the various dive bars and colorful cafés that populated his Venice Beach neighborhood. He worked long hours at his law firm, so when he played, he played hard.

There were always single women around, and his guy pals were a varied lot. He tended to accumulate people as well as possessions, rarely discarding either. His ocean-view apartment was a cheerful hodgepodge of saggy chairs, beach gear and guy toys like an expensive stereo system and his precious drum set. Frequent guests dropped by to jam or watch a game and wound up sacked out on the couch or even the floor. The spare bedroom was occupied by a stream of roommates who came and went like the tide, knowing that Lex was easy about the rent check being late or girlfriends who staged minidramas in the middle of a Lakers play-off game.

Once every month or so, Lex rounded up the available bodies and held a free-for-all housecleaning event, where they pitched the accumulation of beer cans and take-out cartons, swept the sand off the floor, scrubbed the grunge from the bathroom and decrusted the oven and microwave. Most of his girlfriends had at one time or another tried to inject some design into the rooms, but they usually gave up after buying a few floor pillows, alphabetizing his CDs or separating his suits from his Hawaiian-print shirts.

He propped his arms behind his head. Yep, he'd been a happy-go-lucky guy who wished for nothing more than a satisfying sense of accomplishment from his work and an equally satisfying tumble from the closest available babe. Troubles had rolled off his back.

Sure, there'd been days when the realities of his job got him down. Along with the repeat offenders who always swore that this time they were innocent, he'd seen a lot of hard-luck cases who deserved a break that he couldn't always deliver. But his natural optimism was a strong force and when his mood had threatened to turn blue, he'd beat the hell out of the snare drum or head out to the beach to let the surf toss him around. The powerlessness of man versus nature had always adjusted his perspective.

What he hadn't been prepared for was being powerless against Rafael Norris, a truly amoral man who'd do anything to avenge the death of his son.

But Lex—*Alex,* he reminded himself again with a soft oath. He had to think of himself as Alex now, even to himself.

Alex Anderson was not Mark Lexmond.

Alex was solitary. Abrupt. Defensive. Closed. He avoided eye contact. He made no small talk. He had no friends. Needless to say, no lovers of any duration.

Thoughts of Karina Sutter immediately filled his head. When a man was a virtual prisoner, even the smallest connection, especially one that included the touch of skin on skin, became hugely important. He'd replayed her visit in his mind all afternoon until the minor episode was magnified to outrageous proportions.

He got up and stalked around the studio, from the bedroom nook to the living room, past the galley kitchen and the bathroom door, following the route he'd taken a hundred times today. Soon a path would be worn in the floorboards.

Karina had been expressing a bit of interest, that was all. She'd run if she knew what she'd be getting herself into with him.

Lights went on across the street. Alex moved closer to the window, cautiously keeping away from the glass as he pulled the blind down. The sky was the color of steel. It was early for Karina to be home from work.

Peering from the side of the blind, he did his usual scan of the street, then the nearby windows. Normal activity, picking up as the day grew short and people either returned home or prepared to go out. Karina's apartment was dark downstairs, but the lights upstairs were on. He wondered if she had a date with another of the smooth operators he'd seen arriving at her door over the past three weeks. There'd been two or three of them—interchangeable in their handsome, clean-cut looks. Even in his incarnation as Mark Lexmond, he hadn't been her type. He'd worn goofy ties and had used his briefcase as a basketball hoop, dartboard and waste can combined.

Still, envy slipped past Alex's defenses. He'd begun to think of Karina as *his.* Which was both stupid and dangerous, not to mention delusional.

Shiny glass flashed across the way. Karina's bathroom. He saw movement—a pale body indistinct in the steam of a shower. Excitement stirred in the pit of his stomach. The bathroom window was completely uncovered. Bedroom, too. She had to know that he could see inside.

Had to. Which meant that all along she had known he was watching and she'd liked it that way.

Maybe he'd been slow on the uptake, but he was beginning to get it now. Her move this afternoon had been the next step in their game. Now that he'd rebuffed her, she was going to get to him in another way.

He groaned and reached for his binoculars. The steam had risen, but he could see that she was in the shower, spectacularly nude behind the glass door. Rows of brick sprang into sharp relief when he brought the glasses up, but he quickly adjusted the angle, finding Karina's apartment with a learned skill.

There she was. Showering with the shades up. A first.

She raised her arms, soaping her hair. The curves of her body wavered behind the steamy glass. Alex thought briefly of playing the gentleman and putting the binoculars away, but if ever a woman wanted to be watched…

Her head went under the stream of water. He dropped the binoculars and gave the lenses a quick polish with the hem of his T-shirt, returning in time to see the shower door swing open. Was she actually—

Holy shit. She was. She did.

She stepped naked from the shower. He sharpened the lens focus and saw breasts. Poached pink skin beaded with droplets. A narrow strip of golden pubic hair…

Situated directly across from the shower, the bathroom window extended almost from floor to ceiling, giving him a nearly full-length view as she reached for a towel. *Oh, hot mama, don't cover up yet,* he thought, his pulse jackhammering while he scanned down her sexy body. *I want it all.* He already knew her breasts were perfect—round and firm, big enough to fill a man's hand, but not so large they swung past her ribs like heavy grapefruits. She had a narrow waist, a flat stomach, nicely flared hips. And the sweetest spot of all…

She turned sideways, wrapping the towel around herself. For a moment she froze, gripping the towel to her breasts, slightly hunched over—almost as if she were in pain. A cringe? He lowered the glasses, abashed by his lascivious interest. Of course he had to look. Any guy would look. But he'd feel more at ease if he knew for sure, one hundred percent positive, that she was a willing participant.

Invite me in….

She'd said it, but he'd declined. What she was doing now was only another offer. *Had* to be intentional.

Karina had disappeared from view. He scanned her apartment through the binoculars, suddenly finding her when she came out of the bathroom, combing her wet hair as she walked into the adjoining bedroom. She still wore the towel, so he trained the glasses on her face, catching the furtive glance she shot at the windows before turning on a bedside lamp.

Expecting her to hurry over to close her curtains, he straightened and eased away from the crinkled blind.

The window covering suddenly shot up on its roller with a *whir* and a *snap,* exposing him to the street.

And to Karina.

He didn't need the binoculars to know that she saw him. Their eyes connected over the distance—he was one hundred percent certain of *that.* He might have quickly moved out of the window or at least looked away, but for once he chose not to. He wanted her to know, without a doubt, that he was watching.

Then he'd see what happened.

After a couple of seconds, she lifted her hands to her hair, skimming the wet strands back from her face. The motion did interesting things to her towel sarong, making it gap over one thigh. He imagined ripping it off and throwing her on the bed. Or kneeling at her feet, running his hands along her clean silky body, burying his face in the heat between her thighs….

Instead of going for the curtains, she turned and opened the closet. Hardly believing it, he leaned forward, bracing one hand on the window ledge. Panting like a runner.

With a casual flick, she discarded the towel.

Alex let out a moan, his fingers tightening around the binoculars. No surprise, she had a gorgeous ass. The kind a man wanted to bite into like a ripe fruit. Pert and round, made for cupping. For riding.

He straightened and unsnapped his jeans, slid his fingers inside a few inches, nudging down the zipper. Lex Junior wanted to come out to play, but the idea of jerking off at the window like the neighborhood pervert was just nasty. Painfully, he withdrew. A few more minutes of this torture and he'd be shooting in his pants without having to touch himself.

He was almost glad when Karina slid into a silky blue robe. She wrapped the belt around her waist and left the room, momentarily moving out of his sight. He dropped into the secondhand armchair he'd hauled home from a junk shop, cradling the fullness at his crotch. *Enough.*

But the show wasn't over. Though the light was fading, he was able to see into the first level of Karina's place even without the lights on. She descended the spiral staircase, completely oblivious to the way her robe slid open to flash her long bare legs.

Unless she knew exactly what she was doing, he considered. The visit to his apartment had been engineered. Why not this?

Alex gripped the arms of the chair. "You're trying to seduce me, Mrs. Robinson."

Lights went on downstairs. The shades stayed up. He retrieved the binoculars and followed Karina's progress through the apartment as she went to the inner area he'd deduced was her kitchen. She emerged with a glass of red wine.

"C'mon, darling. What's the plan?" he breathed. She moved out of sight again, but only for a few seconds before she was back, swaying her hips and shoulders, holding the glass aloft as she twirled. Music, he thought, as the robe flared out around her slender legs.

She danced for a few minutes, then gracefully draped herself across the armless couch that faced the windows, making a pretty picture in the golden lamplight with her blond hair loose around her face and her pale limbs and the robin's egg blue of her robe against the ice-blue upholstery. She sipped the wine, staring across at him with one shoulder bare where the robe had slipped off it. He moved the binoculars one degree lower to the silk lying open across her chest, one side of the drooping lapel held up only by the hardened pink tip of her breast. A slight shrug and it would drop….

Alex put the glasses aside and settled himself deeper in the bowed cushion. Karina was showing no intention of getting dressed to go out, and there was no way he could make himself stop watching. It was going to be a very long night.

WAS HE WATCHING?

Yes—he wasn't hiding that. She could see him sitting near his window.

Was he touching himself?

Yes—unless his willpower was made of iron.

Karina's clearly wasn't. She let her hand drift along her thigh. Her skin seemed to reach toward the touch. She could only imagine how sensitive she'd be if it were Alex's hands on her, roaming freely. The pure pleasure of that would be stupendous.

Pure? Not exactly. She'd cheated on Alex with a truffle, though she doubted that he'd mind if he knew.

Several hours had passed since she'd eaten the candies and she was still aroused, even after the long shower. The effects should have worn off by now, and instead she remained hot and primed for action. She told herself that only a powerful force beyond her control could have made her show off for Alex the way she had, parading naked for him—and anyone else with a view. She'd be dying of embarrassment tomorrow, but for now, the ache was too sharp, the need too great. She could only think about getting satisfaction. And she was becoming reckless enough to accept any kind at all.

Unfortunately, Alex didn't appear to be as driven.

She'd hoped that the sight of her would make him so crazy with lust that he'd have to charge over and bust her door down to have her.

Oh, yesss. Nice fantasy. Her eyes closed as her fingers glided along the seam of her robe, parting it just enough for her nails to trace tingling paths on the surface of her skin. She slid lower on the sofa, raising one leg along the back.

Alex, touching me. She slipped a hand beneath the silk, stroking over her ribs, up to one breast. The weight of it was nice, but not enough. She wanted Alex's hand, his mouth on her nipple, his body covering hers, conquering and dividing as he parted her with a hugely engorged erection....

What the—?

Karina sat up, shocked to find her robe gaping open and her hand between her legs. Heat flared—at her sex, in her cheeks. She didn't dare look out to see Alex's reaction. Head down, she clenched a hand on the front of the robe and ran over to the light switch, then the curtains. She wrenched them shut, but they were too sheer to offer much privacy. She reached for the dangling cords that controlled the shades, trying to keep herself out of the window.

As if it mattered. She'd already gone too far.

She abandoned the cords and peeped out between the curtains. Alex was still there, standing now with his nose practically pressed to the glass. Trying for a better view, she assumed, gritting her teeth against the impulse to give it to him.

The other windows in his building appeared empty, but she couldn't be sure that there'd only been an audience of one. This couldn't all be blamed on the chocolate. She must have been out of her mind.

But so into her body.

"I will never eat one of those truffles again," she vowed. A rash promise. Damn Alex, anyway! *He* was supposed to be the one who couldn't control himself.

Instead he was the safe detached observer while *she* put on a wanton sex show. The worst part was that she was still turned on.

Which was also the best part.

A river of emotion ran through her. Audacity, humiliation. Passion, frustration. *It was the best of times, it was the worst of times,* she said in her head, pressing herself up against the brick wall. She wriggled a little, letting the robe fall open again. The rough texture abraded her nipples and she moved over a few inches to touch them to the glass of the windowpane. The icy cold was a shock against her fevered flesh and yet she liked it. She wanted to be startled. Blown away. Scandalized.

"Alex," she pleaded. He saw her.

He was watching.

After a few seconds she deliberately put her hand over her pubic mound so that he would know what she was about to do. Fading back a few steps, she let the curtains that she'd brushed aside drop between them again. Her figure would show through the sheer fabric, but the view wouldn't be as explicit.

She stroked two fingers between her labia. *Let him see. Let him know.*

As she fingered the hard bump of her clit, a little smile found its way to her mouth—a teasing pout. Her head lolled, weaving from side to side as she pleasured herself. Alex was watching, frustrated, knowing that he could have been inside her, but also that she was perfectly capable of coming without him. Her hand moved faster, rubbed harder. Jolts of sensation shot through her and when her knees started to go out, she lurched forward, barely keeping herself upright with one palm pressed to the window as a sharp, short climax burst beneath her fingertips.

"Aghhh." She flopped around so that she was leaning up against the brick again, limp and quivering from the vaguely disappointing orgasm.

Never mind. At least she'd taken the edge off. Although she couldn't see Alex, she was sure that he was riveted. Eventually he would eat one of the truffles and know the hunger and the longing that had built up inside her for the past few weeks and ultimately driven her to such incredible lengths.

Then *she* would be the one in control. She could say yes or even *no*...if she wanted him to know exactly what it was like to suffer.

4

DURING A LONG, sleepless night, Alex had decided that it was time to try to be a normal person again. He would bank the memories of his life as Mark Lexmond, banish memories of Florida and the horror and guilt of seeing an innocent person killed one foot away from him, rein in the paranoia, and start fresh.

He had to believe that he was safe. Especially if he wanted to approach Karina.

Which he did. No denying that.

He showered and shaved, ran a comb through his hair and made a mental note to find a barber, put on his least wrinkled clothes, and headed out with only a brief detour to the window to check for loiterers—and Karina. There'd been no sign of her since the previous evening's awe-inspiring performance.

On his way to the door, he noticed the abandoned box of chocolates. Cockroaches would swarm if he left them out. He fitted the lid and tucked the box into the roomy pocket of his long coat. Maybe he could find someone who'd enjoy them—a neighbor, a street person.

Outside, a delivery truck blocked his view of Sutter Chocolat. The back doors were hanging open. Alex stepped off the curb between the truck and a car with its nose nudged into the loading zone, giving the door a shove so he could get by.

Thunk. "Hey!" barked the driver, backing out with a loaded dolly. He rubbed his nose. "Watch what you're doing, man."

"Sorry." Alex held the door. "Let me give you a hand."

The driver pushed the dolly over a few feet to give them room to swing the doors shut.

Alex eyed the boxes, prominently marked with perishable contents labels. "Sutter Chocolat?"

"That's right." The driver shoved his hands into his jacket pockets. "That store—" He shook his head. "Uses one helluva lot of chocolate for a small business. Seems like I'm here every other day."

"It is a busy place."

Wheeling the dolly before him, the deliveryman looked for an opening in traffic. "You ever been there?"

Alex shook his head.

"They've got great chocolate. The girls slip me free samples every time I come by." The man winked. He was young, muscular and full of jaunty bravado. "Can't afford the stuff on my salary."

Alex remembered the truffles in his pocket. "Maybe you'd likc these." He offered the box. "As an apology for your nose."

"Hey, thanks." The delivery driver popped the lid. "One's missing."

"They're leftovers, if that's okay."

"Doesn't bother me." The guy tossed an entire truffle into his mouth. "Thought you've never been to the shop," he said thickly.

"The candy was a gift." Alex raised a hand to signal for an empty cab that was crawling by in the bumper-to-bumper traffic that was apparently a constant during the holiday season. He usually walked, for the exercise and for the illusion that he was getting somewhere fast when his life was stuck in a holding pattern. "I'm allergic."

"Your loss, my gain."

"Happy holidays." Alex jumped into the cab, giving the deliveryman a casual wave goodbye. He wanted a hearty breakfast for a change, then a haircut. Maybe a little shopping. He'd left Florida with nothing but his life.

KYLE MURPHY GAVE UP on cutting across the street and wheeled the dolly to the crosswalk, licking chocolate off his teeth as he went. He patted the foil candy box he'd stuffed into his jacket pocket. Good stuff. Nice of the guy to share.

By the time Kyle reached the chocolate shop, he was feeling unusually warm despite the chill wind. He set the dolly out of the way of pedestrians and paused to unzip his jacket. The sweetness of the chocolate lingered on his tongue, and he would have sworn he felt it moving through his bloodstream if that hadn't been dippy enough to sound like something his psychic-healer sister would say. The warmth rising from his skin was just good old-fashioned sweat. Those bricks of bulk chocolate weighed a ton and he'd had to lift out three boxes of them.

The store was still closed—didn't open till eleven. He knocked at the heavy oak door, peering through the small square panes of the inset window. From previous visits, he knew the kitchen staff was operating in the back. A worker he didn't recognize came to let him in.

"I know the way," Kyle said when the man started to show him toward the back. "Thanks."

He wheeled the dolly through the swinging doors that led to the working side of the store. The new office assistant gave a start when he arrived, pulling out of a file drawer like a kid caught with her hands in the cookie jar. She was a flighty one.

"Delivery," Kyle said. He pulled the signature board out from its holster at his waist. "Sign here, please."

"I've seen you before," the girl said. She scribbled her name on the electronic pad. "I'm Janine Gardner."

"The new girl," Kyle said, giving her a friendly smile. She wasn't bad. Actually sort of cute, he decided, tugging at a too-tight uniform collar as the unusual warmth crawled up his throat. Women flocked to him like gulls to a fish; he didn't usually get nervous around one unless he seriously liked her. The strange thing was that on previous visits, Janine hadn't struck him as particularly special. Kind of prissy and stuck-up, even.

"Can you take the boxes to the storage area?" she asked.

"Sure." Reluctantly, Kyle left Janine behind and pushed the dolly toward the porthole door that led to storage shelves lining a wide corridor adjacent to the kitchen. With what he hoped was a debonair flair, he executed a neat swivel and backed through it, raising his brows at Janine. He even flashed a dimple. She leaned across her desk, watching him with suspicious eyes until the door swung shut.

"Slow down, Fred Astaire," said a female voice from above. Sharply.

"Huh?" Kyle looked up at the same moment that he backed into a sliding ladder positioned to reach the highest bank of metal shelves. It was a heavy ladder, set in place, but he was a big guy and he must have given it a good jolt because suddenly the woman perched halfway up it was flailing her arms and falling backward.

Kyle put out his hands and caught her. She landed squarely in his arms with a solid *whump*. "Whoa," he said, knocked off his game but not off his feet, even though she was a plentiful armful.

He looked into her surprised face—bright blue eyes, a snub nose, pinkened cheeks—then hefted her higher against his chest. "Don't worry, missus. I've got you."

Her eyes widened. "You certainly do."

"I know you," he said. "You're the cook."

"The *confectioner*." She wriggled, wanting to get down.

Instinct made him tighten his arms to keep her close. "I'm Kyle Murphy."

"Yes, I know. You're the delivery guy."

How come he'd never noticed her before, either? She was *much* cuter than Janine. Curly hair the color of a Hershey's bar and a fantastic rack judging by the cleavage showing above her apron. The full curves below were pillowed against his chest. There was a sauciness in the way she met his eyes without blinking. And she smelled like chocolate. A big plus in his book.

His temperature soared even higher. Damn if he wasn't getting hard. "What's your name?"

"Debby Caruso."

"Oh, yeah." The girls out front invoked the name when they gave him extra freebies: *Don't let Debby see. She'll scorch our hides.*

Kyle wasn't scorched—not yet. But he had a very nice sizzle happening.

"You might want to put me down," said Debby. She patted his bunched shoulder. "Although I really do appreciate the display of manly strength."

Before setting her down, he showed off by levering her like a barbell. She whooped, then tottered a bit on her heels when she touched ground. He kept a hand on her waist to steady her. Well, technically on her hip. Maybe her backside. The firm curve of it under his palm was lust-inducing.

"Careful," he said, with an unusual constriction of his throat.

"Kyle," she said, and he found himself mesmerized by the sound of his own name. "Kyle," she repeated, looking as if she were almost as dazzled as he, "would it be too cheesy of me to say that I think I've fallen for you?" She laughed, her eyes bright with a catchy sparkle. "Oh, my. I'm just kidding of course."

Kyle didn't answer. He only smiled and put his free hand on her other hip—okay, backside—and gave her a lusty squeeze.

She widened her eyes again, but didn't seem at all offended. In fact, she planted her hands on his chest, rocked forward on her teeter-totter shoes and gave him a short but exceptionally tasty kiss in return. "Thank you for rescuing me."

The thickening sense of pleasure that had started outside on the sidewalk had completely enveloped him now, as if he'd been dunked into a vat of the richest, warmest fudge sauce in the Willy Wonka factory. There was only one word to define Debby Caruso's kiss, and he said it out loud with an exhilarating, almost triumphant emphasis: *"Sweet!"*

DEBBY BARGED INTO Karina's office without knocking. "He's here," she hissed, holding the door.

"Who's here?" Karina said automatically, her eyes

going to the clock on her desk. Quarter past eleven. The store had barely opened. Alex usually didn't go out for at least another hour or two. Not that she was going to be watching for him today. After the way she'd behaved, she'd prefer never seeing him again.

And what a big fat liar we are.

"Alex, of course," Debby said. "He's *inside* the store!"

"Inside?" Suddenly Karina felt unhinged.

She'd risen that morning, wincing at the memories of the night before, and had only managed to come to work because the thought of staying cooped up in her apartment—the scene of the crime, so to speak—was even worse. She'd kept to her office all morning, telling herself that she must feel ashamed even when, strangely, she wasn't. Not completely. The effects of the chocolate had eventually lessened, but she still didn't feel quite like herself. Masturbating in front of a virtual stranger, even behind a curtain, would normally have made her want to curl up and die.

"He must be looking for you." Debby didn't know what Karina had done to ensure that Alex had seen plenty of her already.

Karina considered. "Maybe he already ate the truffles and wants to buy more." That would be huge. If Alex was jonesing for chocolate, and therefore sex, didn't she want to be there?

"If he ate *all* the truffles he wouldn't be decent to make a public appearance for some time," Debby said with a knowing chuckle.

Karina stood and straightened the white cashmere sweater she'd worn over a black turtleneck and pants. "Do I look okay?"

"Perfect as ever."

"Except when I'm inadvertently flashing my boobs," Karina said, trying not to think of her advertent full-body exposure.

Debby grabbed her by the arm and hustled her from the office. "Hurry up. Either he's going to leave before you get there or end up being molested by one of the customers."

"Hold my calls, Janine," Karina said over her shoulder as she allowed herself to be escorted to the front of the store.

Once they were through the door, Debby gave her a little shove. "Go get him."

When Alex saw her and his expression changed from slightly bored to intense, the embarrassment that Karina had been waiting for hit her all at once like a tidal wave. She put a hand over her face. Good God. She'd done things in front of this man that had never happened with anyone else, and yet the amazing truth was that they'd barely spoken—or touched. How was she supposed to carry on a conversation with him when she knew what images were running through his mind?

Karina forced herself forward, bypassing the clerks shoveling up candies and serving take-out cups of the store's popular hot chocolate. She halted at the corner of the long display cabinet, away from the registers, and threaded her fingers until they were interlocked, a physical reminder to get a grip.

"Hello." *Alex.* "May I help you?" Her voice was as stiff as...well, she didn't want to think about what that comparison brought to mind.

Alex had followed her on the other side of the case, sliding one hand along the top of the glass. His hair had been cut, making it look darker without the shaggy bleached ends. At first she wasn't sure she liked the new style because most of the men she dated were well shorn, but one look into Alex's eyes and she knew that nothing so superficial could make him like the others.

But it was impossible to define why. He was an enigma.

She raised her brows, a light flush creeping into her cheeks. He didn't speak.

"Did you want more of the truffles?"

"No." Another long pause before he made a motion with his head toward the display window. "Can we talk?"

"Outside?"

He moved over a step. "Right here."

Without the counter between them. She didn't know if she liked that idea, but it certainly made her flutter inside. She couldn't blame the chocolate either, unless she'd become sensitive to fumes. She didn't think so. Her most potent stimulant was Alex.

"All right." She nodded, shooting a wary look at his serious face. *Please don't mention last night. I will die.*

She met him near the windows and plunged right in, keeping to an I'm-just-a-happy-shopkeeper expression. "Did you try one of the truffles the way you promised?"

"Did I promise? I don't remember."

"I think you did."

He looked past the top of her head. "The truffles were delicious."

"Don't eat too many at once," she warned. *Blink.* "Um, they're too rich for that."

"Not a problem."

She determinedly held her bland smile. "Well, good."

"I, uh..." Alex rubbed a couple of fingers across his

clean chin. No more stubble either. "I wanted to apologize for being rude yesterday, at my door. I'm not usually—" He stopped, a deep groove etched between his eyebrows.

"But I interrupted you." Karina glanced across the street at his building. "You work at home?"

"Sort of."

"On the computer, I suppose."

"Yeah. I'm a writer."

He said that with no hesitation, but for some reason she didn't believe him. Possibly because she'd seen him sitting near the window with a laptop computer but he'd never seemed particularly absorbed. Weren't writers supposed to lose themselves in their work?

Unless he had writer's block. That might explain his irritability. She gave him a warm look to show that she could be sympathetic. "Published?"

"A *frustrated* writer," he said.

"I see. Then you've found the right city. New York is filled with frustrated writers. You can see them on the street, staring bitterly at stacks of bestsellers in the window of any Barnes and Noble superstore."

Alex almost smiled. "Do you want to go for coffee?" he blurted.

She didn't know why she was surprised. Had she expected him to waltz over and service her on the closest available surface?

Or maybe she was supposed to substitute the word *nooner* for *coffee.* That would be bold of him, but then she'd given him good reason to believe she might say yes.

"I guess you can't leave work," Alex said.

"That's not a problem. I'm the boss."

"Right. Sutter Chocolat."

"The thing is..." How to put this? Unless it was a euphemism, coffee sounded like a date to her, and that meant becoming acquaintances, friends, boyfriend and girlfriend, la la la, the whole enchilada. She had that with other men.

Granted, part of her wanted to get to know Alex, peel away a few of his layers. The good girl that up until yesterday had been prominent in her was loudly demanding it, bolstered by the notion that only tramps had emotionless one-night stands.

And sexually confident women, Karina told herself. Women who knew what they wanted and went for it. She could be one of those women, especially with another dose of chocolate courage.

She took a deep breath, preparing to suggest that they skip coffee and get straight to business, and then copped out as soon as she opened her mouth.

"Sorry. Now's not a good time." She couldn't be positive that coffee didn't mean coffee. As hard as it sounded, not to mention unlike her, getting into a relationship with him wasn't her goal.

Alex's eyes were the color of blue-gray slate, and suddenly just as flat and cool. "Oh."

"We're so busy..."

"I understand." He thrust his hands into his coat pockets and began edging away. "This wasn't one of my better ideas anyway."

She wanted to put out a hand to stop his retreat, but she didn't know how to explain what she wanted from him. She'd already given him a gigantic in-your-face clue.

With a jingle of the old-fashioned bell over the door, he left the shop.

Debby rushed up, wailing. "Oh, crap, Kare. What didja do wrong?"

"He invited me out for coffee." Karina's eyes were on the window. Alex had paused outside to turn up the collar of his coat. He flicked a sidelong glance at her, then hunched his head onto his shoulders and strode away.

Debby was asking why she hadn't gone.

"I couldn't, that would be…" Karina brushed Debby aside, losing her train of thought as she impulsively raced for the door. The brisk air hit her like a slap, but she gulped the cold into her lungs and charged off, waving a hand. "Alex! Wait up!"

He was already at the corner, but he'd heard her. The light changed and the crowd surged into the crosswalk. Karina's stomach dropped, until she realized that they were parting around Alex like a rock in the river. She crossed her arms, hugging herself as she jogged to catch up.

"Alex." Her breath puffed vapor into the air. "I—umm…"

For a moment he looked at her with the same hard eyes, but then he relented and said, "What are you doing?" while he pulled off the gray scarf that had been hanging inside his jacket collar. He wound it around her head with a certain carefulness that made her chin lift and her cheek turn toward his touch.

Abruptly he removed his hands. "Go back inside."

"I came to say…"

"You didn't change your mind." He was certain.

"Not about coffee," she admitted. "But…"

She bit her lip. Why was she having such trouble finishing sentences around him?

"You're shivering." He put his arms around her, but not as if he relished the chance to hold her. A purely gentlemanly action. "Go back to your store."

"Tonight," she said, into the buttons of his shirt. He was *warm.* And solid. She wanted to melt all over him.

He gave her a quizzical "Huh?"

"Eat one of the truffles tonight," she whispered in a husky voice.

Alex frowned, setting her back a little to study her face. "Why?"

"Just do it." She held his scarf under her chin with one hand while she reluctantly backed away into the stream of pedestrian traffic. Impatient shoppers jostled her this way and that, but she didn't take her eyes off Alex. If he could only look into her and read the desire that had taken over, he would know how good they could be together.

This once. Only once, to last a lifetime.

"Eat one of the truffles," she said, having to raise her voice as the crowd pushed against her, bumping her with shopping bags, "and I'll meet you. Tonight." Her knuckles pressed beneath her chin. "At the windows."

"The windows?" she saw him mouth, before she was caught up in the crowd and had to turn to make her way to the door of her shop. If she hadn't started out in search of a fling, if there weren't lingering doubts about Alex's situation, she'd have accepted his invitation in a heartbeat.

But with all that had happened, it was too late for that. He was no more than her one-night-only mystery man.

No regrets. Think of the truffles and how they'll make you feel. She ducked her nose into the folds and scent of Alex's scarf. She hoped that Debby had made extra candies, even though it was possible that she might not need one. She was already aroused…and even daring. All on her own.

KARINA'S LIFE HAD BEEN normal up to now, and after Alex, it would be normal again. This was what she told herself while molding marzipan with Debby in the kitchen an hour later. The rest of the kitchen staff was on lunch break, so Debby had snagged Karina for a private chat. An entire rack of assorted candies ready for boxing sat nearby, scenting the air with the aroma of melted chocolate and fresh vanilla beans.

Karina had expected to get grilled. But Debby seemed distracted. She hadn't picked up on Karina's lie about what she'd said to Alex, and she was not a good liar.

"That's all?" Debby rolled a lump of marzipan into a pear shape. "You ran out of the shop only to tell him that you'd love to go for coffee another day?"

Karina was forming bells. She flattened and molded a ball of the malleable candy to create the curved lip. "I could tell he hadn't tried the truffles yet. He told me he had, to be polite, I suppose, but it was obvious he hadn't. He wasn't all that interested." Certainly not in comparison to how aggressive she'd become.

"Oh, make no mistake—he was interested." Debby nodded encouragement. "You got him to come into the store, for one."

"Yes, wow. What a major step."

"He asked you out." Debby pinched off a tiny bit of the green marzipan to form a leaf and stem, then set her finished pear on a tray covered with waxed paper. "Only a hundred to go."

"This is like Play-Doh."

"I used to always try to eat my Play-Doh."

"Always? One taste didn't teach you?"

Debby flexed her fingers before rolling out the next

pear. "Nope. I'm a gobbler, not a thinker. Not like you." Her smile was smug. "When I find an interested man, I make my move right away."

"But I didn't want to go for *coffee*."

"Then why tell him you'd go another time?"

Karina sliced off another chunk of the red marzipan. "Because sooner or later he will eat one of those truffles, and when that happens I want him to think of me first." True enough.

Debby chuckled. "Can't let some other woman reap the benefits."

"I…" The entire story was ready to burst out of Karina, regardless of her usual reserve. She was losing her inhibitions right and left. No way could that be blamed entirely on the chocolate. The idea that some of this was coming from her unadulterated self was a bit alarming. What happened if, afterward, she discovered that she was dissatisfied with her normal life?

So what? she answered herself. People evolve.

She would cope. As long as it was a natural process, and not as the result of an aphrodisiac. She must not forget that this *was not real*.

Alex could not be more than a fling.

"You're mashing that bell into a pancake," Debby said mildly.

Karina tossed the overworked candy into the trash. "There's something I haven't told you. I've been flirting with Alex."

"Yeah, if that's what you want to call flashing your boobs."

"Not that," Karina said, although Debby had no idea how correct she was. "At night. From my apartment windows. I've seen him watching me."

"Oh." Debby made a baby-doll face—mouth in a circle, lids blinking up and down. "Like…peeping?"

"Kind of. Except that he knows that I know he's watching."

"Everyone does that in the city." Debby shrugged. "Window-watching is the New Yorker's favorite spectator sport. There's this guy across the air shaft from me who yells over to me to pick out his ties. And of course Whitney and the Strangler."

Their friend Whitney had a telescope in her office on the twenty-ninth floor and swore that one night when she was working late she'd seen a man strangling a woman on his bed. The police had treated Whitney like a crackpot but ever since she'd been obsessive about tracking the Strangler's movements. She even kept a log.

"This isn't like that," Karina said, her voice sounding funny even to her own ears.

Debby noticed and glanced up sharply. "What do you mean?"

"I've, ahh, enticed him."

"Ooh. And…?"

"And last night I took a shower with the shades up. I stepped out naked, no towel. He saw everything."

"Nuh-uh. You *di'n't!*"

Karina buried her face in her sticky hands. "I've become an exhibitionist."

Debby exhaled, flabbergasted. "It was the truffles."

"I'd like to think so, but the truth is that I liked it. I felt—" Karina dropped her hands, smiling a little to herself "—wild."

"Ohmigawd. Look at you." Debby reached across the worktable and playfully slapped Karina's arm. "Hell on wheels."

"You're right. It was the chocolate, not me. Not the real me, anyway."

"The chocolate can't make you do something *that* out of character. You know, like they say a person who's been hypnotized wouldn't commit murder."

"Hmm…you think?"

Debby pushed the tray of marzipan miniatures aside and leaned her elbows on the marble-topped island. "So what happened then?"

"I put on a towel."

They laughed. "But what did Alex do?" Debby insisted.

"Well, nothing. He watched. And after a while…" Karina cleared her throat. "I pulled the curtains and went to bed."

"Disappointing." Debby frowned, then brightened. "Except now we know why he came into the store today. He was here to continue the game."

"By asking me for coffee?"

"He could hardly say he wants to do you dirty two ways from Sunday."

"But that's what I want, in a manner of speaking."

"Kare, only you could be prissy and horny at the same time."

"Am I being prissy?"

"'In a manner of speaking'? What *is* that?" Debby dug her fingers into the brick of marzipan. "Girl, you've got to shed your inhibitions and grab life by the balls. Or grab Alex by 'em, at least."

"That's what I'm trying to do." Karina blushed. "The first thing you said, not the—"

"Ha! Maybe that's why he looked so constipated."

Karina was incredulous. *"Constipated?"*

"Kind of tight and inflexible, like he was scared to—I don't know—to live."

"He says he's a writer."

"That explains it, then. Writers are just one big glob of neuroses and insecurities."

"How would you know?"

"My ex, remember?"

"Oh, right." Debby had been married at twenty-one to a fortysomething writing instructor she'd met at school.

Early on, she and Karina had been a little awkward with each other since they were so different, but they'd eventually bonded over a late night kirsch-infused fudge cake. Debby had confided how everyone thought she was marrying a father figure when it had turned out that it was her ex-husband who'd wanted a mother, nursemaid, housekeeper and cook all rolled into one. She'd enjoyed only the latter position, so she'd dumped the husband after five years, four of which were spent in couples therapy, and enrolled in cooking school with a vow to live for herself from then on.

In the spirit of sharing confidences, Karina had talked about her background, growing up in exotic locales with an industrialist-turned-diplomat father and a mother so devoted to being the ideal hostess she'd molded Karina into the perfect party accessory. Her father had retired from diplomacy midway through her teen years, and she'd been able to finish out high school in a ritzy New Jersey suburb. Since then, her parents had moved back to Switzerland, the country of her father's birth. She saw them two or three times a year on exchange visits. They thought Sutter Chocolat was an amusing trifle to keep Karina busy until she settled into her *real* life.

"Where's he from?" Debby asked.

"Alex? I don't know. I didn't ask." She hadn't had much chance, but the less she knew about him, the better. Sharing stories would lead to sharing feelings.

Would that be so wrong? she wondered. Maybe the chemistry she had with Alex was there for a reason—the ignition key to falling in love.

Bad idea. Think of his sneaky ways, his isolation. There was something wrong with a man who lived the way that Alex did, even considering that he may have just moved to the city.

"I met someone, too," Debby said, interrupting Karina's inner debate. "This morning."

Karina blinked, surprised her friend had managed to hold out for so long. "You did?"

"His name is Kyle Murphy. You've probably seen him bringing our supplies." Debby named the parcel service and quickly told how she'd fallen into Kyle's arms. "I don't know how big his package is yet, but I'm pretty sure he can deliver the goods."

Karina groaned. "That was really bad."

"There's got to be a million of them. I'll try to think of better puns for the date."

"He asked you out?"

"Dinner," Debby said. "Nothing fancy—he says he knows a little place that serves good food for less than the national debt. I'd offer to split the check, but I don't think he's that kind of guy. We'll see how he feels after I order my usual."

"You don't order more than the average wo—"

"C'mon. You know I don't stop at salad."

"There's nothing wrong with that."

"Yes." Debby sighed. "A healthy appetite for a

healthy girl. Fortunately, Kyle is a big man. Not fat. He's built like a tree trunk with muscles. He lifted me like I was a feather." She sighed again, with appreciation. "Maybe not a feather. But it wasn't like I threw his back out, either."

"Of course you didn't! I'm so excited for you. When do you go out?"

"Saturday night."

"New clothes?"

"Absolutely."

"Shopaholics Anonymous!" Karina and Debby rapped knuckles over the marzipan. There was nothing they liked more than their weekend shopping excursions with Whitney or one of a rotating roster of women friends whose availability was subject to credit card limits.

"We could pick you out a peekaboo bra," said Debby.

Karina laughed. As usual, a girl-to-girl talk had lightened her tendency for serious introspection. She would follow Debby's lead—enjoy the flirtation with Alex for what it was and not worry about the consequences. "Thanks, sweetie, but that's not necessary. I've already mastered the art of revealing myself."

"I just realized that there's a flaw in the plan," Debby said, dropping her voice as two of her assistants came in from their lunch break. "You know the Shopaholics Anonymous rule: new affair, new clothes. That doesn't work if all you want to do with Alex is get naked."

"For one night only," Karina pointed out. "That doesn't even qualify as an affair. Exception to the rule."

"I guess."

"In this case, new sheets would be more appropriate than wardrobe." Karina crossed mental fingers; she was making a lot of assumptions about Alex's willingness.

"Satin sheets?"

"Uh…"

"Covered with rose petals."

"Hell, no! This isn't about romance, Deb."

Karina made herself sound cynical and proud of it. Even though a piece of her fluttery female heart wished for just a little bit of romance.

5

FRANK WHITMAN.

Alex sat on the counter of his galley kitchen eating a ham and Swiss on rye, kicking his foot against the cabinets like an antsy kid on a car trip, and thinking about Frank Whitman. He didn't really *want* to think about the man, particularly after his decision that morning to be a normal person again, but it was the one sure way to get his mind off what Karina was doing to him.

According to the newspaper reports Alex had looked up after the fact, Whitman had been a sixty-three-year-old parks administrator vacationing in the Florida Keys with his wife Joanne. They were planning to buy a condo for their retirement, but on the last day of Whitman's life they'd been merely enjoying their vacation, taking a walk along the harbor after lunch at a sidewalk café. He'd worn sunglasses and a flamingo T-shirt, and had just bought an Italian ice from a street vendor. The ice hadn't even begun to melt when he'd been shot through the neck by a sniper's high-caliber rifle from a boat in the harbor.

For those first frantic moments, nobody but a man going by the name Chris McGraw had known what was happening. There were screams, panicking tourists, spouting blood. Alex aka Chris had thrown Whitman's wife to the ground behind the vendor's cart and covered her with his body even though she'd struggled to rise, to go to her husband and hold him in her arms.

Frank Whitman had died on the spot, clutching his throat, his hands red with blood, two years from retirement and a life in the sun. His only crime had been being in the wrong spot at the wrong time, just as Alex's misstep had been believing that all defendants deserved representation.

His stomach revolted. He threw away his sandwich.

The cabinet door bore a scuff mark. He could sand that off. Make it a project and sandpaper all of the doors, taking away years of grime and the nicks and scratches. Prime and paint, good as new.

Starting over was easy.

Remembering was hard.

Alex swore. He jumped off the counter, drawn to the window like a fly to honey. Steel to magnet. Man to woman. All those clichés that he hadn't experienced for too long now.

The sky had darkened while he'd huddled in the kitchen. Lights went on in the row of brownstones further along the block, where rows of chestnut trees turned the street into an allée. Nice in spring, he imagined, wondering if there were any chance he'd still be in the city by then.

Although the teeming masses were supposed to give him a sense of anonymity, he'd discovered that Manhattan was a series of neighborhoods. Granted, a man could be unknown even in his own neighborhood, but in time that would wane. Stay long enough, and he'd become recognized by the denizens as the grouch, the lone wolf, the watcher in the window. If he weren't already. While he'd been tracking their patterns, they'd been learning his.

Humans were herd animals, filled with the instinct to meet, socialize, mate. They said hello at the fruit market. Waved from adjacent windows. Bumped into each other at the Italian-ice stand, where it was a natural friendly impulse for one guy to bend and retrieve the change the other had dropped, especially when the other guy's colorful shirt had been so familiar in a nostalgic way.

A scooped up handful of nickels and dimes had saved Chris McGraw's life from the assassin's bullet. What would save Alex Anderson's?

Not Karina Sutter. He couldn't ask that much of her. Still, he searched her empty windows. Too early...or had she backed out?

The city had left its grime on him. He went to take another shower. The pounding water felt good, even though it was a weak substitute for the scouring salt water of the ocean he craved.

He'd grown up in the surf, a California native who'd thought he'd always live in the state, where most of his family and friends were located. But his mother had passed away some time ago and after that his dad hadn't wanted to live in the family's rambling redwood house anymore. As the only child, the place was passed to Lex.

When the Norris murder trial had gone so wrong and he'd had to tell his dad that he was disappearing into the Witness Protection Program, he'd given back the keys at their last short meeting.

He didn't know what had become of the old place, but he thought of it now and then. He'd even dreamed of returning, but in the warped visions his subconscious conjured up, the house was empty, offering little comfort or shelter.

He vigorously shook his head as he emerged from behind the yellowing shower curtain, spraying water across the fogged mirror over the sink. Ignoring the stubborn arousal that had kept him semi-erect even though he'd tried everything to *not* think of Karina, he quickly dried himself and wrapped the towel around his waist.

His face was indistinct in the mirror. Like Karina last night, behind the curtains....

"Oh, hell. Can't you stop?" His fingers grazed his chin, wondering if he should shave again.

He snorted. For what? His date with a window?

Karina was impossible to figure out. He'd offered her the normal guy he'd been sure she'd prefer and she'd turned him down flat. For what? A truffle and a promise—an *implied* promise—of further titillation.

At a distance. No touching, no talk. Appropriate, but terribly ironic.

"This is what I've come to," Alex said out loud as he stepped into a pair of dark blue sweatpants. He added a pair of socks and flannel shirt, also new.

Technically, all of his clothing was new. The stuff Chris McGraw had been wearing on the day Frank Whitman had been murdered were spotted with arterial spray. He'd known better than to risk a return to his rented room to gather even a change of clothes, so he'd bought a T-shirt and a pair of cheap cotton drawstring pants from a street vendor, then dumped his stained clothes at the bus station before buying a ticket north.

Although he'd lived in Big Pine Key for five months, he'd moved on in five minutes. He consoled himself with the knowledge that the people he'd met there probably hadn't remembered Chris McGraw past a couple of salty margaritas and gaudy sunsets. The long-haired guy who'd spent his days at the beach and worked off the books as a bartender in a rinky-dink outfit called The Nautilus had had *drifter* stamped all over him.

Maybe that was why Karina didn't want to get involved. She saw that he was no prize.

"But I'm good enough for kicks," Alex said, his interest rising sharply when he saw from across the room that her lights were on.

His blind was already up. He grabbed the binoculars, giving no thought to checking for suspicious characters. His attention was on Karina, and Karina alone. They could shoot him through the heart if they wanted; he wasn't taking his eyes off the apartment across the way.

"Damn." That carelessness was what he'd been afraid of when he'd first laid his eyes on her. But for the moment, he couldn't make himself revert to caution.

Colored lights flashed, illuminating Karina standing before a device of some sort. Alex zeroed in with the binoculars. He'd noticed the figurine before but he hadn't realized exactly what it was. A fortune-teller—a carnival booth. Karina was proving to be more whimsical than he'd assumed.

She walked across her living room, looking at an item in her hand. When she looked up and saw him standing in his window, the item—a card—fluttered from her lax fingers. For a moment, she stared at him with big eyes, then collapsed onto the blue sofa as if she couldn't hold herself upright any longer.

Weak in the knees, Alex thought. *People are always falling for you.*

Not funny.

Karina did nothing for a couple of minutes, except stare at him watching her. He did not back away. This was almost a confrontation. A staring match.

Eventually her lids lowered slightly. Involuntarily, he took one hand off the glasses and put it on himself, following the path of her gaze along the strip of bare chest that showed from his unbuttoned shirt. He stroked himself, widening the gap, then let his hand rest at the drawstring of his sweats, fingers inside the waistband, touching below his navel.

Karina slid her arms out of her coat, then lazily reached up to undo the buttons of her blouse. Slowly, deliberately, one right after the other, without moving from her slumped position on the couch. She pulled the tails out of her waistband when she was done, but stopped there.

Alex studied the inside curves her breasts, molded by a white bra. Tantalizing, but not enough.

"Come on, baby, show me something," he crooned.

She sat forward, making the blouse hang loosely, but did no more except continue to stare at him.

A challenge, huh? Alex whipped his shirt open all the way, to see what she would do.

She followed suit, except her bra was still on. "No fair." He passed his hand up over his bare chest, across his right nipple, then shrugged off the shirt entirely.

Karina's head inclined. She dropped her blouse. Skated a hand upward over her torso as he had, but paused to cover her breast, hesitating, or…

She undid the clasp, sitting with the bra loosely covering her breasts before she straightened with a snap and pushed the straps off her shoulders. Naked from the waist up, she sat on the edge of the sofa with her hands folded in her lap and her hair up in a bun. A proper lady, displaying her breasts. Defiantly?

He looked, burning the sight of her into his brain for the lonely cold days ahead.

Karina didn't move. He dropped the glasses, rubbed his eye-sockets where the binoculars had pressed, then refocused, and still she hadn't moved except to swipe a hand across her eyes.

So that was it. Monkey see, monkey do. He put his hand into his damp hair, ruffling it up.

She raised both arms, lifting her breasts even higher so the primal surge of his blood became thicker, swelling in his groin. She pulled pins from her bun like a secretary in a fifties movie and her hair dropped around her shoulders, shining like white gold in the lamplight. She gave it a shake, then settled with her hands in her lap, motionless once more.

After another minute of simply looking at the provocative picture she made, he put the glasses aside and moved right up next to the window, standing with his legs slightly spread and his hands on his hips.

"That's it," he said when Karina stood. "Come closer."

But she didn't. She stayed back from the window, by the couch, her hands resting on her hips in imitation of him.

He beckoned with a finger and she put up the corresponding hand, palm out, telling him no. He noticed that her curtains were drawn except in the living area, and he supposed that she felt less exposed, keeping away from the one uncovered window.

He moved back. She had a point.

What now? He let his hands decide as they splayed

across his hip bones, pushing the sweats down a few inches. He was fully aroused and that was as far as he could go without exposing that fact.

Karina unzipped and rocked her hips a couple of times, sliding her pants past her hip bones. He took up the glasses and saw the edge of her underwear. White, to match the bra. She would always match, he decided. But did she prefer panties or a thong? Easy enough to find out.

He did a quarter turn and lowered one side of his sweats as if a nurse was coming at him with a needle. Karina's head shook with laughter, but she copied the movement, turning and displaying one smooth cheek to him, cut into a quarter moon by the elastic of her bikini panties.

Was that fair? He had no underwear to drop. Feeling ridiculous, he tapped his ass. Karina's face lit up with another bout of laughter, though she obediently slapped her butt for him, making the flesh jiggle just a little.

"Oh, man, oh, man," he said with a groan, pressing the eyepieces into his sockets again. "You are fan-frick-ing-tastic, lady."

But what now? He'd have to expose himself if he wanted to see more.

He rested a knee on the seat of the armchair that sat beside the window, facing front again. Without lowering the binoculars, he put his other hand down the front of his pants.

Karina did the same, stretching out the elastic of her underwear. He held himself, felt the pulse of desperate need but ignored it to watch her face as her fingers moved inside her panties. Her eyes closed, her head tilted back. She bit her bottom lip.

After a couple of seconds, her eyes opened. She must have forgotten about her worries about others seeing because she only looked at him. The color in her face had risen so that she looked feverish. Bright-eyed and needy, but waiting for his cue.

He dropped the glasses on the chair and jerked at the knot in the drawstring of his sweats. As soon as it loosened, the pants slid down and he cupped both hands over his erection, holding on to his last thread of decency, as if it mattered anymore. He was a goner.

Karina shook her tail so her pants dropped. They caught on her boots, but were loose enough to step out of. A couple of tugs and the panties followed, skimming down her smooth thighs. Her hands pressed flat over her pubic triangle, but she lifted one foot and put it on the couch behind her, raising her knee, separating her thighs.

Alex looked at his own leg, having forgotten it was propped up that way. He smiled to himself. Brilliant. Just brilliant. Now all he had to do was show her his and she would show him hers.

A thought flitted through his mind—how miserable he should be that he'd completely lost contact with humanity and had to find his satisfaction this way—but he dismissed it. He was Alex now, not Lex, who had formed no lasting bonds with women, either, so what did it matter? There were friends who missed Lex, no doubt. They probably raised a glass to him still, although even that would soon die off as the old crowd disintegrated, with different jobs, new addresses, marriage and children to keep them occupied.

He would have none of that, unless he went ahead and built a life based on a lie. That thought was a lot sadder than sharing a mutual sexcapade with a woman who wanted only that.

Take what you can get. Enjoy her.

Karina was waiting. He couldn't see her face because she'd dropped her chin to her chest, her shoulders hunched so her arms pressed into her breasts, making them full and round. She still held one hand flat for cover, but he could see the slight movement beneath it, the strain in her body as she kept to small secret strokes.

He'd clasped a fist around himself and was making movements of his own. What the hell, he thought. Now or never. He took one hand off, then, with a wince, the other, and his erection swung free, so rigid by now that it curved against his belly.

Karina had seen. She stared at him for a moment and he had to clench his hands to keep from touching himself, the need for completion was so great. She seemed to be equally tortured, her face contorting as she raised her hands up, sinking them into her hair and holding her head, her elbows almost meeting in front of her face.

Alex wanted to look at her through the magnifying lenses, see if she was swollen, or open enough to show her glistening wetness, but he was too stricken to move.

Was this the best he could expect from now on? The sadness and frustration of that bleak future rose up to overwhelm him and suddenly his control burst, slicing away the tight bands that had been wound around him, keeping him safe since Whitman's death, but also so cold. So alone.

The hell with caution. He wanted to feel again.

KARINA HAD THOUGHT she was torn between her arousal and her old inhibitions, but when Alex suddenly disappeared from his window she was struck with only one thought.

Come back. I'll do anything—anything....

And it was true. She'd eaten another of the Black Magic truffles and the clawing need inside her was so strong she was ready to plaster herself against the window to lure him over.

And he'd just *stopped?*

"You bastard," she said, sinking onto the couch and covering herself with her blouse. She pressed her thighs together so tightly she could have crushed apples into cider. *How could he leave her like this?*

She'd exposed herself, offered herself, and he'd seemed receptive. Still, his window remained blank.

Never again. With a screech of frustration, she kicked her pants away, then scooped them up, along with her underwear, and went to drop the linen shade with a vicious wrench. *Never. Again.*

The door buzzer went off. She dropped her clothing.

Alex?

A chill raced over her skin, drawing a hot flush behind it. She shivered, clutched herself, wiped the back of her hand over her damp forehead. Oh, God...*Alex.*

What did she do now?

Bzzzzz.

She had to answer. Feeling ridiculous, she ran across the living room wearing only the knee-high black leather boots that looked like something out of *The Matrix.* Or a bondage video, she supposed, crossing her arms over her naked breasts. She pressed the button of the intercom without saying a word.

"It's Alex," came the disembodied voice. "Let me in."

Another shiver raced up her spine, but it couldn't

touch the fever burning her up inside. She stabbed the button to release the lock on the downstairs door, then slid open the bolt on her apartment door before backing away.

He'd sounded dead serious. How many truffles had he eaten? She imagined Alex barreling up her stairs with one hand wrapped around his erection like a sword. Her head buzzed. Was that her, giggling? And how had she gotten all the way across the room? Should she grab her clothes?

She couldn't think. She shook herself, tweaked her nose, hoping to regain a few shreds of common sense. When Alex got here, she'd have to say something—an explanation, a come-on, a throwaway line—anything at all to make the situation more acceptable.

Impossible. There was no way to make their game socially acceptable. She was standing naked in an apartment with an unlocked door.

The door crashed open. Alex stood in the opening, six feet of hard-charging male. Panting, intense, bright-eyed and wild. His long coat hung open. The shirt he'd thrown on was misbuttoned. The outline of an erection showed beneath his sweatpants.

Wow. She backed up a step to lean against the brick wall, forgetting that she was nude, except for her boots. Then Alex's eyes swept over her like strobes. Her nipples and fingertips and toes tingled as if she'd been plugged into an electric outlet.

He said nothing. Just reached back and slammed the door, then strode toward her.

She literally quaked in her boots. The old saying rang in her head. *Be careful what you wish for....*

Alex grabbed her face in his hands and kissed her. It was a whirlwind of a kiss, and she was sucked into it, powerless. He filled her mouth with his hot tongue whether or not she wanted it, but she did. She did. She wanted all of him. This would never happen to her again, so she'd better enjoy the hell out of it.

The kiss was unapologetically rapacious, thrilling Karina. Her dates were always so gentlemanly. Who'd have known she wanted a dangerous man like Alex, one who didn't stop to say *please, may I?*

You knew, she thought, even if it was only subconsciously. That was why she'd started on this path.

Alex sucked on her tongue, slowly drawing back until she was left panting. As she stared into his hard, stormy eyes, the knowledge hit her that she was about to have sex with a man she barely knew. They'd exchanged no more than fifty words!

He put a hand over her mouth. "Don't talk."

She made a muffled sound of argument, pushing her arms against him where he'd trapped them against his chest.

"Shh." He exhaled against her neck. "You know it's too late to back out," he said silkily into her ear, just before his mouth opened to kiss and suck at her throat and neck, her collarbone, and—*oh my, oh my, oh my...*

She rose to the tip of her toes, following the drag on her nipples as he drew on them with wicked teeth and a hot suctioning mouth, the pull so strong in her body it was like being lost to the ocean's undertow.

As if he sensed her yielding to the inevitable, he reached around and lifted her high into his arms, right off her feet. After the first instant of disbelief, she let her eyes close and her head fall back, giving herself up to the dark world of pleasure and sensation. She was ready for anything.

ALEX KNEW THE WAY to the bedroom. Surging with a triumphant strength, he swept Karina to the spiral staircase. Heading straight upstairs to the proper door, he opened it with a kick of his boot.

The room was shadowed, but not so dim he couldn't see. There was a carousel horse in one corner. A full-length dressing mirror leaned against an interior wall. Opposite was the bed, a contemporary platform low to the floor. He spied an armless chair, upholstered in pink silk, similarly low to the ground.

He lowered Karina just far enough for her toes to touch the carpet, but kept an arm around her waist so she couldn't quite stand on her own. With his other arm, he dragged the chair to the foot of the bed.

"What are you doing?" A nervous thread ran through her voice.

"I told you not to speak." She wanted nothing but sex games; he would comply. That was better for him, anyway. An ongoing relationship would make him vulnerable and put her at risk.

She flinched beneath his grip. Started to insist, and then took one look at his face and closed her mouth.

He wanted to smile to reassure her, but instead he buried his face into her hair, inhaling the clean citrus smell, drugging himself with the beauty of her lithe naked curves as he ran his hands over her skin. She'd gained her balance, so he reached around and put a hand between her legs. Not to feel her up—though that was a nice benefit—but to urge her to rise an inch or two.

As his fingers sank into her softness, she let out a squeak of alarm, jerking herself taut again. He looked into the mirror, liking to see her that way, pale hair in disarray, body naked and quivering for his touch. Her eyes were wide, the pupils gone so large that only a golden rim showed around them. A hundred questions must have been lined up on the tongue peeping from between her parted lips, but she didn't say a word.

"Good girl." This time, he let her see the smile. It became wicked. "Now bend over the chair."

Even with the sounds of city traffic that drifted up from below, the room was quiet enough that her indrawn breath was obvious. Her buttocks clenched. After a tense pause, she wet her lips to whisper. "I can't."

His fingers moved inside her. "But you like showing yourself to me."

Her shoulders twitched, neither agreement nor denial.

He flicked his thumb over her clitoris and she arched back against him, air hissing between her teeth. His other hand cupped her jaw, elongating her neck to receive his kiss.

"Please…"

"I said that, too." He nipped at her nape. "While I watched you tease me. Do you know what torture you put me through?"

She made a humming sound as he slipped his fingers out from between her legs and dragged them across her belly, leaving a telling sheen of her lubricant. "So wet. I know you want to do what I tell you."

The instant of surrender showed in her eyes. She nodded.

He pressed the small of her back. "Bend over."

She had to stretch forward to grab the back of the chair, putting her body on perfect display. "On your toes," he reminded her, giving her rounded behind a light squeeze. "And put your hands flat on the seat." She strained to reach, sliding her arms down the backrest while keeping her ass elevated.

So tempting. He took a long, relishing look before he stepped closer. With a moan of pleasure, he ran both hands along her taut flesh, up to her back, bending over her so he could catch her head between his hands, her tousled hair like a skein of raw silk. He tilted her face up so she had to look at herself in the mirror. Her breasts were pushed forward, resting on the padded back of the chair. Her soft mouth quivered.

"I could take you this way." His erection was pressed into the intimate crease between her buttocks. He nudged against her and she had to widen her stance to keep her balance, giving him even better access. The juicy heat of her made his balls draw tight. "Hard and fast. Would you like that?"

Her chin jerked higher, resisting as he manipulated her head to nod. "Say yes, Karina."

She refused, forgetting that she'd already surrendered herself to him.

"You're right." He studied her defiant face in the mirror. "That would be too easy."

She blinked, worried now.

"I want you to know exactly what you did to me." He guided her to stand upright, but before she could regain her senses and offer resistance, he boosted her over the back of the chair and pushed down on her shoulders until she sat, still facing the mirror.

Her eyes immediately closed.

"Open them," he said. "And your legs, too."

"I can't."

"Oh yes, you can." He pulled her head all the way back so her nose was aimed at the ceiling. Her mouth opened instead, perhaps to protest, and he covered it with a long deep kiss. She swallowed convulsively, struggling a bit against him when he slipped his tongue between her lips. He stroked her soft cheeks, then her throat. Eventually she relaxed. Slowly he drew away, releasing her. She didn't move, except to gasp for breath, and he wondered if she'd take his cock as easily. But he was as hard as an iron bar, and though she didn't know it, he could never be that forceful. The play-acting could go only so far.

He stripped out of his clothes, flinging them carelessly aside, and when he looked up Karina was watching him in the mirror with her eyes dark and her lips curved into a satisfied smile. She wasn't as reluctant as she put on.

For a second, an idea ran through his mind—that she might have been enlisted to seduce him, to keep him occupied. But that was absurd. No more than his overworked paranoia.

Whatever the risk, she was worth it.

"Think you've got me?" he asked in a gruff voice. He sat on the very edge of the bed, directly behind her chair, spreading his legs wide and circling her with his arms. "We'll see how you feel after I show you what happens to naughty little teases."

Her eyes opened wide. She started to answer, then bit down on her bottom lip.

He grazed his mouth along the slope of her shoulder, breathing in her scent. He felt primal, stripped bare. Circumstances had already robbed him of the conventions that normally would have kept him from being this way with a virtual stranger. There was a grim satisfaction in knowing that he was finally receiving some benefit from his expulsion from society.

In the mirror, he lifted his eyes to Karina's. "Touch yourself."

Quivering, she touched her breast with a delicate finger.

Very nice. He copied her, tracing one finger around her pebbled areola. Her nipple was distended, colored a deep pink. He held it between his thumb and forefinger and squeezed, urging her to follow with her own hand.

"Feel that?" he whispered.

She nodded and let out a throaty sigh, rolling her nipple beneath her fingers.

"Where do you feel it?" He reached to put his free hand on her thigh and felt the ripple of her instinctive reaction. She was all nerve endings, aroused by the slightest touch.

Their heads were together. Restlessly, she moved her cheek against his and whispered, "You know."

"But I want to see." His fingers crept to the inside of her thigh, digging into the soft muscle.

She resisted his pressure for a moment, then suddenly wrenched her legs apart, planting her heels on either side of the chair. Another deep rippling shudder went through her. Her hips tilted, giving him a better view. "Is that what you want," she said, a note of near-hysteria in her voice.

"Also what *you* want," he quietly answered.

She tried to calm herself, but the frantic edge remained. "I didn't know what I was doing. It was the choc—"

"Hush. No excuses."

Her head dropped forward.

"Uh-uh." He took his hand off her leg to tip her chin up again. "I want you to look."

She did, with snapping eyes, chin held high on his fingertips.

Their image in the mirror was one of the most erotic sights he'd ever seen. All that pale skin framed by his brown arms and legs. Their two hands covering her breasts, light and dark, fragility and power. The sinuous grace of her elongated torso, the blatant positioning of her thighs, the tall black boots with steep heels that kept her knees elevated. The gleaming rosy-pink of her vulva, opened like a flower. And especially the look in her eyes as she absorbed the sight of herself, explicitly exposed, so aroused, vulnerable, wanting.

"Beautiful," he said.

She nodded.

He let her chin go and caught the hand she'd placed over her breast, dragging it lower. "Now you'll touch yourself for me," he said, "just like you did before."

Although she squirmed a little, she let him slide her hand beneath his, caressing her flat stomach, the patch of honey-colored fur. Fingers interlaced, he slid them along her swollen lips to dip between the wet folds. She made a sound in her throat and rocked her bottom in the chair, the muscles in her legs clenching and flexing as she fought against the conflicting desires that he easily read in her face. There was still a modicum of modesty in her, even though it was obvious that she also craved a wildly shameless release.

He urged her head around so he could kiss her. "Do you need me inside you?"

"*Yes.*" Her breath was hot and sweet.

"You should come first." Their slippery fingers tangled. "But I can't quite reach. You'll have to do it for me."

She whimpered, lifting her hips off the cushioned seat, offering herself, but he was already pressed as close as possible against the back of the chair, entwining her in his arms.

"No." He grasped her wrist. "I want to see you do it. Give me your hand."

"But I want—"

"You'll get it." She let out a soft grunt as he guided two of her fingers into her tight passage. "That's good, isn't it?" He felt her tremble beneath his arms. Her body strained, bowing upward again, trying to tempt him into losing control. "Don't take them out," he ordered.

"But I want—"

"Impatient little hussy."

A sharp inhale. "I am *not* a—"

"Tell that to the mirror. You're a bad girl and you know it."

She moaned, working her fingers in and out. "Yes."

He brushed his finger across the prominent pearl of her clit. Trapped against the back of the padded chair, his penis jerked in response. "Yes, what?"

She threw her head back. Total abandon, complete submission. "I'm a bad girl. And I want you to watch me. I want you to make me come."

"We'll do it together." And hope that he could contain his own orgasm for a while longer.

He'd been circling the hard knot of exquisitely sensitive nerve endings, flicking it occasionally, but now he touched squarely and rolled the nub beneath his fingertip, making her cry out with pleasure. Several strokes and she was vibrating beneath his palm as a climax ripped through her. Her hair whipped his face as she tossed her head from side to side, little yelping sounds flying from her open mouth. He stretched forward one final millimeter to feel the spasmodic clenching as she rode her own fingers to completion. He cupped her, stroked her, dipping into the moisture seeping out from between her fingers.

Finally, her body gave one last shudder and went lax. After a moment of silent shock, she buried her face against his neck. "I can't believe…"

"Don't get skittish on me now," he said, and with a great heave, dragged her limp nude form backward onto the bed. "I have other plans for you."

6

KARINA WAS TOO WEAK to object when Alex dragged her onto the bed, not that there was any reason to. Every bone in her body had turned to liquid and her mind to mush, but she was cognizant enough to know that she wanted more. The effects from the truffle she'd eaten earlier were still there—a light-headedness that kept the thinking part of her brain disconnected from her base instincts, the itchy warmth of her flesh, the urge to rub up against the closest male body, the hollow ache that cried out to be filled.

Clearly, one orgasm wasn't adequate.

She was lying on top of Alex. His hands were on her breasts, moving in slow circles that kept her nipples trapped beneath his palms. His hot rigid penis pressed between the cheeks of her bottom like a branding iron. A small repositioning and he'd be sliding up into her, giving her what she craved.

Think what you're doing, said a distant part of her brain. *He's a stranger.*

"Too late," she mouthed, resolutely keeping her eyes closed so she wouldn't have to confront the reality of the situation. Tonight was all about fantasy. Sex was always a risk, but at least this time her heart wasn't involved. She could take what she wanted and walk away tomorrow morning without regret, knowing that Alex had done the same.

As long as they stayed away from the truffles, there'd be no future complications.

A perfect scenario for her first—and only—one-night stand.

She moved atop Alex, rubbing her butt into his groin. He sucked air through his teeth. "Watch what you're doing or I'll be doing you," he teased.

She laughed lazily. Her hand drifted along his flank. "What's the holdup?"

"You really are the most impatient—"

"But you must be, too," she interrupted, giving another squirm. "Even more than me."

"I've learned self-discipline in the past few years."

She opened her mouth to ask what he meant, but instantly tamped down the curiosity. For the plan to work, she had to keep him strictly in the dream-lover category. Having him living across the street might be a problem, but as long as he continued to remain remote and uninvolved, they'd be okay.

But how did she tell a guy that she wanted only sex, not talk?

Well, there were ways—ways that had nothing to do with words.

She slid off him, rising to a sitting position so his hands had to drop from her breasts to her waist. Out of the corner of her eye, she saw his freed erection bob up. The size and brazenness of it made her breath catch in her chest.

Other lovers had always been moderate in the bedroom. In response to her own behavior, she supposed. Lights dim, or off altogether, a self-consciousness about the lovemaking being a part of the developing relationship, tissues and a robe at hand. And always, always, consideration for the partner's feelings and preferences.

Not like Alex, with his unapologetic commands. Yet somehow, everything he'd done had been just right. She'd never lost herself in the blatant pleasures and sensations of pure sex, but he'd made that possible. As if he'd known every secret fantasy and had come to sweep in and out of her life and fulfill them.

Of course, there was also the effect of the truffles. She mustn't overlook the truffles.

Alex had propped his head up on his crossed arms. He nodded at the mirror. "You've always liked to watch yourself?"

Karina looked up from unzipping her boot. The room had darkened so that the mirror reflected only vague shapes, shrouded in shadows. "No."

He chuckled.

"I'm being straight. I've never used the mirror…that way." She peered into it, watching her shadow-self slowly draw her leg up. There was a languid grace in the way she extended her arm, a certain eroticism about the contrast between her pale skin and the leather boot she unzipped. Hmm. "It's for dressing."

Alex captured her between his legs. "And now it's also for undressing." He tugged on her arm. "C'mere."

"My boot." She twisted to peel it from her calf.

He tapped her hip. "Now."

"Stop giving me orders," she said, but she gave in, kicking away her boot and stretching out to kiss him, lying side-by-side. After a minute, his hold on her softened, became an embrace, a caress. The sexual energy still hummed, but there was something more building beneath it with every gentle kiss. Something dangerous, in an entirely different way.

Karina pulled back. Alex's eyes were open and watching her. They were no longer slate-hard. Still indecipherable, except that she sensed the secretive longing in him.

She grasped at straws. *It's the truffles. They're making us needy.*

But it was too late. Her emotions had shifted and when she touched his chest it was with a genuine caring. "What do we do now?"

His lower body nudged her. "You have to ask?"

She kissed his chest, licking at the salt and musk of male skin. Springy hair smoothed beneath her hand, darker than the hair on his head. Muscles ridged his flat stomach; she felt his ribs through his skin. He was even leaner than she'd expected, but wiry and taut. She found a few small scars. Everything about him said he was a man who'd lived hard and rough, but there remained her first impression—his casual beach-bum appeal. Confusing. Could have been a false lead.

Did it matter?

He'd remained motionless under her explorations, but it was obvious that he couldn't wait long, regardless of the formidable self-control he'd mentioned. His erection twitched against her stomach, begging for attention. Tentatively she ran her fingers along the swollen length, tracing the pulsing vein, then around the edge of the flared head. She loved the sense of life and power that thrummed beneath her touch.

"Karina..." Almost begging.

Even though they were supposed to be living a forbidden fantasy, she liked hearing him say her name.

She smiled and kissed his shoulder, closing her eyes as she steered him toward the crevasse between her parting thighs. He took her leg by the back of the knee and pulled it up to wrap around his hip. She wormed closer. Open for him.

"Do you have a condom?" he asked in a husky whisper.

"*Oh.*" She was startled out of her daze. She never forgot. She was *always* responsible. But it had been a while since she'd been tempted by any of the men she dated. "There are some in the bathroom."

"Never mind." Alex had reached over the side of the bed and found the sweats he'd tossed aside. He took a strip of condoms from the pocket, keeping his arms wound around her as he busily ripped off a packet and tore it open. "Move up an inch," he said, his fingers gliding through the moisture that had gathered at her entrance.

She was so tender and aroused, even that light touch sent her head spinning. "I want to feel you inside me," she heard herself saying from a distance. "But go slow."

"Anything you want." Sheathed, he pressed against her, teasing her with his fingers first and then the advance and retreat of his swaying erection. She hunched her hips at him, slinging her top leg even higher around his waist. How could he be so cool? The secret-recipe chocolate had made her molten and greedy. She wanted only one thing and—timid words aside—she wanted it now.

Alex took hold of her butt and tilted her to receive his thrust. For a moment the pressure was too much. She almost cried out in relief as finally her tissues gave way, allowing the head of his erection to push inside. He was so big she stretched to accommodate him. Thankfully he allowed her a moment to adjust before giving her another inch.

She sighed at the sense of fullness, ready for more. She wanted him deep. But they weren't in a position to gain full penetration, and another part of herself was savoring the intimacy of lying in his arms, watching furrows carve into his brow as he filled her degree by degree.

When they were joined as deeply as possible, she brushed a hand over his forehead and kissed it, feeling more tender emotion for him than she'd expected. Almost as if he'd opened her heart.

This was trouble, she realized with a frisson of worry, but there were too many pleasurable sensations rolling through her to concentrate on what was only a fleeting thought.

They rocked together like a dinghy riding the waves. A familiar sweet warmth lapped inside her, flushing her face and chest.

He murmured. "Is this good for you?"

"Really good."

He had managed to work one arm beneath her. Both his hands pressed against her backside, urging her closer. They squirmed together, panting, sweating, striving.

"Ungh." He grunted. "I have to—"

"Yes," she said as he hunched his shoulders and pushed her onto her back. Her thighs fell wide open. He dug one knee into the bed and drove into her, desperate now, using every muscle and sinew in his body to thrust repeatedly. The rhythmic motion set off vibrations in her that escalated until she was shaking from head to toe. With one last push, she tipped over into the long, liquid free fall of her climax, losing herself in the whirlpool of sensation.

Alex rose up to his knees. He lifted both her legs and flung them over his shoulders, pulling her hips off the bed too as he plunged even deeper, touching off another orgasm that broke over her. He rode her through it, until she was gasping, and then finally he dug deep and let go of his own climax with a hoarse shout that seemed to echo inside Karina's head. The lashings of pleasure gradually diminished to waves, then soft ripples, leaving them floating again in a gently rocking sea of contentment, their slick bodies entwined.

Karina was sprawled on her back, with Alex collapsed partway on top of her. Instinctively, she reached for him, winding an arm around his heaving shoulders, but he brushed her away, flipping over—and away from her—instead. They lay side by side, panting.

"You ate the truffles," she said after a minute or two.

"Umm."

He couldn't talk yet; she smiled. "Several of them, I'll bet."

"Mmm."

"They're incredible, aren't they?"

"Shh."

She pressed a couple of fingers to her lips. Tasted *him.* Better than chocolate.

After another little while, she said, "I don't normally do this," then cringed at the apology in her voice. She was a sexually confident woman—trying to be, anyway. There was no need for her to make excuses. Not even the chocolate could account for tonight. She'd wanted Alex from the first time she'd seen him, *before* she and Debby had ever thought of using the truffles to snare him.

The aphrodisiac took the edge off her nervousness,

the way some people used alcohol to loosen them up. No difference.

"What I mean is I don't, ahh…flash my neighbors. As a habit. You're the first." She cringed. "And the last. I'm not into kinky sex, is what I'm trying to say."

"Pity."

Oh. Her eyes widened. "Pity?"

"We could have had fun."

"But this is a—" She faltered. It was a fling, at least it was supposed to be. Naturally, because of the way it happened, he'd probably believed she was always this wild. He'd be wrong. She was not ready to get into a weird sex thing with him, even if the very thought produced a throbbing between her legs.

She inched away, rocking her butt on the mattress, then caught herself. "Are you…" She shot a wary look at his profile. "Are you some kind of freak? Whips and chains and leather?"

"No." His laugh was indolent, and not entirely reassuring.

"You're sure?"

He glanced at her. "Do you think that I'm leading a double life I'm not aware of?" There was such an ironic tone to the question that she still wasn't reassured.

"Well, you are mysterious. To me, anyway. I don't know much about you except that you claim to be a writer."

He looked at the ceiling again. "That's right. You don't know anything about me."

Except that you gave me the most powerful orgasms of my life, she said silently, feeling the bottom drop out of her stomach at the mere thought of how much she'd loved having him inside her. Even more—how the first delicious tremors of fear and desire had become a strangely sweet emotion before evolving back into pulse-pounding sexual energy.

She was wrung out, but she hoped he wouldn't go. Not yet. There was something wrong with her. Weren't participants in one-night stands supposed to be eager to leave the scene of the crime? Had to be the residue of chocolate in her system.

Whatever the reason, she wanted him again, and they were still within the boundaries of a fling so there was no reason she couldn't have him. As long as she maintained her detachment. But she had to clean up first before a damp spot formed beneath her. Maybe she could lure him into the bathtub.

That would be too intimate, she instantly decided, picturing them up to the chin in bubbles, all warm and cuddly. Then she had to chide herself. They'd already been more intimate than she'd intended. She didn't seem to be very good at having sex with no prospect of emotional involvement.

Alex was supposed to remain cool, even if she didn't. And he'd started off being all about the sex. But there'd been that moment, when they'd been positioned face-to-face, gently touching…

Karina squeezed the tip of her nose. *You're conjuring up a deeper meaning where there is none, to give yourself "permission." Think straight. It would be best if he leaves now. Don't prolong the situation.*

"Where are you from?" she blurted. Damn!

His upper half jackknifed off the bed. "My last stop was Arizona."

That explained the tan. "Phoenix?"

He shrugged, his back to her as he removed the condom. "Yeah, sure."

She swung her legs over the other side of the bed and found the box of tissues on the low shelf attached to her bird's-eye maple headboard. "If you want to shower…"

Alex didn't answer, just raked a hand through his hair and let out a sigh. He probably wanted to get out as soon as possible.

She glanced at the topography of lean muscles in his shoulders and back, reminding herself that technically she had a stranger in her bedroom. She should know at least a *little* about him, in case…

Her heart squeezed. She was on the pill and they'd used the condom, of course, but there was always a slim chance of pregnancy or STDs. Practical matters, she decided. She was being responsible, just in case. That she could satisfy her curiosity at the same time was a bonus. "What did you do for a job in Phoenix?"

"Wrote…ad copy."

So he was a regular guy after all. No big mystery. "And you quit to become a writer?"

"Yep."

"Fiction?"

"More or less."

"Do you have family in Arizona?"

"No. They're all gone."

"I'm sorry." She paused, but he didn't explain, nor express any curiosity about her.

She volunteered. "My parents live in Switzerland. They're retired. I have an older brother, Ralf, who's an attorney in San Francisco, specializing in international law. He has a wife and two kids, and we all try to get together at least once a year at my parents' summerhouse in the Rhône Valley. I thought I might see them this Christmas, but it turns out that Ralf's involved in a big case—"

She halted her babbling. Even though they were sitting on opposite sides of the bed with their backs to each other, she sensed that Alex was disturbed by something she'd said. About her brother? Could Alex have lost his family? That would explain his air of sadness and desolation. But not his penchant for binoculars.

She licked her lips, suddenly nervous. "Were you…"

Don't ask, don't get involved. Just let him go.

"…ever married?"

She was doing a terrible job of listening to herself.

"No," he said, exhaling so forcefully his shoulders slumped.

Her questions were annoying him. She leaned down and grabbed the pieces of clothing she could reach, dropping them in a pile on the bed.

"I'm a wanderer," he added abruptly. The silent message was: *So don't count on me sticking around.*

How could she respond to that?

She couldn't. "You're not intending to stay in New York, then?"

"Probably not for long."

"Long enough for a lease."

"A sublet." He shrugged. "Any contract can be…"

"Broken," she finished for him. *Like hopes and dreams and hearts.*

Go ahead. Really *finish for him.* She stood. "Well, it's been interesting, but now I really need to take a shower. You know the way out." Her clothes were scattered downstairs and her robe was hanging on the bathroom door. There was always the option of dragging a sheet off the bed, but that was so ungraceful. A fully confident woman would saunter from the room, giving her lover one last look at what he was about to lose.

Karina forced her hands to relax and hang at her sides. With a shake of her head, she tossed her hair over her shoulders. Pinning her gaze on the bathroom door, avoiding both the mirror and Alex, she strolled across the room. All jumpy nerve endings and goose bumps, so aware of his eyes on her that they felt like a laser beam cutting into her skin.

She was about to safely shut herself in the bathroom when Alex appeared in the doorway. His eyes were hot and alert. "Maybe I'll take that shower."

Her heart leaped, but she remained cool. "You can go first then."

Surprise flickered on his face. "I thought we'd do it together."

"That would be so intimate," she purred, giving his body a sloe-eyed perusal. She resisted licking her lips. "You were giving off 'keep-away' vibes out there."

"I've never been good at the post-coital thing—cuddling and calling each other pet names."

A small grin twitched at his mouth, though, and she wondered if he was being completely honest. There were flashes in him of another sort of man, which confounded her at every turn. She couldn't seem to get a firm grip on his personality.

Except that *way,* she thought, glancing at his swelling penis.

"Cuddling?" She made a fake cough. "Any one of the Central Park statues is better at cuddling than you."

He laughed. And stepped close enough to wind his arms around her. His hands went to her breasts, lifting them with gentle fingers as his thumbs took a lazy sweep over her nipples. Back and forth until the flesh had drawn into tight, tingling buds. "See?" he said into her hair. "I can cuddle."

She wanted to resist, but desire was looping and swirling, entwining her like silk ribbons. "That's not cuddling, that's second base."

He began to pepper her with light, ticklish kisses. The back of her neck, her shoulder bone, the inside of her elbow, behind her ear. "And what is this?"

"Seduction," she said, although there was no need for it. She was already thoroughly seduced.

"Not if I stop before it goes farther." His hands skimmed over her backside, one finger tracing the seam. "Do you want me to stop?"

She slid a foot along the tumbled-marble tiles, opening her legs for him just a little bit. "Third base," she said as his finger teasingly stroked her without actually entering.

"What's with this baseball obsession?" he muttered into her neck.

"Don't you like baseball? I became a huge fan when I was twelve and we got satellite TV."

"It's okay. Surfing is my sport."

"In Arizona?"

"*Was* my sport. I've moved around a lot."

His voice was casual. If her hands hadn't been on his shoulders, she wouldn't have realized just how tense her questions were making him.

"I like the feel of water on my skin," he said, pulling away from her to twist the taps on the walk-in shower.

"We could use the bathtub instead." She indicated the claw-foot tub that sat below the tall window overlooking the street. During the apartment renovations, she'd splurged on every deluxe fitting in the book. The friends who considered her so restrained and disciplined were flummoxed when they saw the positively sensual setting of her private bath.

"Have you ever tried sex in a bathtub? It's not easy. The water washes away the natural lubrication."

The insistent pulse between her legs had returned. "I thought this was about cuddling, not sex."

Alex sent her a narrow look.

She raised her eyebrows.

He relented without an argument, shutting off the taps. "All right. Just don't expect me to call you cupcake."

"Please." She got the apothecary jar of bath salts. "I have more dignity than that."

"Pookie."

She chuckled. "Spare me."

"Don't tell me you want to be called cuddle-buns," he said with a low growl as the tub filled.

"God, no." Karina could hardly believe they were laughing and teasing like a regular couple. She'd been prepared to boot him onto the last train to One-Night-Standville, if only to beat him to it before he ran out on her.

When she bent to sprinkle the eucalyptus salts into the stream of water, Alex ran his hand along her derriere and she reminded herself that this was still about sex. They hadn't burned through all of the aphrodisiac yet, and even if they had, well, there was plenty of natural combustion to keep the flame alive.

One-night stands could end in the morning just as well.

THE ROSY-GRAY DAWN was creeping past the curtains before Alex could make himself ease away from Karina. He did it by increments, because—or so he told himself—she was lying on his arm. The numbness of the sleeping appendage was preferable to the guilt and regret gnawing at him for leaving her this way. Men who ducked out were chickenshits in his book. Not that he hadn't had his share of brief affairs over the years, as long as the woman was on the same track. Even then, he almost always had waited to say a cordial goodbye in the morning, and he'd made sure they had his name and number, too.

This time, leaving unannounced was the only way to go.

It was bad enough that he'd given in and come over to ravish her the way he had. Pile on the complications—that he'd put them both at risk, how emotional he'd been for a few minutes in the middle there, the awkward interrogation, the much less awkward but all the more troubling scene in the bathtub...

With Karina warm, naked and wet in his arms, his defenses had splintered like shale. Luckily, she'd been silent more than she talked, with no more of the probing questions. She'd chatted a little about the pleasures of New York at the holiday season and he'd bitten down on his tongue to stop from asking if she'd share some of it with him. She'd mentioned her shop, making comments about the potent product that he hadn't understood, but put down to the female obsession with chocolate. Maybe he should have confessed up front about his allergy, but she'd seemed so damn proud of those truffles. It was not as difficult for him to lie as it had once been.

The bath had stayed fairly innocent. He'd held her, caressed her some, aching with gratitude for the feel of a supple female body nestled against his chest. Her serene voice, soft touch, sweet scent. At one point, tears had even prickled at the back of his eyes, and he'd had to lay his head on the tub, blinking and swallowing until the lump in his throat had gone, hoping like hell that she hadn't noticed.

They'd finally climbed out of the tub, raided her kitchen for crackers and cheese, then got back in bed with the food that went mostly untouched after he'd realized that there were only so many hours until morning. He'd made love to her again, intending to keep it simple and fast, but after a few minutes of kissing she'd started working her way down his body and at that point the only polite thing to do was to reciprocate.

Alex gathered up his clothing and stood in the doorway for another minute, filling his eyes with the sight of Karina, smiling in her sleep. He was certain of only one thing: *normal* guys didn't slip out in secret and leave a woman like her behind.

But he had to do it. He couldn't be absolutely positive that no one had trailed him from Florida. He might *never* be sure.

Karina deserved better.

He moved silently to the loft area that opened off the staircase and slipped into his clothes. The spiral stairs creaked a little as he descended, boots in hand. By the time he got to the bottom, he was halfway expecting Karina to have awakened and be glaring at him from the landing, but when he looked up she wasn't there.

His getaway was clean. *Unfortunately,* he thought, which gave him a blip on his internal radar screen. *You're getting too close, man. Back off before you're drawn in so deep you forget the risk. One moment of inattention is all it'd take.*

The floors were hardwood with seagrass area rugs. Deciding to put his boots on out in the hall, he padded to the door. The fortune-teller in a glass booth caught his eye, and he stopped to stare. What an odd item for Karina to own. Didn't seem to be her style at all. Although there had been that carousel horse in the bedroom, he vaguely recalled.

Aha. The machine lights up, he remembered. He'd seen it from his windows. Karina had taken a card from the device and dropped it…somewhere….

Curiosity got the better of him. He listened for sounds of stirring upstairs, then went to the living room to look for the fortune.

The card was on the floor beside a glass-topped coffee table. Alex picked it up, turned it over in his palm. Beware The Man Bearing Gifts.

His gut clenched, for no reason that he could see. The men he had to look out for came bearing guns. The fortune meant nothing. Nothing at all.

7

"STEP AWAY FROM the low-riders," Karina said in a monotone. "This is a matter of ego security. Please, ma'am, step away from the low-riders."

Debby looked up, guilt splashed across her face. Her fingers were poised near a rack of low-slung leather pants with lacings and nail-head detailing. "I just wanted to look. I wouldn't actually try any on." She gave the soft leather a lingering caress. "Not after the last time."

Karina was relieved. Several months ago, Debby had wiggled into a pair of hip-hugger pants on one of their Saturday retail therapy sessions. One look at her tummy bulge in the merciless dressing-room mirror and she'd plunged into a rigid seeds-and-weeds regimen. The diet had wreaked serious havoc with her culinary inventions for Sutter Chocolat. The line of carob candies had not been a big seller. Armed with chocolate temptation, Karina and the other employees had been forced to stage an intervention for the sake of the business—and Debby's sunny personality, which had taken a nosedive into her edamame salad.

"Don't give the pants another thought," Karina said. "Confectioners aren't meant to wear low-riders."

Debby stuck out her lip. "*You* could wear them."

"I'm management. You're the creative one."

"What does that mean?" asked Whitney Smythe, the third participant in the day's Shopaholics Anonymous outing, who was frequently oblivious. A natural brunette with curls, her hair was so straight and blond she had a standing appointment with her stylist to maintain the look. She spent more on its upkeep than rent, but then she shared a studio apartment with Japanese twin sisters and slept on a single-bed mattress in a room so small there was only room for her and an overstuffed clothes rack.

Karina steered Debby away from the leathers and toward the feathers. Deb was a boa type of girl. "It means that she's free—"

"Fat," Debby said cheerfully.

"Free," Karina emphasized with a push at her friend's back. "Arty and original. Unfazed by sizes and rules."

"So then you're the opposite?" Debby looked skeptical and Karina hoped she wouldn't bring up the contradicting proof with Whitney around.

Instead Debby reached back and snatched up a pair of the leather belly-pants. "Let's see *you* try these on."

Karina sailed ahead. "Not my style."

Debby handed the pants off to Whitney, who gave them an interested examination, being both arty and managerial in her job as a features editor at *Hard Candy,* a racy lifestyle magazine for men. She'd been trying to talk Karina into an article about her chocolate shop, but the publicity was the last thing they needed.

Debby caught up to Karina and gave her a nudge. "Are you sure about that—your style? Seems to me you've been undergoing a radical shift in philosophy. Depending on what happened last night, that is."

"Last night..." There were no words to explain. Fortunately, Whitney interrupted before Karina had to think some up.

"*I* will try them on," she said, waving the pants. "I have an invitation to an MTV bash next weekend and I need to look hip and funky."

"Will Funkmaster Z-Row be there?" Debby handed Whitney a burgundy velvet top. The bodice was criss-crossed with ribbon and buckled leather bands, the price slashed by fifty percent.

"Who?" Whitney frowned. "The rapper? He's so a hundred-and-five minutes ago."

"Z-Row's a classic," Debby said. "He's big and cuddly. I just want to squeeze him."

Cuddly? The coil of restraint in Karina loosened at the reminder of her conversation with Alex. It was hard to act like she was normal when she began feeling so loose and loopy inside.

Loopy about Alex, even though she'd awakened to an empty bed and all the shades drawn in his apartment. She'd told herself that his early departure was convenient, not disappointing. They'd avoided all the fumbling weirdness of acting like they were cool with each other, that engaging in a night of illicit sex meant no more than changing clothes.

She had no business feeling abandoned. Imagining they'd shared something special, wishing to see him again—that was so predictable, so female. The chocolate courage was supposed to have carried her past those conventions.

"But I am not the unconventional type," she muttered, and Debby's head came up from her tussle with a pile of feathery sweaters.

"The leather," Karina explained. Whitney was still lurking nearby. "All wrong for me."

"Sounds like you're trying awfully hard to convince yourself of that."

"Maybe so." The warm throbbing she felt between her legs whenever she thought of Alex was merely the aftermath of being very well laid.

"Oh?" Debby's curiosity was engaged, but Whitney hailed them from the doorway to the dressing rooms. Debby waved her off, calling, "Give me a couple of minutes to find my size." She hooked her hand around Karina's elbow and hauled her toward the Lady Bountiful section of the boutique, where they'd be assured of privacy. Not many fashionistas would be caught dead lurking past size eight.

Debby squinted an eye and looked Karina up and down. "Did you hook up with Alex last night?"

"I can't say anything around Whitney."

"How come?"

"You know she'd tell everyone we know. I don't want to get a bad reputation."

"Hah! That's about as likely as Santa delivering crack door to door."

"That happened. The police arrested a ring of street-corner Santas on drug charges." Karina straightened a cuff on her suede jacket. "Prepare to be astonished."

Debby rubbed her hands together. "Now we're getting to the good stuff."

"We're not getting anywhere because I can't go into it here. Wait until lunch, Whitney's got her hair appointment and can't come with us."

"No fair keeping me on pins and needles." Debby eyed Karina with dawning suspicion. "The truffles. You tried the truffles again. Damn! I should have recognized the post-cocoa-bean glow."

"I'm not glowing." Karina pointed to her face. "That's good old-fashioned embarrassment."

"You're so Victorian. It's adorable. Just tell me—was it the truffles?"

Karina nodded. "I told Alex to eat one and then I—" She felt her cheeks heat at the memory of their window assignation. Okay, so Debby was right; she was glowing like the Rockefeller Plaza Christmas tree. "Let's just say I invited him over."

Debby's voice rose to a peak. "A-a-and?"

"The truffles really are magic."

Debby did a cha-cha in a little circle, pumping her fists like maracas. "Karina got some, Karina got some," she sang in tune to "La Cucaracha."

Karina gave in to her giddiness and joined the dance. "And it was hot stuff, it was hot stuff," she sang. Silly, but she loved it. The last time she'd been ga-ga over a guy had been…never. Maybe when she was thirteen and so in love with Patrick Swayze she'd watched *Dirty Dancing* on video every day after school.

"Hot stuff?" Debby halted. "This I've got to hear. Is it time for lunch yet?"

"We've barely begun to shop. We have to find you an outfit for your date with Kyle, and Whitney has the MTV thing—"

On cue, Whitney wailed from the dressing area. "Kare, Deb—emergency consult. I look like a velour pirate!"

"Coming." At random, Debby grabbed a few garments off the racks and they made their way to the curtained cubicles, where they squeezed in with Whitney and gave the holidays-in-bondage top a quick thumbs-down, while the decision on the pants remained pending, per their pairing with the right top.

The holiday shopping season was at its zenith. Chatter rose all around them, in various accents and languages. Next door, a Korean mother-daughter team were in a hissing debate over the girl's wish to wear a dress with cutouts. Farther down, a snappish woman with a surgically chopped Pekingese nose threw garments over the curtain of her stall, screeching that the size fours had been altered in the past month.

Whitney shimmied into a spangled tank. "Not buying anything, Karina?"

"She's only into taking clothes off, not putting them on," Debby said, making a face while Whitney wasn't looking.

Whitney blew strands of bleached hair out of her eyes. "Huh?"

"I'm here as your advisor," Karina said from her position on a ledge seat in the corner, out of the way. "That top would be better in red." She swept the feathered sweater out of Debby's hands, leaving her in a gray wool skirt and a bra. "Yellow, Deb? Are you planning to audition for *Sesame Street?*" She gathered the rest of the rejected garments off the floor. "Your delivery guy sounds like a good prospect. I'll go find you something slinky and sexy so you can really wow him."

"God, I wish I had your breasts," Whitney was saying as Karina picked her way toward the curtain.

"You can have them in return for your butt. That thing is teeny-tiny, even in a thong."

"Pilates classes," Whitney said, a smug sylph. "Karina comes, why don't you?"

Debby giggled. "I'll try to—tonight."

Karina made a choking sound and was just barely able to exit the changing room before she blew a gasket.

"There are no classes tonight," a befuddled Whitney was saying as Karina trotted away, snorting into her hand. She dropped the clothes on the sales counter and went off to find Debby a dress that would set her up for a magical evening. No one deserved it more.

"I'M ALWAYS SHOPPING with you." Debby tucked her shopping bag under the table. They'd dubbed her new dress Black Magic. "For richer, for maxed-out credit, in sickness or in health, till sample sales us do part."

Karina gave a modest shrug. She'd found Debby a little black dress that hugged her curves without turning them into bulges, dipped in low *V*s front and back to show off her friend's flawless skin, and yet had wide crisscrossed straps that concealed her upper-arm trouble spot. "'Twas nothing. The gods blessed us."

"Serendipity," Debby said with a dimple, which was why they'd chosen the popular restaurant despite it being packed with screaming kids. That, and to sample their competitor's hot chocolate.

"But now that Whitney's gone..." Debby sipped her chocolate, then leaned toward Karina with a foam mustache above her salacious grin. "Tell me about Alex."

Karina touched her upper lip. "He was...I mean, *it* was..." She sighed. "Just fabulous. He swept me off my feet."

Debby licked the mustache. "Details, please."

"There aren't a lot to tell. We hardly talked. He was smoldering."

"Smoldering?"

"That sounds over the top, I know. But he was. He, um, kind of took charge and…you know. It was just overwhelming. I had no control over myself and the sex was shockingly good."

Debby nodded as she dabbed with a napkin. "Why am I not surprised? It figures you'd like having the decision taken out of your hands."

"How do you mean?"

"Put him in charge and you can have the hot, sweaty jungle sex experience while still maintaining your good-girl standing. Otherwise known as having your cake and eating it, too."

Karina frowned. She wasn't sure that she liked the sound of that. "Don't forget—*I* instigated the affair."

"True. Baby steps."

"But I'm not stepping out again. This was a one-time thing, remember?"

Debby smirked. "I always figured you'd change your mind if the sex was really good."

"Well…" Karina dunked her spoon into her cup of hot chocolate, stirring the disintegrating whipped cream. "The thought has crossed my mind."

"Do tell!"

"I'm tempted," she admitted. "He's right across the street, and it's not as if I have to worry about us developing a relationship. He was clear about not wanting that. He even pulled out the standard 'I'll be moving on soon' line that guys use to keep marriage-minded chicks at bay. So I have no expectations in that area."

Debby grinned. "But an endless supply of truffles."

Which all sounded good, if not reasonable, but Karina knew that continuing the affair would be asking for trouble. Common sense prevailed and she shook her head. "No. It's smartest to stop now."

"Aw, that's no fun. How about when the truffles run out?"

Karina considered. "I gave him a half dozen, but I ate one on the day I delivered them. And he ate at least one last night, if not two. That leaves four truffles at most."

"And four fu—"

"Four's too many. I might get feelings after four times." Pfffft. She had feelings after just *one.* It was bothersome, having to tamp them down all the time. Four more nights with Alex and she'd be thinking about ways to turn him into a proper boyfriend, which he clearly did not want to be.

And the truth was that she didn't consider him a very promising prospect anyway. His actions were mystifying. His personality was mercurial. He was a wanderer. He didn't even have a job, aside from being a wannabe writer—if that was even legitimate. There wasn't much to recommend him.

Except the sex.

And…yet some small, impractical part of herself still believed in fate.

She swallowed a large gulp of the hot chocolate. "He left me. I woke up this morning and he was gone."

"Yeah, I hate when guys do that." Debby flashed an irreverent smile. "The only thing worse is if they leave cash on the nightstand."

Karina laughed; Debby could always get her to do that. "Okay, so it wasn't that bad. I'd given him no reason to believe I wanted him to stay."

"And it's not as if you don't know his name and where he lives. He didn't *vanish.*"

"Somehow, though, I got the feeling that he might do exactly that." Karina flicked her fingers in the air. "Poof."

"Use your powers of persuasion, along with the truffles. Trust me, he won't leave."

"I don't want to keep him by artificial means."

"You're so naive, Kare. Women have been using their wiles to keep men since Adam and Eve. The lugs don't know what they want. We have to tell them. That's why biology made it so they think with the little head—for our convenience. The little head is easy to control."

Karina shuddered. "Ugh. I can't do that. When I get serious—and it won't be with Alex—I won't play games. It will be an equal partnership of love and respect."

"What a bore. You've turned marriage into a social studies exam." Debby grinned. "No wonder you needed a little fun first."

Karina felt sheepish. Trust Debby to be blunt while pointing out a few hard truths. "I never said the relationship couldn't be fun, too."

Except the model that came to mind was her parents, who'd been a partnership first, always working to put forward her father's career in industry and then diplomacy. They weren't the kind to show each other much public affection, but at least they were still together and seemed content enough. Many of the lovey-dovey couples she knew were either divorced or in the throes of marital disharmony. Being practical-minded had worked for her up to now.

Karina moved her cup aside as the waiter arrived with their food. According to the Shopaholics Anonymous code, they must always order substantial lunches to keep their strength up for the fray. "Enough about me. What about you and Kyle?"

"Is there even a question?" Debby picked up her cheddarburger, momentarily confounded by how to get her jaws around it. "We're *all* about having fun."

"Why not more?"

"I'm not getting remarried anytime soon." Debby mashed the burger together, with oozing results.

"Yes, but what about a long-term relationship? It would be nice to have a guy around for the holidays at least." Karina became wistful as she rearranged the filling in her Ultimate BLT. "Someone to help decorate a tree and exchange gifts with, take to Christmas parties, sip mulled wine by the fire. You know."

Debby nodded with her mouth full. "Even though the only fire I have is the pilot light that's always going out on my stove," she said after she'd swallowed.

"You could give Kyle a truffle." Karina winked. "He'd light your fire."

Debby got a happy look on her face. "The man seems to have arrived already ignited."

"Lucky you." Karina's ego winced over the lengths she'd gone to with Alex. "Imagine when he sees your new dress."

Debby gurgled around her burger. "Oh, yeah, baby. I'm *really* looking forward to that."

"You said he's a bodybuilder. What if he's all into himself, going on about how his body is a temple, blah, blah, blah?"

"I'll ask to worship at the shrine." Debby shrugged. "But I don't think he'll be like that. For sure there were a lot of muscles when I was in his arms, but he didn't have that arrogant way about him. No preening. And I might have even felt a tiny hint of a love handle." She smacked her lips. "'Course, most of my attention was on other areas of his anatomy."

Debby's eyes were shining beneath the curly fluff of her bangs. "How come it's so easy for you?" Karina asked.

"I don't expect perfection from the men I date," came the quick answer. Debby smiled to soften the implied criticism. "After all, I'm not perfect, either, and I wouldn't even want to try to be." She flipped her hair, acting cavalier when Karina knew that there was a real hurt lingering there. "Call it low expectations. Failing at marriage the first time out tends to revise your standards about what men are capable of providing."

"Aw, Deb. Someday you'll meet the guy who'll give you everything you want."

"Maybe, but for now all I expect from Kyle is a hot meal and a good time. Or vice versa." Debby lifted her burger high. "Here's to getting what we want."

Karina did the same. "And wanting what we get."

She neatly bit into her BLT, mentally castigating herself. Why couldn't she be as easy and uncomplicated about Alex? *Carpe diem,* grab for the gusto, put off her concerns until tomorrow. With another of the mindless throbs pumping endorphins into her veins, she thought of the remaining truffles.

Chocolate was a terrible thing to waste.

"HERE WE ARE. Welcome to the little place I like to call my humble abode à la mode." Debby tossed her and Kyle's coats on the back of a chair. Luckily, she'd remembered to fold the futon into a couch, in between tugging a pair of tights past her hips and cooking homemade chocolate pudding so she could lure Kyle to her apartment with the offer of dessert. Not that he needed much convincing. He'd been more than agreeable.

"It's big," he said about the two-room space, which only a New Yorker would understand. One room opened onto the other without doors, so she'd turned the first into her lounge and the second into her kitchen and dining area.

"Big enough for me. Make yourself at home. I'll get our dessert." Feeling very Donna Reed, minus the apron, Debby click-clacked in her high heels to the bare-bones kitchen that she'd dressed up with tangerine paint and a row of old wedding-gift appliances. She took the pudding out of the fridge and at the last minute decided to add chocolate shavings as a garnish. Only a few, from her personal stash of the special chocolate.

She popped one of the dark curls into her mouth. Kyle had been extremely attentive all evening, looking across the table at her as if he couldn't wait to eat her up. But a little insurance never hurt. Karina would be proud that Debby was thinking so pragmatically.

She took two spoons from the utensil drawer and arranged a tray, stopped to make a quick adjustment of her breasts inside the strapless bra that was the only style that worked with the new dress, then returned to the lounge. Eyes avid, Kyle stood as she entered and took the tray from her so she could sit. She was pleased with his continued display of gentlemanly manners. Call her narrow-minded, but she'd expected a blue-collar deliveryman to be the kind to get marinara sauce on his chin and burp after dinner. Kyle *had* dunked a shirt cuff in the wine carafe, but only because he was passing her the bread basket, with the most adoring look on his face.

Not once had there been a hint that he thought she should cut down on carbs or order the salad instead of the baked ziti. After her husband, who'd memorized nutritional labels like some men did baseball statistics, there was no quicker way to win Debby's heart than to enjoy good food and encourage others to do the same. For a time, she'd wondered if she could possibly be friends with a woman like Karina, who ate chocolate only for dessert. Eventually she'd understood that it wasn't about calories with Kare, it was about moderation and self-control. Some people were just wound too tight.

Debby kicked off her shoes and curled up on the futon. She held her hand out to Kyle. Nothing tight about him. He was big and solid, but as huggable as a stuffed animal. "Come cuddle with me, teddy bear."

Kyle put the tray on the coffee table and eagerly dropped down beside her, at least two hundred pounds of luscious male. With a blissful sigh, she put her arms around him and squeezed.

Aha. She'd been right—he had love handles. And, boy oh boy, did she love to handle them. A nice, warm feeling spread through her, almost as if she'd gorged on the aphrodisiac chocolate instead of only a single curl. There were times the extra help wasn't necessary.

"Thanks for a lovely evening," she said, leaning into his massive chest.

He let out a soft grunt, like a contented grizzly. "Thanks for going out with me. Want to do it again sometime?"

"Anytime." Time after time, if they were as good together as she suspected they would be.

"I never thought I'd meet a girl like you."

She blinked. "Me? I'm nothing special."

"Yes, you are."

"How so?" she asked, not intending to fish for compliments. She wanted to know, considering her ex had said she'd never find another man willing to overlook her many flaws.

"Your smile," Kyle said. "And your eyes." He grinned. "You make me laugh, and you feel—" he ran his hands along her arm, down to her hip "—real soft."

Debby moved closer.

"You smell good, too," he added before he began nuzzling her ear. His lips moved toward her mouth. "Like a chocolate cake."

They kissed for a while, until Debby was so out of breath she had to suck air like a racehorse. This made her boobs heave, drawing Kyle's entranced gaze. Oh boy. She shimmied against his chest. "Two scoops. Want a bite?"

"Yum. Looks delicious." One hand moved up and clasped her breast. She closed her eyes, letting herself sink into the caress, willing to overlook the fact that Kyle was not a sparkling conversationalist because what he did say was completely genuine. He had marvelous hands, so large and strong. When he held her, she believed that she'd finally found the man with whom she was the perfect size.

And so is he. Impressed by the wood pressing against her thigh, she reached behind her back for her zipper.

"Oh, wow," Kyle said in a shaky voice as he watched the fitted bodice of her dress peel away to reveal her breasts bursting out of the skimpy strapless bra. He put a thumb to one nipple and stroked until it popped past the elastic. Debby went for his mouth, throwing her arms around his shoulders as he tilted her back onto the futon, burrowing into her.

"You haven't tried the dessert," she said as he clambered between her open thighs, kissing and squeezing every inch of her at once.

He hadn't eaten any of the special chocolate, either, she realized as Kyle worked his hand inside her tights. After that, she stopped caring.

THE TRAIN THRUMMED beneath Alex, returning him to the city, filled with both anticipation and his constant low-grade dread. He knew he was making a mistake, coming back when it would have been easiest to keep on going. But there was no reasoning with his heart.

After leaving Karina, he couldn't bear the idea of returning to the comfortless cage of his studio apartment, so instead he'd walked. And walked. Block after block. Thinking of Karina with such intensity that he'd lost track of his surroundings, startled to find himself at the East River near the Williamsburg Bridge.

Struck by the realization that he'd forgotten to watch for trouble, he'd looked wildly around him. One of Rafael Norris's hired guns could have picked up his trail and followed two steps behind.

The wind had been so bitter off the river that not many people were out. A burly man bundled in a thick jacket with a fur collar had been walking a puffball dog across the frosty ground of the riverside park. A couple of guys huddled together, smoking.

Cursing his lapse of attention, Alex had quickly headed into the shelter of a large brick warehouse. After making sure—as sure as he could be these days—that he hadn't been followed, he'd strode briskly to the nearest subway station. Reaching Penn Station, he'd taken the first train departing, without caring about his destination. All he'd known was that he had to get away.

Not from the danger of being found.

From Karina. His feelings for her were dangerous—for both of them.

And yet, twelve hours later, he was returning, unable to convince himself to leave her. In fact, the day apart had made him want her even more.

He was losing it. Being stupid. Rash.

Letting his guard down and making the kind of mistakes he'd feared.

His one comfort was that there'd been no sign of surveillance during the train journey, which there would have been if Norris's men had picked up his trail from Florida and thought he was trying to escape again. He didn't quite dare to believe, but it was beginning to look like he might be free. Really free, this time. Three weeks and counting, ever since he'd arrived in New York. That hope, that one slender hope of a fresh start, was all he had.

It was enough to send him back to Karina.

For now.

ABOUT NOW, KARINA DECIDED, lurking near the windows of her darkened living room, Debby was probably rolling around on her futon with Kyle Murphy, without a qualm. While *she* was driving herself crazy, waffling back and forth in her mind over what to do, what to do.

The hell with that. She grabbed the weighted cords of the linen shades and yanked them open, one by one. She went around the rooms, turning on every light so the place was lit up like a Broadway stage. Then she stopped in the center, hands on hips, breathing hard, glaring at Alex's dark apartment. She'd checked frequently since getting home from her shopping excursion and there hadn't been a single sign of him. But where else could he be? He had no friends. Nowhere to go.

She stalked to the windows. "Hey, Alex—here I am! Come and get me!"

Nothing.

He must not have eaten another truffle. She had, on impulse, after stopping in at the store to carry a couple of them home for emergency use.

Why she'd done it, she didn't know. She'd been plenty aroused, just from thinking about Alex.

So, okay. It was obvious that her physical needs were real, not manufactured. Alex's, too, she supposed.

Maybe he had this type of affair all the time, but for her, this first taste of wild, ravenous sex had given her a surprising need for it. A craving. Even without the chocolate, she was constantly feverish with the desire to have Alex's hands on her, his mouth, his tongue...she wanted his tongue licking inside her, tasting her....

Frustrated, she rapped her fist on the cold glass. For a couple of seconds, she didn't realize that the resultant knocking was coming from the door.

"Karina." Alex's voice. "Let me in."

With her heart in her mouth, she went to open the door. He stood with one hand on the jamb, out of breath, a light dusting of snow melting into his hair. His cheeks were ruddy and he seemed weary and spent, yet filled with a raging energy that crackled in the cold air that clung to him.

"What are you doing here?" she demanded, forgetting that she'd been begging him—challenging him—to come.

"I don't know. But I couldn't stay away."

She glanced toward his apartment, still undisturbed. "Where have you been?"

"All over. I left here around 5:00 a.m. and I walked out to the river. Then I took a train out to Long Island, all the way to Montauk. End of the line. I've been walking on the beach. The waves were wild. I found a coffee shop…."

He seemed broken up. As if he didn't want to be there, with her, but had come anyway.

A nameless fear nipped at her already crumbling composure. She fingered the lapels of his coat. "Alex. What's going on with you?"

He didn't answer, just took her face in his cold hands and kissed her with a sudden hot, pounding hunger that was almost too much for her to bear. Yes, too much. She'd always thought she was strong, but one wrenching kiss from Alex and she felt herself entering a dark maelstrom where there was no restraint, only the driving need to be consumed.

They staggered together, getting Alex inside, tearing off his coat, slamming the door, all without breaking the contact of their mouths. She fumbled with his shirt, the same one from yesterday, but gave up halfway through, leaving it hanging open, partially unbuttoned. Getting naked took too much time when she had to have him right now, right here.

Right or wrong.

They continued kissing, locked together with their arms and legs as they twisted and rubbed and clung. Alex's hands were everywhere at once—tangled in her hair, diving under her sweater, tugging at her jeans. He got them open, pushed them down her legs, stripped off her panties, and with each brush of his fingers she felt deep throbbing as her desperate craving built to a fever pitch.

Alex lifted her up, pushing her back to the wall. She shivered uncontrollably as he reached down to drop his pants and release himself. His thick penis sprang up, nudging between her open thighs. Reluctant to break contact, but too frantic not to, she unwound her legs from his waist and found her balance. "Condom?"

He made a sound of frustration. "I left them in your bedroom. From now on, we keep them always at hand. On a string around your neck, if we have to."

"It's okay. I stuck one in the pocket of my jeans…." Karina sank to her knees in front of him, searching through the tangle of her discarded clothes. "Here." She held up the packet, then changed her mind and snatched it away. "Let me," she said, another wave of passion surging through her as she saw his hard-on rising proudly from his open zipper.

"Fast." His panting breaths rattled in his chest.

She worked his pants down a little. When she touched him, scooping her palm beneath his testicles, he moaned and hunched forward, keeping upright by slamming his hands against the fortune-telling booth. The mechanism whirred to life, flicking on the bulbs. They were bathed in garish blinking colors as she licked her tongue around the head of his penis until it glistened.

He banged a fist against the booth. The carnival music started up, followed by the monotone voice: "Give me your hand."

Both hands. Karina skimmed the condom down the length of Alex's shaft, rolling him between her palms.

"I will tell your fortune," said Esmeralda.

A sharp cry tore loose from Alex's throat and he

dropped to the floor, giving Karina no time to react before his hands were on her hips, dragging her bare bottom across the floor toward him. He plunged directly into her. She grabbed onto his shoulders, taking him with her as he tipped her over onto her back and began to thrust, pushing a little deeper each time, each lunge edging their bodies along the floor until they were butted up against the fortune-telling machine.

Esme repeated. "Give me your hand."

Oh, yes, give it to me! Karina flexed against Alex's hard body, holding herself taut for a moment of incredible, transfixed sensation as he pulled almost all the way out, then drove deep again, his hands locked on her hips, holding her steady even as she shattered under the impact, lost again to the wild pulsing rhythm of their mutual release.

"I will tell your fortune."

But I know exactly what's coming, Karina thought, flowing inside as the pleasure swept through her over and over again in slowly diminishing waves.

Heartbreak.

No matter what she told herself about chocolate-induced flings, she knew in her heart that she was involved. And that Alex was too tortured for this to be an easy ride.

8

A SMALL WHITE CARD emerged from the fortune-telling booth and fluttered to the floor. The bulbs shut down and the mechanism hummed to a stop.

"What's with this thing?" Alex asked, twisting to look at it.

Karina stirred against him. "That's Esmeralda, the fortune-telling Gypsy Queen. I got her at an auction."

"Why?"

"For fun." She lifted her head and looked levelly at him. "You don't like fun?"

"Depends what kind of fun." He moved his fingers against her bare backside.

"Hmm. Yes, I see. There's that kind, and then there's the other kind. You don't seem like a guy who'd enjoy a carnival."

She was wrong, he thought. Lex would have been shooting down rubber ducks with a water gun, whirling upside down on the roller coaster, gorging on greasy hamburgers and popcorn. But not Alex. Sunny days and happy crowds only made him think of Frank Whitman and the thin line between life and death.

"Except..." She splayed her hand over his chest and rested her chin on it. "Didn't you say you surfed? I'm trying to picture that." She grinned. "Say, 'Yo, dude,' for me, and maybe that'll help."

He wanted to joke with her, but instead he shut down. "I'm not that guy anymore."

She hesitated, then pushed up to sit with her legs pulled in tight. Disconnecting. She pulled her sweater down, modestly covering up as much of her bottom half as she could. "What happened to him?"

He was blindsided by his idealism and belief in the system. "He grew up."

"Of course."

Alex was not ready to move, although he did yank his pants up over his hip bones. His knees were abraded from skidding on the wood floor, and the hard surface wasn't exactly comfortable to lie on either, but for some reason he liked being here with Karina, their bodies relaxed and loose from the sex, no worries on his mind because they were inside and safe.

Another ten minutes. He could give himself that.

She made a move to get up, and he put his hand on her leg to stop her. "You don't seem like the kind of woman who'd enjoy a carnival, either."

"I don't?" She straightened her hair. "How come?"

He shrugged. "Too restrained. Demure. More the type to go to the opera or the theater." He pronounced it *thee-uh-tuh* to egg her on.

"I like those, too, but…" Her eyes shone with umbrage. "Restrained? Demure? I can't believe *you* would say that. I've never been *less* restrained—"

"Outside of—" he flipped a finger back and forth between them "—this."

Suddenly she was crestfallen. "So you think that, um, *this* is…out of character?"

"That'd be my guess." He shrugged. "I don't know you well enough to say for sure."

Her chin went up. "You know me. You've been watching me for weeks now."

If she was going to call him on that…

"You're a beautiful woman," he said quickly. "Any man would watch you."

"Through binoculars?"

"Any way possible."

"Seriously, Alex. What are you doing with them? I know you're not only looking at me. You're sneaky about it, but I've seen you studying the street. Even the rooftops."

Damn. He'd allowed the distraction of her to make him overlook one of the cardinal rules of staying safe: keeping himself nondescript, avoiding notice, blending in. He'd been beyond obvious with Karina.

"Just keeping track of my surroundings," he bluffed.

Her eyes narrowed, but she didn't continue the questioning even though he was sure he hadn't convinced her of his harmlessness.

"I just can't believe—" She shook back her hair. "You think I'm demure. What's a girl got to do?"

He grinned. "When's the last time you went to a carnival?"

Her lips compressed, twitching to one side while she thought. "Not in ages," she conceded.

"Then why the fortune-telling machine?" He patted the booth looming over him. "And the carousel horse in the bedroom?"

"Only a collection. There's also a genuine Ringling Brothers Circus poster in my dining room, and a popcorn maker in the loft."

"They don't fit in."

She gave him a narrow look. "Maybe there's more to me than you can see through your binoculars."

"I suppose that's true." A pang pinched his gut at the knowledge that he'd probably never get to really know her. He'd never had one, but a lasting relationship was built up over time, made up of fun and fights and the quiet times in between. It wasn't only about hot sex.

Though that was always a good starting point.

"I don't know what it is," she said, "but I'm drawn to carnival pieces. There's no psychological significance. It's not that my only happy childhood memory was going to the carnival, or that I was abandoned by my mother when she ran off to join the circus…." Karina laughed. "Maybe I just like the surprise of it, and how my guests react. I don't want to be pigeonholed as easily as you just did." She threw him a look. "Restrained and demure. Huh."

"Says the woman who sets her alarm at the same time every day, even on weekends, and follows the same routine every morning and night—" He stopped. Too late.

Her eyes had gone wide. "You really have been watching me."

"You should close your curtains more often."

A pink blush inched into her face. "I usually do."

"But not lately."

She swallowed. "Okay. Yes. I knew you were watching all along."

He went up on one elbow. "I could tell."

"Alex." Her voice had dropped to a whisper; she avoided his eyes. "What are we doing?"

"Having a little fun with each other, that's all."

"Yes, of course." Then she shook her head, contradicting her words.

"What do *you* think we're doing?"

"I don't know. It started as—" She stopped abruptly. "You said you were gone all day."

"Yes. After last night, I was too restless to stay cooped up in a small ap—"

She interrupted. "You didn't go back at all, you didn't eat anymore of the chocolate."

That again? "Uh, I'm not crazy about chocolate. I'm sorry if that hurts your feelings. I'm sure it's very good."

"Oh, that's okay." She was smiling. "Very okay. I kind of like it that we're doing this the natural way."

"Natural? What do you mean?"

"Never mind," she said quickly. "You must be hungry. I haven't had dinner, either. There's leftover ravioli, if you like. It's not homemade, but I only order in from the best." She'd started to get up, but stopped again and sank back to her knees, giving him a lofty look. "That is, unless you have to cut out on me. Or do you prefer to do that when I'm not awake?"

So. She was not pleased with his silent escape. There was a slight tremor of uncertainty in the way she bit down on her bottom lip, waiting for his explanation. He couldn't tell her the reasons behind his hesitation. But he wanted to stay, holding on to his last hope of a normal life.

He stood and gave her his hand. "I'm not going anywhere." *Tonight.* "Leftover ravioli sounds good."

"I shouldn't forgive you so easily."

"Oh?" He lifted his brows. "I'm forgiven?"

A wry smile flitted across her mouth. "I guess so—against my better judgment. This is a very weird re-ro-rendezvous."

Relationship? Romance? *Hey, now,* he wanted to say. *Hold on.*

"Oh, look!" Karina said, seemingly as glad as he to seize on a change of subject. "You have a fortune." She swooped down to retrieve the little card that had been spat out by the fortune-teller.

He held up his hands. "Oh, no. Not me. It must be for you."

She glanced at their scattered clothing and tugged self-consciously at the hem of her sweater. "I'd say it was for both of us, considering..."

He remembered the card she'd received the previous evening. "I don't believe in that stuff."

"I'll keep it to myself then." But her demeanor changed when she read the fortune. Rolling her eyes, she crumpled the card in her palm. "Pretty silly."

Alex couldn't help himself, which was beginning to be a familiar state when he got near Karina. "What did it say?"

She shrugged and moved past him. "You don't believe in it, so what do you care?"

"I don't." He buttoned his shirt as he followed her, admiring the sway of her hips and the way her sweater cupped her sweet ass. He was hoping she'd drop the card into a wastebasket, but she kept it.

When he got to the kitchen, she was already dumping a Tupperware container of ravioli into a saucepan. The small slip of cardboard was tucked under the edge of an Emmett Kelly cookie jar that sat on the corner of the countertop. He caught himself drumming his fingers on the granite and quickly slid both hands into his pockets, avoiding the temptation to take a look at the card. His fortunes were unpredictable, at best.

"You can set the table."

He glanced up and saw that Karina had been watching him eye the cheesy card of fortune as if it were a scorpion. She wore a smug little smile that he wanted to kiss away until they were back to the chemistry that he found easier to accept.

Relationship?

Romance?

They had their dinner on china plates, with real silver. Wine in goblets. Cloth napkins.

Alex offered to clear and she let him, even though she must have known he only wanted a few seconds alone in her kitchen. When he came out, she had Diana Krall on the CD player, a couple of candles lit, the curtains closed. She was stretched out on the couch with her legs bare and a bemused smile of invitation on her face.

He was torn. The day spent being all tormented and dramatic in Montauk had done him no good at all because he was right back where he'd started. Endangered if he did, damned if he didn't.

"I'm making no promises," he said, and bent over the back of the sleek sofa to slide his arms around Karina and bury his face in her silky hair.

"I don't expect any," she said.

But the fortune card had read After The Darkness, Comes The Dawn. A Brighter Future Awaits.

MONDAY AT WORK, Karina had trouble concentrating on her tasks. She was irritable with Janine, whose eagerness to know every aspect of the business seemed more like butting in. When the girl had hovered over Karina's shoulder at the computer for the third time, she'd finally sent Janine out of the office on a make-work errand, just to get rid of her for a while.

But even then she couldn't seem to get her head straight. Coming down off a sex-and-candy high with Alex was like dealing with a hangover. They'd separated first thing Sunday morning, but had been back together that night, when he'd come knocking on her door once more despite having said nothing about continuing their affair.

Although they weren't exactly having a meeting of the minds—or hearts—there was also no way to pretend that the one-night fling hadn't become a lot more. She couldn't even claim they were turned on by the truffles. He seemed to have no particular taste for them, and she only popped one when she was feeling unsure and wanted the boost of sexual confidence.

Which left them…where?

Karina threw down her pen. All she knew was that she'd never been so engrossed by a man. If only he'd open up just a tad, give her a little something to work with, a hint of his feelings for her.

Then what? Was she ready to accept a stranger in her orderly life on the basis of little more than their combustible chemistry?

Deciding she needed to work with her hands and give her buzzing brain a rest, Karina went to check activity in the kitchen. The scent of melted chocolate had permeated even her office, making her queasy. Too much chocolate lately…or maybe it was the emotional push and pull that she'd intended to avoid.

Karina glimpsed Debby through the porthole window and pushed open the swinging door to the corridor. "Deb, I've had either too many sweets or too much sex—"

Debby whipped around, tugging at her skewed apron. A large, muscular man with thick blond hair and a goofy hound-dog grin stood behind her. Beneath an open, quilted vest, he wore the khaki uniform of their delivery service.

Karina blinked. "Excuse me."

Debby slid a finger beneath her smile to rub away lip gloss smears. "Oops. You caught us. Kyle was just leaving."

"Yes, of course, Kyle," Karina said, giving the guy a nod hello. Not that there'd been any doubt this was *the* Kyle. Debby had phoned in that morning to say she'd be an hour late to work as Kyle had just left her house.

Karina looked at her watch. Apparently a measly four hours was too long for Kyle and Debby to be apart. They had her and Alex beat by a full working day. She wondered how many truffles Debby was using.

"I know, I know. Time to get back to work." Debby shot Kyle a double-smacking air kiss. "See you tonight, huggy bear?"

"As soon as I clock out, creamcake." He lumbered past Karina, doffing the bill of his uniform cap.

"Nice to see you again, Kyle." As soon as the door swung shut, she rounded on Debby, comically shaking a finger at her. "Kissing in the corridor. What are you, teenagers?"

Debby dimpled. "Ohmigawd, yes. I could make out with him for, like, hours."

"If he can keep it up for hours, you must be feeding him truffles around the clock."

"Nope." Debby reached under her apron to retuck her blouse. "It's really amazing. I haven't fed him *any* of the chocolate. We're falling for each other the old-fashioned way. No cocoa beans necessary."

"Oh." Karina blinked in consternation, contrasting them with her and Alex. They would have never got together had it not been for the truffles. Perhaps that meant they weren't meant to be.

"Congratulations. I guess it's the real thing," she said,

trying to beam, and failing. Not wanting to bring her friend down, she turned and fled the corridor, almost bumping into Janine, who hadn't even taken off her coat.

"I got the new candy thermometers you wanted," she said, but Karina rushed past without stopping, one hand lifted to block her face from view as she gave her nose a wicked pinch.

She burst into the front room of the shop and stopped there, while she rubbed at her stinging nose and prickling eyes. It was ridiculous to be jealous of Debby and Kyle when she'd got exactly what she'd bargained for from Alex: a strictly sexual affair without attachment.

Several customers waited in line at each of the cash registers. Karina glanced over the operations, then moved to the hot-chocolate machine as one of the workers reached for the take-out cups they kept stacked nearby. "I'll take charge here for a while. You see to the customers."

The employee gave her a grateful nod. "One French hot chocolate, double on the chocolate, please."

The shop had several signature hot-chocolate drinks, including Aztec made with a dash of chili pepper, and the rich chocolate cream of the French style. Karina got the container of heavy cream from the fridge and dropped in two healthy dollops. She set the cup and pushed the lever on the machine, releasing a hot stream of pure dark chocolate.

The sweet smell went straight to her head, evoking memories of the past three nights with Alex. She flicked the lever, trying to shut off her thoughts as well, but that was not easy. Being with him had changed her in a fundamental way. She'd become so tuned in to her surroundings—inhaling the sweet smells, caressing the embossed copper of their logo, relishing the warmth of the cup in her hand.

That was all real, wasn't it? Then why not Alex?

She passed the hot chocolate to the waiting customer, jolted from her own thoughts by the middle-aged man's familiarity. The shape of his face reminded her of someone she knew.

Perhaps he was a regular. She said hello. "You look familiar, sir. Are you a frequent customer?"

The man's eyes sharpened behind a pair of thick glasses. "Of course not," he huffed, before grabbing the cup and scurrying away.

Karina shrugged. The city was filled with oddballs.

Needing the mindless work, she continued making drinks and boxing small orders for the next hour, until the next shift of part-time employees reported to work. Karina drifted off to her favorite spot near the windows, where she could check Alex's apartment.

He was there, but the casual observer would have missed him. A narrow opening along the side of the blind was the only sign of his presence. This time, he wasn't looking for Karina. The binoculars appeared to be trained on her customers.

She looked them over. A young woman with a lustrous mane of shiny sable hair sat at the table nearest the front window, writing in a notebook with an array of chocolates on a plate in front of her. Pen poised, she picked one up and nibbled at the edge, stopping briefly to swoon with appreciation before she resumed her note-taking.

Karina scoffed to herself. Probably another rival, hoping to duplicate the Sutter family recipe. Except they usually weren't so blatant that they'd plunk themselves at one of the shop's own tables to attempt their research. Nevertheless, the young woman was a beauty and certainly worthy of Alex's attention.

There seemed to be nothing of note about the other customers. At the farthest table, the man she'd thought she recognized sat with his face buried in a newspaper. Occasionally the aphrodisiac effect prompted a male customer to become enamored with one of the clerks. Store policy was that they must urge amorous customers to direct their attentions elsewhere.

Although Karina made a mental note to ask her employees about the lurker, she couldn't see any reason for the man to catch Alex's attention. No, it had to be the stylish young woman he was studying so closely.

I'm not ready to lose him. Karina slid a finger along the glass doors of the display cabinet, searching the contents.

"What are you looking for?" Debby asked, coming up from behind. She put a hand on Karina's upper arm and gave her a squeeze.

"We're out of the truffles?"

"Black Magics? You know we don't stock many of them up front."

Karina's voice rose. "But you have some in the back?"

"We may be sold out. There were a couple left over from the last batch. They seem to have disappeared from the refrigerator." Debby winked.

Karina flushed. "Yes, I took them. But my spectacular weekend of wall-to-wall sex was worth it."

"I'll say." Obviously, Debby was eager to hear more. "Come in the back and help me make another batch."

"Yeah, I could." Karina bunched her fists on top of the display and took a deep breath. "Except I'm falling into a trap here. Kind of a damned-if-you-do situation, exactly the one I meant to avoid from the beginning. But now…" Her shoulders dropped. "How will I ever know what Alex really feels for me if I rely on the double-strength chocolates to ease us along the way?"

"Why do you have to know?" Debby asked. "Enjoy the sex for what it is." Karina looked at her with a bleak expression and she added, "Uh-oh. You're getting serious."

Karina nodded.

"What happened to the short-term fling?"

"I should have realized that wouldn't work for me, but I wanted Alex so much I persuaded myself I could pull it off."

"I know what you mean." Debby nodded. "Sex is never only sex, at least for women. Some women." Debby paused, considering. "Exactly how close are you two?"

"Aside from the physical, not so very. I still don't know much more about him than I did at the beginning. But that just doesn't matter. There's something between us. It's small, barely a beginning." Karina smiled to herself. "As hokey as it sounds, we transcend words."

"Uh-oh," Debby said again.

"I know. Ridiculous, huh?"

"Maybe…maybe not."

"I'm fooling myself." A starker version of the truth hit Karina when she looked at the lovely young woman who'd so easily captured Alex's attention. "I can dress this up all I want, but the reality is that he can't get away fast enough, come morning."

Or even before morning, she added silently, since

Alex continued to disappear while she was sleeping. Not once, but twice.

Debby slung her arms around Karina's shoulders and made a consoling sound.

"After the aphrodisiac and the lust has worn off, we're so awkward with each other," she confessed in a low voice. "Transcending words? Who'm I kidding? Alex doesn't talk to me because he's not interested in getting to know me. This isn't a great love affair. It's a booty call."

A booty call, Karina repeated ruthlessly to herself, trying to crush the romantic notions she'd acquired to keep herself from seeing the blunt, naked truth of it.

As always, Debby was quick with reassurances. "Aw, no, Kare—it's more than that. Has to be! Even the Black Magic truffles aren't *that* strong—"

"Excuse me." The dark-haired girl at the table near the window tentatively waved a hand. "I didn't mean to eavesdrop, but..." She rose, skidding the lightweight wire bistro chair across the floor. "I'm Nikki Silk."

Karina was too startled to respond.

"Nikki Silk," Debby mulled. "I know that name from somewhere."

"*Hard Candy,*" Karina said, remembering. Oh, damn.

"That's right." Nikki approached, her expression hopeful. "I'm a staff writer there. Whitney Smythe said she'd mentioned my name to you? I'm looking for a good story for my next feature in the magazine, and I think Sutter Chocolat is it!"

Karina greeted the announcement with less enthusiasm than Nikki obviously expected. "Thanks, but we don't need the publicity. I've told Whitney that several times." Unfortunately, Whitney was known for missing a lot and forgetting the rest.

"She said I might have to persuade you." Nikki smiled a winning smile.

Karina remained wary. "What were you thinking of?"

"Aside from the story about the most fantastic chocolates I've ever tasted, I was interested in, well..." Nikki pressed closer to the display cabinet, leaning an arm on the green marble top. "What's this about them being aphrodisiacs?"

Debby and Karina exchanged a look.

Karina winced. "You heard that."

Nikki wagged a finger. "Off the record, until you agree otherwise."

"How do we know we can trust you on that?" Debby asked.

Nikki blinked blue eyes. "Because I'm so charming and guileless?" She grinned. "For a reporter, at least."

Almost involuntarily, Karina returned the grin, then introduced herself and Debby. Nikki Silk was tall, thin, gorgeous and outfitted in designer labels, but there was something eminently likable about her. Which didn't mean she would trust the girl with her darkest chocolate secrets. "Sorry. That was a private conversation you overheard. I'll consider the story on the shop, but I won't share personal information."

"But that's where the real story lies. Chocolate aphrodisiacs! I'm dying to know more."

Karina wanted to disappear. "You know enough already."

"How about a bargain?" Nikki said. "I won't ask you questions about your, um, personal experiences, but in return you do let me explore the possibilities regarding the chocolate. And just so you know, I didn't get that from your conversation alone. People are talking about your store. At first I thought this was just about good chocolate, but I've been sitting here for an hour now, listening to the customers. Quite a few of them seem to be well satisfied by more than the chocolate." Nikki arched her pencil-thin brows. "I know you know what I mean."

"We sure do," Debby said, making Karina drag her away.

They put their heads together, consulting in whispers. "What do you think?" Karina asked. "My instinct is not to do this. We certainly don't need an influx of customers."

"Why not? You could make out like a bandit when the story hits the stands. Customers would be lined up all the way down the street, begging you to take their credit cards."

"But we're already at our production limit."

"So we carry our regular recipe chocolates and keep the special recipe to limited availability."

"Wouldn't work," Karina said stubbornly. She'd always worried about how to keep the shop small and personal. The potential profits weren't a prime concern when she already had made more than she needed, with a family trust fund untouched except for the capital she'd used to fund her start-up costs and make the down payment on the building.

"Nikki can write a story even without your approval."

Another worry. "Yes, but what if..."

"She exposes you?" Debby shook her head. "Whitney won't let the article get out of hand."

"It's too risky."

"But participating is the only way you can keep some control." Debby turned to Nikki. "Can Karina make it a condition that you don't identify the store?"

Nikki frowned. "The *Hard Candy* readers would demand to know."

"Tough marshmallows." Debby put her hands on her hips. "The publicity would deluge Sutter Chocolat and possibly force us out of business—"

"Ha!" Nikki tossed her hair. "You could expand into a million-dollar success story."

"Not interested," said Karina. "We want to keep the place as a storefront operation."

"Look at it this way," Debby coaxed. "New Yorkers love to be in the know about an exclusive source for their goodies. There are all those restaurants with unpublished numbers and the underground clubs and the invitation-only guest lists."

"Hmm." Nikki's head tilted to one side. "I suppose I can try to come up with an interesting angle that doesn't include your store by name, but it'd have to be provocative to sell to my editors."

"Whitney's our friend. We'll put in a good word and she'll support you."

"All right." Nikki returned to her table and got a couple of business cards out of a quilted leather pocketbook. "Here's my number. I'll be calling you. But in the meantime—" With a sassy wink, she hurriedly stuffed the remainder of her candy selection into a copper take-out bag. "I'll be calling one of my boyfriends, if you know what I mean."

Karina watched her go, then walked around the counter to clean off the table. Most of the customers had cleared out, including the familiar-looking man. Alex had disappeared from his hiding place near the window. No coincidence, with Nikki's departure.

Karina shook her head at Debby. "I don't know about this article. Seems to me we're asking for trouble."

"Yeah!" Debby clapped. The confectioner was almost as gleeful as when she had a new shipment of bulk chocolate from Brazil. "Isn't it fun?"

9

A BITTER WINTER WIND whistled along the street, making banners flap and rattling the bare-branched trees against their cages. Pedestrians kept close to the shelter of the buildings as they hurried for home in the growing dusk. The sky was heavy with leaden clouds.

A good evening to be home in bed, Karina said to herself as she locked up the shop. A week ago, she would have finished that thought by adding *with a good book.* Now, she had Alex. Sort of.

No more sort of *about it,* she decided. *I've had just about enough.*

A vehicle double-parked outside of the store. The horn blatted three short, seemingly exuberant blasts. Debby waved from the curb. "See you tomorrow," she called to Karina as she climbed into Kyle's delivery van.

Karina smiled, watching as Debby leaned toward Kyle with puckered lips despite the honking horns and irate drivers stuck behind them. After a thorough kiss, he put the truck into drive and the stalled traffic got moving again.

Karina shivered. The warmth inside her door was only steps away, but her eyes went to Alex's windows instead. Chances were he'd come over tonight. She could go home and wait. But…

"Screw that," she said.

Gathering up the proverbial head of steam, she jerked her Peruvian-knit hat down over her ears and marched straight across the street, paying no mind to the horn blasts and colorful variations of the F-word that erupted. It was time she set things straight with Alex.

He buzzed her in with only a moment's hesitation. Climbing the two flights of stairs, she readied her case. She would say that she didn't expect a lot from him, but that it might be nice to say hello before they had sex, or even go out for dinner. She'd have to make it clear that he wasn't being turned into, God forbid, an actual *boyfriend,* but just a…a….

Was there a word for this? They weren't friends with benefits, because she couldn't rightly say they were friends.

Strangers with benefits. Ugh.

She rang his doorbell, having reached no conclusion. Alex, and the way she felt about him, were indefinable.

The door opened. "Hi," he said, looking far too good in jeans and a red sweatshirt that had faded almost pink.

"Hi." She pointed at the Syracuse logo. "Did you go?"

"I've been—" He looked down. "Oh. The shirt. Uh, no."

"Where did you go?"

"To college?"

"No, last night." She had intended to be sarcastic, but the instant the words slipped out she realized how true they were. "Of course I meant college," she corrected hastily.

Alex frowned. "Does it matter?"

"I'm not asking for your PIN number."

He rested his hands on his narrow hips, dragging the

unbelted waistband of his jeans down just far enough so a strip of flat, tanned belly was revealed. She wanted to slip her fingers inside the snap, popping it as she pulled him to her for a kiss. But that would be a very distracting direction to go.

"I went…" He closed his eyes for an instant. "I went home because staying would make this too complicated."

"This? What's *this?*" Karina blurted, making the awkward jump from his mystery past to their mystery future.

"Us."

"Is there an us?"

"Not in the conventional way."

She sighed. "Yes. Indeed. Don't you think it's time we figured out what we're doing?"

A wry grin. "I knew you weren't really the spontaneous type."

"Despite evidence to the contrary, you're correct," she said, keeping her gaze low and her hands jammed into her pockets.

He raised an arm and she thought for one moment that he would caress her cheek, but instead he plucked off her hat. "Come on in, I guess."

Not much of an invitation, but she grabbed it, curious to inspect the inside of the apartment she'd only caught glimpses of.

There was little to see. She ducked a head into a narrow slice of a galley kitchen, where all the doors were off the short bank of cupboards and stacked against the wall, revealing meager rations. A round cardboard canister of oatmeal, a jar of peanut butter, packets of single-serving soup. No sign of the truffles, but he might keep them in the fridge.

She followed Alex to the living space. It wasn't two rooms as she'd expected, but only one, L-shaped, with his mattress and box spring on the floor in the nook. Neatly made, with one lone pillow.

One was his motif. One catch-all desk, with a laptop computer and printer, a short stack of papers, one pen, one cup and the carafe from his coffeemaker with a half-inch of coffee so old the sediment had settled. One folding chair. One lamp. One TV, on the floor near the bed, the cord snaking to an outlet that was pulled halfway off the wall.

One window, with a grungy armchair nearby and the binoculars resting on the sill.

Alex had slid his hands into his pockets. He gazed into the space above Karina's head, detached from her survey.

She walked to the window to see her apartment from his viewpoint. In the growing darkness, not much was revealed, but she could imagine the difference once the lights came on. And the show began, she thought with a residual shiver of disbelief.

She cleared her throat. "So…what do you do in here, all day?"

He shrugged. "Not much."

"What about the writing? How's that coming along?"

"Actually, I, uh—" Suddenly, he looked almost bashful, and was avoiding her eyes out of too much emotion, not lack of it. "I have a chapter."

"Oh! That's great."

"Not really. I'm sure it's garbage."

She pressed before he could withdraw again. "May I read it?"

He appeared to think that over. When he came up

with no immediate reason not to, she decided to get even pushier and stepped over to swoop up the stack of printed paper.

He made no move to snatch them back. She ruffled the pages under his nose. "Please?"

"Go ahead."

Surprise. "Right now?"

"You might as well, before I trash them."

"Oh, you creative types. Such drama and angst." Chuckling to herself at how decidedly *un*dramatic he was, she pulled off her coat and dropped it on the armchair before collapsing there herself. She laid the pages on her lap and pushed up her sleeves. "You know, I almost thought you were misleading me, about being a writer. It's one of those things that people say—" She mimicked, *"I'm an artist, I'm an actor, I'm a writer...."*

He went to the card table and snapped shut the laptop. "About this, if I'm misleading anyone, it's myself."

"I'm sure your work's not that bad." She rattled the pages. "Chapter one."

Alex put up a hand to silence her. "I'll go make coffee."

Karina nodded. "I could use a cup."

"Yell when you're finished."

She followed him with her eyes. How cute. He was neurotic about her reading his work in front of him. She'd dated a writer once in college, but he'd been the type to make ten photocopies of his work in progress and try to fob them off an anyone with a sniffle of interest or a connection to publishing, however remote. The fledgling relationship had crashed and burned when she'd mildly suggested that using eight adjectives in every sentence was at least a half-dozen too many.

Sixteen pages of double-spaced type didn't take long

to read. At one point, Alex brought her a cup of black coffee and she held it in one hand, balanced on the arm of the chair. As she turned the final pages, she was aware that he'd wandered into the room again, but he didn't sit until she'd finished.

He perched on the folding chair, his elbows on his knees, looking a question at her.

"Wow," she said, then took a sip of the coffee, which had been sweetened with so much sugar she almost choked. She swiped a knuckle over her lips. "I didn't expect a thriller."

"No?"

"I thought maybe a brooding intense character study…"

"We're always wrong about each other."

She looked up from fingering his pages. "Do you think so? Why, because you couldn't understand my carnival collection?" Alex's writing was swirling in her head. "The first chapter was intense. But the violence, coming so quickly—" She shuddered.

In the story, a young criminal lawyer narrowly escapes death when masked killers burst into his office and take out his client, a Mob figure. The chapter ended with the lawyer out on the streets of New York running for his life.

"You didn't like it," Alex said.

"No, it's that I'm surprised. The story was very involving."

"The writing's rough. It's just a first draft."

"Yes, but so visceral. My God. I could *feel* the lawyer's—Mack's—fear. And the description of the shooting. I don't know how you could imagine all of that out of the blue. But then I'm not the creative type."

She took another sip of the awful coffee. "Have you experienced violence like that firsthand?"

Alex straightened. "Of course not." Each word clipped.

"You should get a package together and find an agent. Maybe you'll be the next John Grisham or Scott Turow—"

"Don't jump the gun."

"That would be a great title. *Jump the Gun,* by Alex Anderson." She laughed. "How does that sound?"

"Like you're jumping the gun," he said, but he looked pleased.

"You'll need a female protagonist."

"A blond confectioner?"

"Nah. A blond assassin with a heart of gold and a mean karate kick." She leaned over to put her coffee cup on the floor. A reasonable guess occurred. She slanted a glance at him. "Unless this story is autobiographical…?"

His eyes, previously alight with his involvement, quickly shuttered. "Why would you think that?"

She shrugged, acting nonchalant because she instinctively felt that she'd hit the nail on the head. "Because it's so real."

"Fiction," he said.

She attempted to tease him. "Then your real name isn't Mack Chessler?"

Alex answered so ultra-casually she believed he was covering. If not his name, then *something*. "Nope, 'fraid not."

"Do you have any more written?"

"Not yet."

"Keep going. It's very good." Perhaps he wasn't actually relating his own story verbatim, but she suspected that each chapter would give her further insights into the enigma that was Alex Anderson. Eventually, she hoped, he'd be able to trust her with his real past.

"More coffee?" he asked.

She wrinkled her nose. "How many sugars did you put in it?"

"Three." His mouth twitched. "Another wrong guess?"

"Uh-huh. Despite my business, I don't have a strong sweet tooth. I like my coffee with one Splenda and a touch of cream."

"I had milk, but it was chunky so I dumped it down the drain."

"You don't keep food at home? No wonder you're so thin." Rangy was more like it. She'd felt the muscles and sinew of his body rippling under her hands, honed to a fine whipcord athleticism. Like the character Mack, he could flee, if he needed to.

"When do you eat?" she asked, glancing over her shoulder at the bed on the floor. They'd made progress this evening, but the possibility of sex loomed in her mind. How easy it would be to walk into Alex's arms and lean down to kiss him, and within minutes they'd be shedding clothes and tumbling onto the bed....

But I didn't come here for that.

He hadn't answered. "Do you have any of the chocolate left?" she asked idly.

"What was that about your lack of sweet tooth?"

Was he evading the question or only teasing? She couldn't tell, just as she couldn't tell about a lot of things with Alex.

She rested her head against the back of the chair, narrowing her eyes at him. "Gosh, you're dense. I'm hinting for sustenance, here."

"I'll go grab us some takeout."

"We could call for delivery," she said. "Or even go out."

"Out?" he repeated, as if he'd never heard the word.

"Yes, *out.* Putting on coats, walking to a restaurant, sitting at a table and ordering off menus like normal people. Thousands and thousands are doing it all around the city at this very moment. We don't have to call it a date. Just dinner."

There was a long silence. She watched him silently debate with himself before he quirked one corner of his mouth, attempting to charm her into doing this his way. "Seems like a lot of bother."

"So is picking up takeout."

"All right. We'll do delivery then. You have a cell phone, right?"

She rolled the sheaf of pages into one hand. "Yes, but this is ridiculous. Is there some reason you don't want to be seen in public with me? Are we supposed to conduct this affair strictly out of our apartments?"

"I told you not to expect much from me."

"Uh-huh. I seem to remember that." She sat forward. "Are you agoraphobic?"

"No."

"A werewolf?"

"Karina." He narrowed his eyes. "Don't do this."

"It's not a full moon, you know." Her laughter had a hard edge. "It's safe to go out tonight."

"I'm not a werewolf," he said with a clenched jaw.

"Are you—oh, I don't know—*famous?*" She gestured carelessly, sending the pages flying. They spilled across the floor. "I'm sorry," she said, immediately getting down on her knees to gather them up.

"Leave them." Alex pulled her up. "I'm not famous."

She rested her forehead against his chest. "I know that. But I'm trying to understand you."

"No, you're asking for more from me. And I can't give it."

"Why not?" she whispered, spasmodically closing her fingers over bunched folds of his sweatshirt.

"I told you. I'll be moving on soon. There's no use in getting involved."

"I'm not looking for a functioning—"

"Yes, you are." His palm brushed across her back, soothing her.

"Only going out to dinner," she continued blindly. "Is that too much to ask for?"

"Maybe not," he conceded, "but what happens after that? We spend more time together, and soon we have a standing arrangement. Then you introduce me to your friends. We fall in love...."

She couldn't believe he'd said that. And although her first impulse was to cling to her mistaken notion that she could have a fling without becoming involved, that would be simply stupid. The sex was getting all mixed up with emotion, and if she was totally honest she'd admit to being halfway in love with him already. Foolish, when she knew so little about him. She'd pinned a lot of her hopes on the way he seemed to be struggling over their relationship, but maybe that was part of his tortured-artist act and in reality all he'd wanted was a piece of her ass. After all, she was making assumptions about his character based on very limited evidence.

"We fall in love," he repeated. She felt his mouth moving against her hair. "And then I have to go. And then your heart is broken. I don't want to hurt you that way."

He cares for me.

"But you don't have to go. You could stay."

"No, it's possible—likely—that I'll leave at a moment's notice."

"Called back to the mother planet," she quipped, although she was in no mood to joke.

Alex kissed her temple.

"You're a spymaster."

His hands moved from her elbows to her shoulders, then around to her back, stroking warmth into her chilled bones. He kissed one eyelid, touching his tongue to her closed lid in a way that made her suck in a breath and go very quiet.

"You're on an undercover assignment," she whispered.

Ignoring her, he kissed the other eyelid. She held still, playing meek while plotting her first move. Except every move she thought of required staying in and getting physically intimate, not going out and coaxing him to reveal his well-hidden thoughts.

"My competitor has sent you to steal the secret recipe," she guessed.

"Yeah, that's why I need to taste you." He licked his tongue between her lips, parting them with delicate precision. She rose up to her toes to return the kiss, squeezing and bunching his shirt in her fists until she'd pulled it taut across his back.

Suddenly his head lifted. "What secret recipe?"

"Family recipe," she said, then cocked her head back. "You haven't noticed that my chocolates are extra good?"

"Of course," he said, kissing her again.

"You don't have to—" She put her hand over his mouth to push him away. "I'm fine with you not eating them. Really. Guys don't seem to have the same appreciation for the chocolate as women. But they learn to." She raised her eyebrows.

"Well, for me, it's not a matter of acquiring a taste—"

"You're already a connoisseur. That's obvious every time we kiss."

Alex looked confused, until she kissed him, and then he knew exactly what to do. He felt very good, very right, in her arms—though there was less urgency, there was also a sweeter tone to their intimacy.

"So let's do it," he said, breaking off a kiss.

Thud. Had she been thinking he was sweet?

"Let's go out to dinner like normal people."

Oh! "Why the sudden change?" she asked.

He wasn't quite meeting her gaze. "It's only dinner, right?"

"Absolutely."

"I don't know why I was opposed." His eyes skimmed her face. "As long as you understand…"

She nodded emphatically. "Yes, of course. It's only dinner."

LATE THE NEXT AFTERNOON, Alex was back at the window. Perhaps he'd been overly paranoid these past several weeks, but nearly being killed did that to a guy.

The previous evening with Karina had been like balancing on his board at the edge of a monstrous wave, racing toward the protection of a distant shore but fearing he'd never reach it in time. Given his situation, his life would always be unstable. Safety could be snatched away at any second.

He'd told Karina good-night at her door. Her bewilderment had pulled his heartstrings, but he'd remained firm. After going over the decision endlessly in his mind for the past few days, he'd convinced himself that leaving her was the courageous thing to do.

Except that leaving is for cowards, he thought, lifting the binoculars. The real test would have been taking up her challenge for more than a dinner out in public. But he was still too wary to open himself up that way.

Early on, in L.A. after Rafael Norris had followed through on the first of his death threats by arranging the execution of the defendant who'd killed his son, Alex had made it his business to learn how to create his own false identity and leave no tracks, independent of the Feds, never imagining how soon he'd use the skills.

Following the attempt on his life in Florida, he'd faced the stark reality of a lifetime of being completely on his own.

His life savings were in a numbered account, but were dwindling rapidly. The original plan for his life as Alex Anderson had been to find a job in the city as soon as he was comfortable that he was safe, keep his head down and hope like hell that he wouldn't be found again.

Karina had changed all that. Like it or not, he was involved with her.

He had two options: kiss her goodbye, and get out while the getting was good, or make the leap of faith that he'd been clever enough about creating his new identity that no one would find him.

It happened. Wanted persons could live for years, happy and unharmed. They held down everyday average jobs, they married, they had families, with no one ever suspecting the truth.

That prospect was tempting. Each minute with Karina made him want it more. The problem was that he'd be risking her to please himself.

No way.

Back to option one.

Alex watched the street, paying particular attention to Karina's shop. Sure enough, here came the man in question, short and slightly round, garbed in a trench coat and muffler, with the lenses in his glasses fogging up as he stepped from a warm cab into the cold air. In the course of Alex's daily observations, he'd begun to notice the frequent customer and wonder about him.

The man always ordered a hot drink, sat and read the newspaper. Nothing particularly suspicious in that, except for the frequency. And, as Alex had noted, the man's preoccupation from behind his newspaper with the goings-on in the shop.

A henchman hired by Rafael Norris—well-funded by his "career" as a Southern California drug trafficker—would be slick and professional. This guy seemed like an amateur. Still, the chocolate shop was a perfect observation point, so Alex had continued to keep track of the bespectacled customer in case the guy was keeping track of *him.*

Even Karina had noticed the man. She thought he was hooked on her chocolates, or interested in one of her clerks. Throughout dinner, she'd chatted in nervous stops and starts about everything that was happening in her life, filling in the blank spots in their conversation whenever Alex managed to dodge another of her questions about his past, his family, his likes and dislikes and on and on. He'd fished for more information on the customer, but she'd had nothing to tell.

Alex focused on the suspicious guy as he entered Sutter Chocolat. As usual, the man waited patiently in line, placed an order, went to sit at one of the tables. He sipped the drink while surreptitiously studying the store. At most, he'd exchange a few words with the employees—the clerks in their aprons, the girl who greeted the deliveryman when he came to pick up an outgoing shipment.

Not once had he revealed an interest in the building across the street. Alex had begun to accept that his suspicions were baseless.

Karina must be right. Still, it didn't hurt to keep an eye on the lurker anyway. Alex lowered the binoculars and got more comfortable in the armchair, settling in to be patient.

HE AWOKE WITH A START a long while later. Bewildered for a moment about where he was, even confused that there was no sea salt in the air. Until he looked out the window and his hellish situation snapped back to him.

Except that it was night. By the looks of the neighborhood, late night. The businesses were closed and gated. He'd managed to sleep for hours, when usually he woke frequently, attuned to every suspect noise.

He stood, stretching to relieve his stiff muscles. Karina's windows were closed and dark. Had she waited for him? Seen his silhouette in the chair and tried to get his attention?

Alex grunted and went to check the time on the clock on the stove. He'd always been a slacker about being on time, and had raced through the L.A. courthouse corridors on countless occasions, tucking in his shirt or knotting a tie. But at least he'd owned a watch in those days, and a clock. Now he'd given up caring, because he'd sunk so low that he'd believed there was nothing left to care about.

Karina might be his last chance at happiness. But only if he were willing to risk her.

"Stop," he said out loud. Why go over it again? The pipes rattled when he turned the faucet on. He splashed cold water on his face and returned to the window, drying himself on the sleeve of his T-shirt.

He'd never be able to go back to sleep. But what was he going to do—sit by the window and stare out at her place like a lovesick puppy dog?

A cab stopped a short way down from Karina's door. A passenger moved in the back seat and for a moment he thought it might be her, until the figure emerged, bundled in a puffy ski jacket with the hood up, a deep ruff of fur trim obscuring the person's face.

Were the passenger's movements fervent? Suspicious?

Alex let out a huff of air. Face it, he was obsessed.

But he continued watching as the passenger sidled along the sidewalk until the cab drove away, then walked briskly to the door of Sutter Chocolat. Alex estimated that it was a man of average build, but he wasn't even certain of that.

The door opened before the person knocked and he slipped inside.

Karina had a visitor, Alex thought.

To her store.

After 1:00 a.m.

With the lights out?

Every instinct that he'd developed in the past year was screaming on red alert. He damned himself for not keeping a cell phone, for not even getting her number.

He wanted to run to her rescue, but he delayed, waiting to see if lights would go on in the store and if somehow the late-night visit would make sense.

When that didn't happen, he yanked his gun out from beneath the mattress, grabbed his keys off the table and left the apartment. He took the stairs at a gallop, slowing only when he paused to tuck the gun into his waistband before stepping out the street door into the frozen air.

Shit. No jacket. That would look odd, if he was being watched. He curled his hands up into his sleeves, hunched his shoulders and took off at a brisk walk, risking no glance at Karina's shop.

Once he was far enough away, he cut across the street and sped to the door that led to the living quarters above the shop. Locked, dammit. Of course. Alex leaned on the button for Karina's apartment, wasting precious minutes trying to raise a response.

No answer. Not home? Or…

There were too many variables. Before he made a move, he had to be sure she wasn't in her apartment. He jammed his fingers down on every other apartment's buzzer until finally a shambling male figure wrapped in a robe appeared on the other side of the glass. Instead of pajamas, a regular shirt and pants showed underneath. The tenant rubbed his eyes and peered out. "Door's locked."

Obviously. Alex's attempt at a smile was pathetic. "I'm a visitor." Discreetly, he pulled out the tail of his shirt to cover the gun at the small of his back.

"Not mine, you're not. Buzz the apartment you want or go away."

"I tried that. No answer."

The tenant's face pressed against the glass, looking him over. "Can't help you."

"Please, just go and knock on Karina's door," he said, straining to keep his voice low. "She should be home, but she's not answering. I'm worried about her. Tell her Alex is downstairs. She'll let me in."

After an agonizing minute, the man nodded and returned to the stairs, climbing so slowly in his flapping slippers that Alex was ready to go ahead and just shoot out the glass. He jogged in place, although the adrenaline in his system was doing a good job of zapping away the cold.

When no response came, he pressed Karina's buzzer again and again. *Please be asleep. Just asleep.*

Finally the intercom crackled. "Who is it?" Karina said, in a sleepy voice. "Do you know how late it is?"

"I know. But this is—" He caught himself, aware that the neighbor could be listening in. Strangely, the man apparently hadn't given Karina Alex's name. "It's important. I have to see you right now."

She inhaled. "All right." She buzzed him through.

Alex ran up the stairs, arriving as she shooed the robed neighbor back inside his apartment. "Sorry to disturb you, Mr. Alonzo. I don't normally have visitors at this time...."

Alex hustled her inside, not caring that Alonzo was watching with some suspicion, holding a cell phone in his hand.

He slammed the door. "Quick, tell me if—"

"Alex!" She went to throw her arms around him. "You came."

"Stop, Karina." He clasped her shoulders, holding her away. "Listen to me. There's someone in your shop."

"Someone in my shop? Oh, come on." It took a couple of seconds for her to process that he hadn't arrived at her apartment for his nightly visit. "What do you mean? Burglars?"

"Maybe not." He stepped back, trying to think of rational reasons for what he'd seen. "Who has the key?"

"Only me and Debby."

"Would she have any reason to be down there right now?"

"Well, no, unless..." Karina looked bemused. "Unless she ran out of chocolate."

"You're not serious." He'd heard of chocoholics, but this was ridiculous. "Hold on, let me explain. I saw a man arrive in a cab, and someone let him into your store. Do you see? Someone was already inside. I couldn't tell who, but it's safe to assume the person had either a key or the alarm code."

"Was it Kyle in the cab? The buff delivery guy," she elaborated when she saw Alex's confusion. "He's Debby's boyfriend, so if it's her downstairs, we'd better not disturb them. They might have stopped by for, ah, dessert."

"What? Wait a minute. This man wasn't built—he was on the short side. I didn't get a good look at him, but he *might* have been the lurker you mentioned."

"How can that be?" Karina let out a yelp, finally realizing that the situation was serious.

"It's no ordinary break-in. The alarm didn't go off." Alex paused. "I think it's an inside job. Maybe one of your employees?"

Unless Norris had managed to track him down again, Alex thought, with a stone-cold horror. But if that had been the case, holing up in Karina's shop made no sense. Even for a sniper.

Karina gasped. "Industrial espionage! They might be after my secret recipe. Alex, we've got to call the police."

He'd rather not have the cops involved lest they ask too many questions, but there was no way out of it. "All right. You do that, and I'll go downstairs. Lock the door behind me and don't come out no matter what until the cops are here."

She grabbed at his arm. "No, Alex. That's too dangerous—"

"It's okay." He reached behind him. "I have a gun."

Karina stared at the illegal firearm he slipped out of his waistband. "Alex—my God. Where did you get that?"

10

"DON'T FREAK. This is my protection, just in case." Alex palmed the small silver gun before reaching for her door. "We don't know what's going on downstairs."

Karina grabbed at his arm. "All the more reason for you to stay here." Let them have her recipe, as long as Alex stayed safe. "You can't run around with a gun. That's crazy. You'll shoot somebody. You'll shoot *yourself.*"

He managed a grim smile. "The safety's on."

An explanation hit her like a hammer. "Were you a cop?" Shock froze her blood. "Are you *still* a cop? L-like on a stakeout?"

"No," he said, swinging past the door. "Stay inside. But give me your keys so I can get in without them hearing me. I'll need the alarm code, in case they've turned it back on."

She'd handed over the keys and repeated the pass code before she had a chance to think it over. He was no longer a stranger, but…

"Alex. Wait."

He looked at her, his blank face showing nothing.

She stalled at his cold efficiency. If he wasn't a professional of some sort—NYPD, P.I., FBI—what was he?

"This is too dangerous," she blurted. "I can't let you go."

"You are not coming with me."

"Then please stay here with me." Good idea. She was determined not to be one of those brainless girls in movies and books who insist on going along, only to end up getting in the way or becoming a hostage of the bad guys. She had more sense than that. But then she never expected her life to feature such drama either.

"We're wasting time." Alex reached for her. In the movies, he would have pulled her into his arms for a brief hard kiss and said he loved her. Instead he pushed on her shoulder, urging her back inside. "Go call the police."

"All right." She gulped. "Promise me you'll be careful."

"Don't worry. It's probably Debby."

"Then don't you dare shoot her!" Karina called after him, even though she knew he was only reassuring her. At first she hadn't believed he was serious about a break-in. But an attempt to steal her recipe made sense. She'd turned down many lucrative offers.

She ran to call 9-1-1, was put on hold for an agonizing minute, then reported her address and wasted more valuable time trying to explain why the shop's security alarm hadn't gone off. "It's got to be an inside job," she said, repeating Alex's assertion, and was poleaxed by the likelihood. How? Who?

She hung up the phone, put a robe on over her pajamas and went to hover in the hallway, listening for sounds of a chase—or gunshots.

Mr. Alonzo appeared, creased with worry. "What's happening?" he whispered.

"There's been a break-in at my shop…we think."

Her neighbor reached inside his open door. "I have a baseball bat. I can go downstairs to aid your young man with apprehending the burglars."

"Oh…no. Please don't do that. I'm sure—" She exhaled in relief as the sound of sirens grew closer. "Thank goodness. The police are coming."

But the sirens faded as the vehicle veered off onto another street. "Any minute now," she added, then it hit her that it could be awhile yet. Meanwhile, Alex was alone downstairs, playing the hero.

"Give me that bat," she said to Mr. Alonzo.

He wouldn't release it. "We'll go together."

Karina shoved her feet into boots and grabbed a ski pole from the back of her hall closet. Some backups they made. But she wasn't willing to wait forever, whether or not her common sense was screaming to leave the thieves to Alex. He'd seemed strangely cool and competent. Why was a question for later.

She and Mr. Alonzo hurried downstairs. "We'll just take a peek," Karina said as they crossed the frosty sidewalk from the apartment door to the shop. The door was open, the alarm shut down, the shop dark and quiet. If there had been a burglary, no damage was visible.

They stood just inside the entrance, listening. "I don't hear a thing," Mr. Alonzo said, lowering the bat.

"But what if—" Karina swallowed. She imagined Alex bludgeoned, bleeding, unable to call for help.

"Stay here. I'll go look in back."

"We'll both go." She remembered her resolution not to be the blundering fool. "But carefully."

They tiptoed across the shop and peeked through the porthole window in the swinging door that opened to the short hallway of the reception area. Nothing to see, except the glow of a light.

Karina put a finger to her lips. Mr. Alonzo nodded and they quietly moved inside, the door making a small sound as it swung shut behind them. She peeped around the corner. The desk lamp on Janine's desk was on. The door to her own office stood open.

Mr. Alonzo hefted the bat as they looked inside. Again, nothing seemed to have been disturbed, but all the lights were on in the windowless office.

"They've been here," Karina whispered, glancing behind the desk to be sure there wasn't a body lying on the floor.

"Don't touch anything," Mr. Alonzo said when she tucked the ski pole under her arm and went to open the narrow coat closet. "Fingerprints."

She stopped. Her eyes went to the wood panel that fronted the wall safe. If the intruders knew the layout of the office, they'd start there in a search for her secret recipe.

Suppose Alex had been wrong? Or led her wrong?

No, that was ridiculous.

But he's been watching you—and the shop—through binoculars.

Only to plan such an elaborate ruse? "Forget it," she muttered.

Mr. Alonzo looked at her, silently questioning.

"The kitchen," she said. "This way."

They passed through the second corridor lined with shelves—at a glance, untouched—and were about to step into the dark kitchen when a hand touched Karina's shoulder.

She let out a yell and whirled with the ski pole raised, but Alex caught it in midair. "You'll put an eye out," he said.

"Alex!" Relief washed through her, pushing out the moment's fear. "How did you get behind us?"

"I went out the back door, looking for the burglars, then I couldn't get back in again and I had to come around." The back exit was a self-locking safety door that opened to a narrow walkway between buildings.

"You didn't catch them." Karina was just as glad, especially when she thought of his gun. It had disappeared again. Her gaze went to his face. He appeared very contained, though breathing hard.

He took the ski pole. "Didn't even see them, I'm afraid, except for hearing the back door close. They must have heard me coming in the front and were able to leave in time."

"Oh, no—the grate." Karina led the two men back to the office and pointed to a decorative grate in the ceiling. "I forgot. My hallway is right above, and voices carry through the grate. It's never mattered because I'm usually here during work hours."

Alex stared at the ceiling. "Damn."

"Seems lucky to me," Mr. Alonzo said, looking greatly relieved. "The burglary was stopped before it started."

If there even were a burglary to begin, Karina thought, in spite of herself. The story seemed absurd, except that Alex had no knowledge of her valuable recipe. And she trusted him, the same way she was drawn to him—instinctively.

He studied her and Mr. Alonzo with eyes as flat as dull silver coins. "Do you see anything out of place?"

"Aside from the lights..." She shrugged. "Give me a minute. I'll check the office."

"Fingerprints," Mr. Alonzo said again.

Alex shook his head. "It's doubtful the police will dust for prints, especially since there's no evidence that anything was touched. And this being—" He looked at Karina again, with a shrug. "An inside job."

Mr. Alonzo was curious. "An inside job?"

"We don't know that." Karina was dismayed at the prospect since she'd been so careful about hiring, especially after a problem with an earlier employee who'd been caught filching from the cash registers. She went to sit behind her desk. "Someone's been on my computer."

Alex appeared to look over her shoulder. "How do you know?"

"The keyboard's been moved. Only a couple of inches, but I can tell." She tapped the key to remove the screensaver. "I don't know if it's possible to tell if they tried to access my files, but they couldn't get in because I have a special password-protected program for documents like my customer addresses and our recipes and suppliers."

"Our voices must have scared them off." Alex didn't sound entirely convinced. "Is my name on your customer list?"

"You're not a customer. Yet. The truffles were a gift." She closed down the computer. "I didn't even know your name at the time."

"The police are here," Mr. Alonzo called from the doorway. "I'll go let them in."

Alex moved away. "Listen…" He paused, shifting nervously from foot to foot. "Don't tell them about my gun, okay?"

She stood with a snap, shooting her desk chair back. "Why not?"

"Just don't."

"I want to know why."

"Later," he said, looking toward the noise at the front of the shop.

"Promise me an explanation," Karina insisted.

Alex seemed reluctant, but he gave her a quick nod before leaving to greet the law. Karina grimaced, not at all sure that she was doing the right thing. Once more, she listened to her heart instead of her head and decided to believe in him.

"YOU'RE VERY CALM," Alex said, some time later after the police had departed. Karina had relentlessly combed her office looking for clues until finally he'd taken her by the hand and led her upstairs to her apartment. He'd sat her on the sofa, wrapped her in a white-fur throw, and gone to make her a cup of coffee with a shot of cognac. He'd taken one swig himself. For the Dutch courage to keep on lying.

"Thinking," she said, holding the mug under her chin.

"About?"

"How a person on my staff could have done this."

"Literally?" he asked, to stall. She'd resisted the idea that she might have been betrayed and had sworn up and down that there was no one who'd do that to her.

"Yes. How would a person get into the shop?" She sighed before answering herself. "They would have had to get a key and the security code, but I suppose that wouldn't be too difficult. I've punched it in with employees standing right there beside me."

Alex sat beside her and she pulled her elbow in, keeping her face turned away from him. He'd had her change the code when they locked up after he'd negotiated the tricky dealings with the cops. "Where do you keep the keys?"

"In my purse. Sometimes in a desk drawer." She sighed again. "Or even on the desk."

"What's so valuable about this recipe?" When she'd mentioned the various files, he'd considered the possibility that the intruders had been after his address. Which only showed that his paranoia was way out of bounds since he was right across the street, in plain view. Particularly if the constant lurker and the night's second burglar were one and the same.

"My chocolate's unique." Karina stirred beneath the synthetic fur. "You still haven't noticed?"

"I've told you. Chocolate's not my thing."

"So you say." She sipped the hot drink. "Trust me. Milton Hershey would die for my recipe, if he wasn't already…" She shuddered. "Dead."

"Would you die defending it?"

She stiffened. "What? I was kidding. No one's going to *die*."

"That depends. Where do you keep the recipe?"

"Don't worry," she said. "It's safe."

"*In* the safe?" She'd opened the hidden safe for the police, who had been singularly unimpressed by their story of burglars who took nothing and immediately departed the scene after hearing their voices through the grate.

"Not in the safe. In a security box at the bank, but…" She gnawed her lip. "It's not only about the recipe. There's also the supplier. I get a special chocolate made from a particular cocoa bean that's sold only to me. Expensive, but worth it. And the contact info for my supplier is on the computer."

"Would a business rival be aware of this?"

She shook her head. "I don't think so. Debby is my only confidante. But other employees, particularly the kitchen help, probably know since they've been instructed to treat the bulk chocolate shipments and the occasional package of the raw cocoa beans with special care."

"These deliveries—they come the usual way?"

Karina shot him a furious look. She shoved the fur down and set her coffee mug on the table. "What are you suggesting? Debby's in cahoots with Kyle? That makes no sense. She already knows the recipe since she uses it every time she makes a new batch."

"It was only a question. I'm trying to look at this from all angles. Who's this Kyle again?"

Karina nodded, but with reluctance. "I already explained. Kyle is Debby's new guy, our regular deliveryman. They suddenly got the hots for each other—"

"Oh."

"Don't go there, Alex. I trust Debby completely."

"But what about Kyle?"

"You said it wasn't him, getting out of the cab."

"What if I was wrong?"

"Do your binoculars often deceive you?"

"No."

"Well, then." Karina's tone was dry. "It seems to me that you're the only mysterious stranger on the scene. But you don't see me accusing you, even though you're the one with the gun." She shivered again. "I hate that you have a gun."

He tried to pull the fur back over her, but she resisted.

He cleared his throat. "Thanks for keeping quiet with the cops." It had been tense, making himself answer their questions with complete nonchalance when he knew that one slipup could collapse his identity like a house of cards.

"Where is it? If you move too suddenly, will it shoot a hole through my couch?"

"Don't worry. I removed the ammo."

"Wonderful," she said with sarcasm, then sank back down onto the firm cushions and pulled the fur up to her chin, absorbed in thought. After a minute, she looked at him, her eyes narrowed to crescents. "And so…?"

He'd been waiting for her to ask. "The gun is only for protection, like I said. I'm not an undercover cop. Not a bank robber, either. I don't fit any of the crazy scenarios you might come up with." Except the only one she hadn't thought of.

"Uh-huh. Then why were you worried about the police?"

He'd have to give her that one. "The gun's not legal."

She frowned. "Why not?"

"Um, because I'm not into paperwork?"

"This is no joking matter. I want to know the truth."

You can't handle the truth. Hell, I *can't handle the truth.*

"You weren't in advertising, were you?" she continued. "Did you even live in Arizona?"

"No," he said, and then couldn't make himself come up with a lie to cover the previous lie. He had to tell her some version of the truth—he owed her that.

She turned away from him, hugging herself beneath the fur throw, and he gave in to the impulse to follow her, molding his chest to her curved back, enfolding her in his arms. She shuddered beneath them and said, "Don't touch me," but he didn't stop. He couldn't.

She didn't fight the embrace. The opposite, in fact. She softened against him. "Did you *ever* tell me the truth?"

For once, he was able to say, "Yes."

A minute, maybe two, passed. Then, quietly: "When were you honest?"

"When I was inside you."

She let out a slow exhale. Her head dropped forward, away from his, but then tilted to rest against his arm. "I've been following my instincts with you, trusting you even when my common sense says I shouldn't. This is very unlike me."

He closed his eyes. Honored.

"But I want you to know, I can't keep it up. Tonight, for instance. I had this thought—" She stopped.

He knew what she wanted to say. "You were suspicious of my story about the intruders. Are you still?"

"I should be. I know I should be." Her hand crept out from beneath the fur and took hold of his forearm, where he'd crossed them across her chest. An abiding affection for her shot through him, pure and strong.

"When will you tell me who you are?" she asked.

The last thing he wanted was for any of that ugliness to stain Karina. But asking for her blind faith was too much to demand.

His head inclined beside hers and he breathed the perfume of her hair. "I'm just a guy who's starting his life over from scratch."

"Mmm." Lazily, she rubbed her cheek against his arm. "That's no explanation."

Saying nothing, he clicked off the standing lamp behind the sofa. The sheen of the white curtains softened the glare of the streetlights. A light snow had begun to fall and the flecks danced in the strange silvery-orange glow that filled the windows.

Karina exhaled, her body growing lax. "You promised me…"

"Sleep," he said, and she did.

He drifted off, too, stirring only when the grinding

rumble of a truck on the street woke him with a start. For several minutes, he stayed where he was, treasuring the gift of holding Karina in his arms. Her hair spilled across his shoulder, one smooth cheek turned up near his face. He kissed it before slowly sliding away.

Moving gingerly, he stood and tucked the fur around her again after she'd murmured and nestled against the sofa cushions. She was out like a light, trusting him in spite of herself. A trust he'd done nothing to earn.

Now was the time for him to decide. After Florida, he'd sworn that he'd leave his next life at the first sign of anything out of the ordinary. But rationally, the break-in—for lack of a better word—couldn't be about him. And Karina needed his help. He had to stay.

"A little while longer," he mouthed. Just until he knew she was safe.

Or…he could truly dedicate himself to living a new life. A real one. He'd made a resolution to be normal, after Karina had come to his apartment the first time, but that hadn't lasted long. To do it right, he'd have to commit to more than a haircut and a shave.

Now wasn't the time to decide, with the threat to at least one of them in play. But if he didn't do it now, would he ever?

He walked out. Took the stairs slowly at first, but then faster as decision prickled in his blood. Picking up speed, he emerged from the building and crossed the ice-rimmed road at a fast stride, his breath coming out in vaporous puffs.

Into his building, up the stairs, his pulse drumming. He didn't bother to turn on the light in his apartment or check for signs of intruders, but went right to the windowsill. The binoculars weren't there.

He found them on the floor. Snatched them up. Damned glasses, keeping the world at bay.

He was so consumed, he left his door hanging open and didn't care. The roof was several flights up. He ascended in lunges, two, even three steps at a time. One thought in his head.

To put an end to his fear.

The heavy black tar of the roof was as hard as cement in the cold. He went straight to the back of the building, where there was an opening among the crowded structures, little more than an air shaft.

He hefted the glasses, shoulder-height. Higher. Over his head.

Rearing back, muscles stretching. *Now.*

He threw the binoculars over the edge. Using all his strength, his arms swinging down as if he wielded a sledgehammer. The glasses hit the pavement with a sharp crack. Splitting the cold gray dawn.

He turned away without looking over the edge. Turned toward the sunrise sending an arrow of light onto the chalky red brick of Karina's building.

NIKKI SILK, KARINA WROTE on a notepad the following day, right after she'd hung up the phone. The magazine writer had called to ask for a tour of the shop. She was collecting background information for her article. Karina had tried to put the tour off, but Nikki wasn't taking no for an answer. They'd finally settled on a date later in the week, but the young woman's pushy inquisitiveness had roused Karina's hackles. Although she couldn't see a connection, she added Nikki's name to her suspects list.

All the employees were there, regardless of her trust

in them. Janine and a part-time clerk headed the list, simply because they were the newest. Next was the one worker she'd had to fire earlier that year for pilfering from the till, followed by the rest of the staff.

Reluctantly, she added Kyle's name. And Debby, as his inside connection. Immediately she crossed Debby out with heavy strokes of the pen, and wrote in Alex, and a question mark.

Alex? No, not him. The incident with the intruders made no sense if Alex was in on it. More cross-outs.

Unless the entire thing was a ruse to gain access to her shop. He'd told her not to follow him. If she and Mr. Alonzo hadn't, an expert safecracker might have had time to get in and out before the police had arrived.

"Ridiculous," she said, stabbing her pen on the notepad. "Convoluted. Impossible."

The familiar-looking customer went on the list, even though there was no way for her to track him down. She would question him next time he showed up, *if* he showed up.

Not likely. She decided that he was her prime suspect. Perhaps he'd gotten to one of the employees, promised them a lucrative payoff if they helped him acquire her trade secrets.

Janine buzzed on the intercom, even though Karina's door was open. "Debby Caruso to see you. Don't forget you have that appointment with the wholesaler in twelve minutes."

Debby leaned past Janine's desk, waving.

Karina made a face at the chef, suppressing the urge to giggle as she pressed the intercom button. She intoned, "Thank you, Janine. Please send Ms. Caruso in."

"How can you stand her?" Debby said before she'd quite closed the door.

"Shh. Janine's not so bad. Very serious, that's all. She's a good worker."

"But she's attentive to the point of intrusiveness. That would get on my nerves."

"Seems to me that Kyle's being very attentive."

"Yeah, funny enough, his attentions tend to soothe me." Debby stretched luxuriously before plopping into the visitor's chair. "I was very well attended over the weekend. How about you?"

"Hmm." Karina turned over her notepad. "How's it going with Kyle?"

"Too good to be true. There have been a few moments where I wondered if this was all about sex—"

Karina raised her brows. "You have a problem with that?"

"Are you kidding?" Debby grinned. "But we haven't been big talkers up to now, so I tried to get him to open up. Turns out he likes making model race cars and lives at home with his widowed mother in Queens. Well, in a studio apartment above the garage. The man's a nerd in a muscle suit. Who knew?"

"Does that bother you?"

"Nope. It was almost a relief. I'm a nerd, too. But…" Debby pushed her bangs back. Her mouth puckered. "He did hint this morning that there may be a fly in the ointment. He said he has something to discuss. He actually said *discuss.* You know that's bad, coming from a man. I think he's keeping something from me."

Karina's skin prickled. "That sounds worrisome. What do you think it's about?"

"Oh, you know…whatever." Debby waved a hand,

wearing her brave-soldier expression. "I'll be sure to have a supply of truffles on hand to cure the problem."

Karina shook her head. "A temporary cure…"

"For a temporary relationship," Debby said lightly, although her mouth turned down.

Certain that Debby was more serious about Kyle than she let on, Karina crossed her fingers under the desk and sent up a quick wish. *For Debby's sake, please don't let him be involved in the break-in.*

"It'll be okay, Deb."

"Sure." Debby brushed at her bangs. "Anyway, what did you want to see me about?"

First thing that morning, Karina had gone to the kitchen to check on a few items. She'd asked Debby to drop by the office when she had a free minute. Alex had advised her to keep the attempted burglary quiet for now, so that they could concoct a plan to apprehend the prowlers. But Karina couldn't be compliant. In the unlikely event that Kyle was involved, Debby should have fair warning.

Karina nipped her lip, searching for words. "There's something going on that I wanted you to know about."

"Ooh. Sounds serious."

"Actually, yes. I believe that an unknown employee has attempted to pry into my computer records. After hours."

"What!"

"Looking for the recipe, I expect."

Debby crossed her arms, frowning. "Got to be Janine."

"Shh. Not so loud. She's probably listening at the door." Karina leaned over the desk. "Why Janine? You're just saying that because you don't like her."

"All right, I admit our personalities clash. But she is

new, and frighteningly professional, like the Stepford secretary. Is there anyone else you'd suspect first?"

"Shelby's new too, and I know much less about her, where I've worked closely with Janine." Karina made a helpless gesture. "But really, I have no idea. The thing is, it appears this person has a copy of the key to the front door. Or maybe lifted one of the spares. I wanted to check in with you since you're the only one who has a set. Have your keys gone missing, maybe?"

"They're always in my purse."

"And your purse is…"

"Always in the kitchen. Oh."

"You see my quandary."

Debby frowned. "Well, what about the recipe? *Everyone* has access to—"

Karina raised a finger to her lips. She shook her head.

Debby whispered, her eyes lighting up. "We could conduct a covert investigation of the likely suspects."

"I don't want the staff all upset, when we're so busy with the holidays."

"But industrial espionage is a serious issue. You can't put it off. What if this mystery person has backers who can buy the Brazilian chocolate out from beneath you?"

"Ugh. I don't want to even imagine that."

Debby was getting excited. "I'm with you, Kare, one for all. What can we do?"

"For now, keep quiet, but be observant. I'm working on a plan."

Debby waited expectantly, but Karina shrugged, giving no more details. She had nothing, except her trust in Alex.

Slowly, a shadow crept over Debby's face. She shifted in the chair, absently running a finger beneath her chin. "Are you sure the suspect is an employee? I just can't believe that any of my kitchen workers would be involved. I know them."

Karina nodded glumly. "Unless someone here thinks they can sell the recipe for quick cash, an outside source is probably the instigator. But we have to face that there might well be an employee connection."

Debby jumped up. "I'd better get back to work." With an almost perfunctory, "Don't worry, we'll be just fine," she departed.

Karina's smile faded, along with her confidence. She sat unmoving for several minutes, various suspicions filling her head, vaguely annoyed by the way Janine crossed back and forth through the outside office, glancing at Karina with each pass.

Resolutely, she turned to the computer, typed in her password, opened the supplier file and removed the contact information for her source in Brazil. Trying not to think of the cliché about shutting the barn door after the cow's run away, she changed the password, committed it to memory, then wrote a fake one—KJSTRSTALEX—on a snippet of paper. She added random numbers that simulated the safe combination. Taped the paper under her blotter.

A totally obvious hiding spot, but that was the point.

11

KARINA WAS CERTAIN she'd fallen into a fairy tale. "I've never seen anything so beautiful," she told Alex, her gaze rising up and up and up to the hand-hewn rafters and the four-tiered crystal chandeliers. Everywhere she looked there was the sparkle and shimmer of lavish holiday decor. Evergreen garlands, twinkling lights, richly colored stained-glass wall panels. Flowers in abundance. The soft glow of heavy silver, etched glass, white tablecloths. The shine of brass. "It's magical."

"I thought you could use a treat," he said. "Take your mind off—"

"Oh, let's not talk about that." She reached for his hand, clasping it atop the table and not letting go. After a moment, he relaxed. He smiled. He could use this too, she thought.

"How did you manage this?" she asked. They were seated among the holiday splendor of the Rafters Room at the city landmark in Central Park, Tavern on the Green. When Alex asked a woman out, he really went all the way. "Don't you need to reserve weeks ahead at Christmastime?"

"Bribery." He winked. "It was a challenge. They wanted a credit card just to make a reservation. I had to come in person and use all my—" he coughed "—persuasion to get us a table for the evening."

"You don't have a credit card?" Suddenly she wondered if his barren existence wasn't merely because of the timing of his recent move. "Never mind. We can use mine."

"Of course not." He used such a firm tone that she said no more on the subject.

The setting was so dazzling, she couldn't stop looking. Windows overlooked a snowy garden filled with trees and topiary animals outlined in thousands of tiny lights. She sighed. "Thank you. I'll never forget this."

His thumb moved across her fingers, saying that she was welcome without using the words. "You've never been here?"

"Once, in spring, many years ago. I must have been nineteen or twenty."

He laughed. "Oh, *many* years ago."

"Eight, then." She smiled. "Seems like a long time to me."

"Life is short."

Ah, one of those enigmatic but meaningful statements of his that she had yet to crack….

She forgot the surroundings to study his face. "You're different tonight."

"It's the suit," he said.

She tightened her fingers on his. "Well, you clean up nice."

"You, too."

"I would have dressed up even more if I'd realized what you had in mind." He'd said he was taking her out to dinner, but she hadn't imagined quite such a splash-out. She wore a simple dress of soft gray wool and her leather boots, with her hair caught up in silver combs.

He had on a new suit—charcoal and conservative. But his tie was a surprising ivy pattern in gaudy holiday colors. It made her smile, to think that there was a bright soul hidden somewhere inside him.

"This is a date," she said, suddenly feeling shy.

"I guess so."

"You *guess?*"

"All right. It's a date."

"About time you made an honest woman of me."

"Is that what it takes? You're easy."

She kicked him under the table and they laughed. "We both needed this," she said as a waiter approached the table with their first-course selections: stone crabs and a mushroom dish made with white truffles.

"How was it, at work?" Alex asked.

"We weren't going to talk about that." After a moment, she gave a small hitch of her shoulders. "It was strange. I couldn't help suspecting everyone. Except Debby." When he would have commented—probably to say that she couldn't be subjective—she hurriedly added, "And I managed to come up with reasons that any of them might have to do it, even though I'm not convinced in the least. Shelby is a poor college student, Tara has a sick mother, Richard in the kitchen has been known to place bets with a bookie…."

Alex nodded. "There are always reasons, if you dig."

"I don't *want* to dig. I had a locksmith in, and I changed the alarm code. Isn't that enough protection?"

"You can continue to work with a mole?"

She shook her head. The treachery would eat at her. "But what else can I do?"

"Don't worry." He gave her hand a squeeze. "I'll

think of a way to take care of it. That is, if you've stopped suspecting me."

She kept her gaze level on his face. "It would help if I knew even one true thing about you."

"You know me, Karina."

"Do I?" She looked down at her fork, moving the food around her plate. "I know of you. I know your body and the way you react to questions, or danger and fear, and—and—other stimuli. But I don't know about you. Don't—" She put up a hand to stop him even though he hadn't made a sound. "Don't tell me that's not important."

"It's better that you don't know." Momentarily, his expression turned bleak, but not in the same hard way from before. He *was* different. She'd have sensed that even without the obvious clue of the very romantic date.

"Tell me something," she insisted, for the first time believing that he might really open up to her. "One true thing. About your interests. Your childhood. Anything at all." She gestured at the elaborately decorated Christmas trees, sparkling like jewel boxes in the crystalline light. "Your favorite Christmas."

A wry grin. "It wasn't like this."

She lifted her wineglass. "Go on."

"I was raised in California. An only child. My parents were—they both had good jobs. But there was always time for family."

"Did you have lots—cousins, uncles and aunts and grandparents?"

"No, not so many blood relatives. Many friends though. We had a big house in—on the coast. One of those rambling redwood structures that were popular in the sixties and seventies. It's probably ramshackle by now."

"No longer in the family?"

"Technically, yes. But my father's renting it out."

"What about your mother?"

"She died. Dad remarried several years later to a very nice lady and moved away. He's happy."

"But you're not close?"

"Not anymore."

"I suppose you won't tell me why."

"Right. You said one true thing, and I've given you several."

"Stickler."

He dipped a crab into a pool of hot mustard sauce. "I had a great childhood. Good parents, loads of friends, long summers on the beach. I did well in school. Went on to college, got the job I wanted after graduation." He shrugged. "I had every opportunity in the world."

"But…?"

He tilted his head back and let the crab slide down his throat. "Life happens, you know? Bad luck, bad timing, the wrong choice. Whatever you want to call it. What went down was out of my control, and after a while, I wound up here, starting over."

Although he was trying very hard to be nonchalant, she wasn't buying it. But he'd given her more than before. "Okay. What about women? Now that I know you really were a beach bum, I'm guessing you had bikini babes crawling all over you."

"Maybe the other way around," he said with a teasing lilt.

"Sure. I can just imagine."

The waiter came to clear their plates and Alex caught her hand again, swinging it between their chairs. "I've always been partial to blondes."

She gave him a lofty sniff, imagining him rollicking in the surf with some *Baywatch*-type babe. “And I’m sure they’ve always been partial to you.”

“Your turn,” he said. “One true thing about Karina Sutter.”

She waited until the waiter had served their entrées. “But you know lots about me.”

“I want to know everything.”

“Mmm, well…” She tasted the cranberry compote that went with her traditional turkey dinner. Tangy and delicious. “I was the best native dancer at the American school in Papua New Guinea.”

Alex gave an astounded laugh. “What?”

“We had sing-sing classes. I picked it right up.” She chuckled at his befuddlement. “I didn’t tell you about my dad? When I was young, we lived in New York while he was a top executive for an international company. Even then, we traveled a lot. I was nine when he retired from that to become an ambassador for Switzerland. Papua New Guinea was his first posting, but after that we lived all around the world for seven years.”

“No, you didn’t tell me.”

“That’s what we get for trying to have a meaningless fling. We’ve missed all the fun getting-to-know-you part.”

“Fun? That depends. You haven’t ever been on a bad date?”

She conceded the point. “But with the right person…”

Alex gazed steadily at her. She became flustered, but she couldn’t look away.

“You’re the right person,” he said.

She touched her lips with her tongue. “So are you.”

They put their heads together and shared a light kiss. She felt the goodness, the four-square *rightness* of Alex, the feeling setting off a tangled mass of hope and confusion and love.

They separated. Alex dabbed with his napkin. "Ahem."

She let out a shivery sigh. Love? If she was falling in love with him…oh Lord. It might be heavenly, but there was an equal chance that it could be a downward trip to hell. There were so many reasons to have doubts, and only one to believe. And she'd never relied on her heart alone to make decisions.

She touched the burning tip of her nose with her pinkie, then gave it a quick pinch before rearranging her napkin and quietly picking up her knife and fork.

He was smiling at her. "Why do you do that?"

Blink. "Do what?"

"Pinch the end of your nose. It's cute."

"Oh. Well. A habit, I guess. You have them, too, like your penchant for drumming on tabletops." She tried to switch the subject. "How's the venison?" He'd ordered it because he'd never had it before, but she'd teased him that the holidays weren't the best time to start eating reindeer.

He wasn't distracted. "No, it's more than a habit. You did it outside my door, that first time we met, when you came over with the chocolates."

Her brow furrowed. "I did? How am I expected to remember?"

"It was after I—" Alex stopped, looking embarrassed.

"Aha. After you dismissed me."

"You were getting to me. I really needed to be rid of you, and fast, so I was rude. I'm sorry."

"It's okay. I understand. Not *why,* but I know about wanting to keep control. That's what the nose-pinch is.

When I'm getting too, you know, emotional or outlandish, losing my senses..." Her face had grown hot. "I always had to be quiet and well behaved at embassy functions, so I learned to temper myself."

Alex had followed her rambling explanation with his head cocked. "Which was it this time?"

"This time?" Her breath came short. She wrung the napkin in her lap.

"Be honest now."

"You're a fine one to talk about honesty."

He leaned closer, taking her hand again. "Tell me one true thing."

All right then. He'd asked for it.

"I was alarmed that I might be falling in love." Her chest was tight, prickly. "With you," she added, in case there was any question.

Alex didn't speak right away. She was certain he would pull away again, but he gave a small nod.

"That would be the best Christmas present I ever got."

Was that all he meant to say? She waited a couple of seconds before batting her lashes at him. Her mouth made a nipped-in smile. "Then we'll have to wait and see what happens on December 25th, won't we?"

She was thoroughly unnerved when he let go of her hand and straightened up. But he didn't withdraw, as he always had before.

He reached up and pinched the end of his nose.

PLEASANTLY BUZZED by the fermented-cider sauce of a shared gingerbread dessert, they exited beneath the red canopy to a thick dusting of snow that had turned the fanciful gardens into a winter wonderland. "I don't want this evening to end," Karina said, entwining their arms.

"It's not over yet." Horse-drawn carriages were lined up near the entrance, waiting for passengers. Bells jingled as one of the steeds, a dappled gray, stamped a foot and snorted plumes from its nostrils.

Alex waved an expansive hand. "Should we go for a ride around the park?"

"That's so touristy." She moved past him, inspecting the carriages before turning back to clap her gloved hands. "I'd love it!"

Alex approached the driver at the head of the line and gave Karina his arm as she climbed up into a carriage. He followed and pulled the robe over their laps before wrapping her up in his embrace and hugging her close. "Not too cold for you?"

"I like the cold. When I was young, my family spent Christmas skiing at Saint Moritz." Her laugh tinkled on the frozen air. "But you! You're the beach baby." She hugged her arms around his waist. "Too cold for you?"

He smiled down at her, snuggled up against his chest. "Not now."

The carriage took them on a tour of Central Park, peaceful as a picture postcard, under a blanket of snow. Antique street lamps cast halos of light. The horse's hooves clip-clopped to the chime of their jinglebells.

"You're so different," Karina whispered into his ear at one point, still wondering over the change. "I don't know why, but I like it. I like it very much."

He couldn't explain without telling her everything. Maybe one day. For now all she had to know was that he was trying. Every move felt like a risk at first, but slowly he had begun to remember what it was to have a life. Most likely, he'd never be without moments of fear and worry, but even a life shadowed by anxiety was better than the bleak emptiness of his days since he'd fled Florida.

Karina began chattering about the annual holiday party she'd been planning for her staff. The event was catered, a casual smorgasbord set up in her apartment. There would be music and drinks, and a Santa to hand out her gifts, along with the packages from the staff's name exchange.

"You'll come, won't you?"

"I'm not sure."

"What's to stop you?" she asked, as if he would tell her. Her look became sly. "This would be the perfect opportunity for you to evaluate my employees as the mole."

"That's bribery."

She nudged under his jaw with her nose. "You're not above it."

He mulled over his options. "Does the party stick to your place, or do you use the shop?"

"My place. Until we want dessert, then we storm the back entrance and raid the shop for chocolate."

"What's this about a back entrance? You can't mean the emergency exit—that leads outside."

"No, there's another door. It's rarely used. In fact, it's usually boxed off, because it opens onto the corridor where the supplies are stored. I open it for the party—convenient for the guests so they don't have to parade in and out the front door."

Alex inhaled too much cold air; it parched his lungs. "Wait a minute. You're saying this door opens—where?"

"Onto the vestibule for the apartments. But it's hidden under the stairs, and always kept locked, I assure you."

"Still, that's very interesting."

"I know what you're thinking, Alex. But the intruders used the front door, remember?"

"One of them did. We don't know about the other."

"It's not any easier getting into the vestibule."

"I suppose." A plan formulated in his mind. "Who all is invited to this party?"

"My employees, and their significant others—husbands, wives, parents, kids. Some of them bring a friend or two. I invite the tenants in the building too, since we tend to get loud and I don't want complaints—or to leave anyone out."

"Will Debby bring Kyle?"

Karina frowned. "I think so."

"And the rest of the names from your suspect list will be there?"

"All except the one employee I fired. And Nikki Silk."

"Who's that?"

"A nosy journalist. Harmless."

"Invite her."

"Alex! What do you have in mind?"

"It's simple enough." The carriage had circled Sheep Meadow and was now returning to the restaurant, a brick and stone edifice that had once been a sheepfold.

"Tell me," Karina said. Her cheeks were blotched with pink from the cold.

"Suppose that you let it be known this back door is open, ready for the guests to storm the shop for their dessert. I'll hide myself in your office. The mole won't pass up the opportunity to slip downstairs during the confusion and make another attempt at your computer or the safe. Then I'll step out and catch him, or her, red-handed."

"What about the accomplice?"

"We'll let the police worry about that."

"Could be dangerous."

"Nah. I've faced worse."

"Oh, really?"

He shook his head, discouraging the curiosity. "I've already said enough for tonight."

"Actually..." Karina worried her lip. "Your plan could work. Especially because I've planted a fake password in my office." She explained about hiding the slip of paper under her desk blotter. "I was only thinking that it would delay and frustrate the person trying to get into my computer files, but if the mole discovers the codes before the party..."

"The temptation will be all the sweeter."

The carriage slowed. "Ride's over, folks," said the driver, tightening the reins to the chiming accompaniment of the silver bells affixed to the harness.

Alex got out and swung Karina down beside him, his hands on her waist. She rested her hands on his shoulders, moving closer into his embrace. "I don't know. Maybe we should take all of this to the police. Let them handle it."

"You saw how much they cared."

"But what if—"

"I'll be fine." He kissed her, struck by how heightened his senses had become, in a new way. Before, it had been all about keeping his eyes peeled and his reflexes fast. Now he wanted each moment to last. The night was all about the sharp tang of pine, the biting chill, steaming horseflesh, tattered velvet and old leather and cold lips that melted into the warmth of kisses that tasted like apple cider and cinnamon.

"Let's go home," Karina said, puffing warm breath against his ear.

"Will I get to unwrap you?"

"You're supposed to wait until Christmas morning."

She laughed, her cheek pressed to his lapel. "But that's still a week away, so I'll make you a mug of the store's peppermint hot chocolate and, mmm, you know how turned on I get after I've been dipping into the special chocolate. Anything might happen."

"Sounds good to me," he said, even though he was never going to get her obsession with chocolate.

Back at home, she showed him the canister of the drink mix made of dark-chocolate shavings and crushed peppermint. Wondering just how he was ever going to tell her about his allergy to chocolate after delaying for so long, he watched her melt the chocolate concoction in a saucepan, pour the rich brew into mugs and add heavy cream. "Too rich for my blood," he said when she urged a mug on him, but she insisted he take a taste.

"I don't want to drink alone." She tipped her mug back and took a big swallow, coming up smiling as she licked her chocolate-coated lips. "Or get naked alone."

"Magic words." He sipped. "Very good, but you'll taste even better."

She came easily, looping her arms around him and sliding her tongue along his bottom lip. "That's what I like—chocolate and peppermint and Alex, all in one."

Kissing her was a distraction that always worked, and within seconds she'd forgotten about the hot chocolate and was leading him to the bedroom. She mentioned still being cold, and he wished he'd let her down the entire hot chocolate when she hurriedly stripped, put on a pair of flannel pajamas and hopped under the covers.

But matters improved. One hand slipped out from under the blankets and beckoned him. "Come warm me up."

He was out of his clothes in record time. After carefully

placing a couple of condoms in easy reach on the headboard shelf, which made her laugh, he climbed into bed.

"Not so fast," she said when he reached for her. "I want to snuggle."

He moved in closer. "You're really pushing this intimacy stuff."

Laughingly, she pushed his chest. He caught her shoulders and pulled her against him, running his palms over her flannels. "We've got to do something about these pajamas."

"But I'm cold."

"Get under here, then." He lifted the heavy bed coverings up over their heads and they nestled side by side in the dark, soft cocoon, only hugging at first, then more. His fingers brushed across her abdomen, under the pajama top. They found the hard tips of her breasts. He strummed. She gasped.

The air got warmer. Her hands grew more adventurous, sliding along his naked body until they'd homed in on the hard-on that pressed between their bellies. His breathing became more labored, but he went for her mouth anyway, wanting the taste of her on his tongue. They kissed and fondled, murmuring sweet nothings to each other.

"This is almost like our first time," she whispered, releasing him to splay her hands across the clenched muscles below his navel, from hip bone to hip bone.

He made a gap at the top of the blankets, took a gulp of the cool air, then dove back down into their nest. "How's that?"

"We're not strangers anymore."

The defensive part of him—of Alex—wanted to brush off the newly forged intimacy. But Lex was reasserting himself, finding ways to meld the old personality with the new. Karina had no idea how right she was. They were starting over.

"Yes, but I knew you before I met you." His hands were under her pajama top again, stroking the satin skin on her back with one hand, raising goose bumps with the other as he tweaked her nipples. A couple of her buttons popped. He burrowed his head deeper beneath the covers, finding the valley between her lush breasts.

She cupped his head, holding him to her as she wrapped one leg around his hip, even the sole of her foot managing to up the pleasure as she rubbed it over his calf. "Mmm. But I've only just begun to know you."

He nibbled kisses along the fragrant curves, making circles until he'd reached the pebbled center. "Nice to meet you," he said, then sucked her nipple into his mouth, rolling it against his tongue for a few moments before drawing hard.

She squirmed, rocking against him, making soft encouraging noises as she shivered beneath his wandering hand. Shivered, this time, with desire. The heat captured between them had become thick and heavy, fragrant with peppermint and chocolate and arousal.

"I want you now," she demanded, reaching for him again.

He laughed softly. "But we only just met." His hands said otherwise and she exhaled with a deep sigh. He would do anything to please her, and this request was no hardship.

The pajama bottoms slipped past her hips with one tug and then she was open to him, so hot and tender that she jerked at his touch. Her grip tightened on his penis, giving it a tug that nearly blew his mind.

She undulated against him. "Quick," she said, "quick," and he made a blind grab at the condoms as she slid the pad of her thumb across the head of his erection.

He rolled one of them on. "I thought we'd go slow for once."

"Next time."

A much-needed draft of cool air breached their cocoon as he rose up, positioned himself between her open thighs and slowly sank into her welcoming body.

Sweet.

Tight.

Heaven.

Once he was all the way inside her, she let out a moan and wrapped herself around him. Her warm body moved like a wave, drawing him deeper into the relentless stream of pleasure. He rocked in and out of her and she matched him instinctively, moving in perfect sync, giving back with as much energy as she received. They locked hands, riding through the crashing pleasure, coming and coming and coming....

Alex collapsed, completely spent. Karina gasped under his leaden body. She breathed hard against his moist skin, reaching up to claw at the tangled blankets. "Oh, man, I'm so hot. I need oxygen!"

He tipped over onto his side and together they thrust their heads out from the covers, gasping with laughter.

After a minute, he rolled onto her, not finished with her yet, but she held his face away. "Wait, Alex." She made a crooning sound and touched a tentative finger to his mouth. "Your lips are a little swollen."

The chocolate.

He shrugged. "Too much kissing."

"Then we'd better stop." But her thighs clasped his hips.

"Nah. I'm tougher than that." With a lusty growl, he pulled the blankets back over their heads and went in for round two.

12

A COUPLE OF BUSY DAYS passed. The shop was overrun with customers, keeping the kitchen staff working overtime. Karina was barely able to manage quick hellos with Debby and the rest of her employees, which she chose to think of as a blessing. She didn't have time to fret over the identity of the mole. There were presents to buy and wrap, party details to confirm and decorations to finish. After staying up late to deck the halls of her apartment, she'd talked Alex into helping her with the final chore, the Christmas tree. She had played the sympathy card and told him that there was no more sad a task than decorating a tree solo, omitting that for the past year she'd had friends over for a tree-trimming, nog-drinking, girl-talking bash.

The day before the party, she took an hour off work to go with Alex to pick out a twelve-foot blue spruce. They wrangled the tree upstairs to her apartment and set it up near the spiral steps, making plans to do the decorating that evening. Mr. Alonzo was hovering in the hallway when they left the apartment, picking stray evergreen needles off the soles of his shoes. Karina apologized, promised she'd sweep up later and reminded him about the party. Alex cleared his throat. She rolled her eyes at him, but remembered to cheerily add, "And we'll be raiding the shop for dessert again this year, so don't forget to come!"

"You didn't say anything about the secret door," Alex commented as they trotted downstairs.

"How obvious do you want me to be? Besides, it's only Mr. Alonzo. I've made sure that everyone in the shop knows, so the trap is set. I have my doubts that it will be sprung—at least not tomorrow night."

Alex was noncommittal. "We'll see."

She gave him a quick hug outside the shop door. "Will you come inside, just for a minute? You still haven't met any of my co-workers."

He seemed reluctant, but finally nodded. "I want to check the layout of your office anyway."

"That again." She sighed as she pushed open the door. The shop was so crowded, customers had to shuffle about to make way for the new arrivals.

As they made their way to the back, Karina waved at the counter girls, pointing at Alex. "This is him! Alex Anderson."

He hustled her along. "Maybe you shouldn't be introducing me so loudly. We don't want to rouse antennae."

"They don't know you're a…" She glanced back at him and made another wild stab. "Interpol agent?"

"Karina! At last." Janine was on the spot as soon as they stepped into the reception room. "I've got a zillion details for you to approve. First, there's the Santa Claus. I handled that—he's booked. All you have to do is initial the expenditure and sign the check I've printed off…." She shoved a register at Karina before she'd managed to remove her hat and gloves.

Karina glanced over the paper and scrawled her signature. "Janine Gardner, this is Alex Anderson.

He's my—uh, my neighbor. He lives across the street."

Janine blinked owlishly, one eye twitching as she clasped her notebook to her chest.

Alex gave her a head-bob. "Hello."

"Alex was helping me with the Christmas tree." Karina shook the tree's sticky needles out of her hat. "It's a monster. Twelve feet tall."

"Will you be at the party, Janine?" he asked.

Janine's gaze went to Karina for approval. "Wouldn't miss it. Will I see you there, um, Alex?"

"Oh, no," Karina answered. "I mean, I asked, of course, but Alex is busy. He's not staff anyway, so he wouldn't know anyone." Alex pressed his knuckles to the small of her back, steadying her before she ran further amok.

Karina resisted the urge to squeeze her nose. She got nervous around anyone who'd made the top of her suspect list, which was irritating. Shouldn't she be angry with the saboteur?

But she was too giddy to maintain her anger for long. Especially now, with the holidays in the air and the promise of Alex on Christmas morning.

"The caterer is confirmed, as well," Janine said, keeping track of Alex from beneath her lashes as he walked toward Karina's office door.

There's certainly a compelling quality about him, Karina thought, admiring him herself. He had retained his brooding intensity, but ever since their dinner at Tavern on the Green there was a lighter air about him that made him much more approachable. Her feelings grew every time she saw him. Love was inches from her grasp, shiny and alluring as a bauble hung from the high branches of a tree.

Practical Janine continued. "And Nikki Silk is here, with a photographer."

"Oh, no! I completely forgot about our appointment." Karina tore off her coat and tossed it into Janine's arms. "Hang this up, please." She frantically smoothed her hair, which was scraggly from catching on the tree branches. "Where is Nikki now?"

Janine brushed a few more of the stray spruce needles off the coat. "In the kitchen, interviewing Debby. I told her you'd be along any minute."

"You said she brought a photographer? Oh, damn." Karina unclipped her hair, shook it out, then smoothed it back into a tight ponytail. "This was only supposed to be a preliminary interview. She mentioned nothing about pictures."

"I wanted candids of the shop," Nikki said from the office doorway. She wore a big smile, a chunky fake-fur jacket and orange vinyl thigh-high boots. "We're here to capture the inside story on candy-making. But we'll give you time to fix yourself up."

Karina rubbed her lips together. She'd applied a glossy balm that morning, but it had all been kissed away.

"And who is this?" Nikki said throatily, taking several slinky steps into the office. Karina turned. The *Hard Candy* reporter's gaze was pinned on Alex, who stood frozen at the threshold of her office.

"The booty call?" Nikki murmured *sotto voce* to Karina, but not *sotto* enough. Everyone heard, including the photographer, a young man with slouchy shoulders and three day's growth of beard, carefully cultivated.

If possible, Alex became even more tense. Karina felt it radiating off him, but she wasn't sure why. One thing was certain. He wouldn't want to be included in the article.

She touched Nikki's arm. "You promised. My private life isn't part of this."

"Oh, sure, sure." Nikki stroked her long dark hair, still looking admiringly at Alex. "But can you blame me for wanting an introduction?"

"Let me take your jacket first." Karina got it off and lobbed the fur at Janine. She turned toward Alex.

He ducked his head, murmured some excuse or other in a gruff voice, and rudely walked straight out of the room, almost knocking the photographer over.

"Alex, wait," Karina called, although she had little expectation that he would stop. Even their past few days of acting almost like a normal couple hadn't worn away all of his rough edges.

She threw a quick apology at Nikki and ran after him. The customers must have parted for him like the Red Sea, because he'd already reached the sidewalk. "Excuse me," she said, pushing through the crowd. "Make way. Coming through. Thank you."

Too late. By the time she got outside, Alex had already disappeared.

"AS GOD IS MY WITNESS, I'll never decorate again," Karina said to herself, resting her head in her hands. She sat midway up the spiral staircase, bone tired from the eventful day in the shop and three hours of tree trimming.

She'd given up waiting for Alex one hour in and had phoned Debby to come and help. They hadn't had any time together lately. But Debby had been evasive, muttering something about plans with Kyle before hanging up rather precipitously.

Trouble brewing there. Karina intended to take a few minutes at the party and pin Debby down to ask her what was up. Maybe it was only boyfriend problems. She'd never believe that her friend was the mole, but Kyle...he was another matter. If only because he was new and thus an unknown quantity, like others on her suspect list.

Karina climbed off the stairs. The tree was spectacular—tall and thick, trimmed out the wazoo with multicolored lights, glittery baubles, garlands of copper beads. All lit up, it filled the space with a festive glow and the unmistakable spicy scent of evergreen boughs.

There was still a mound of gifts to wrap and house cleaning to do, but she'd finish those chores tomorrow. Bed, now. After one more look at Alex's place.

She went to the window. Her curtains were open, the shades up, all lights on. No way for Alex to miss her lonesome tree-trimming session. She'd have been ticked off at him if she weren't so worried. Since he'd walked out of the office earlier in the day, her imagination had run overtime.

He'd been featured on *America's Most Wanted*...had changed his name and gotten plastic surgery...was a runaway crown prince....

More and more absurd.

His windows remained dark. There hadn't been even one sign, not a wrinkle in the blind or a single flash of the binocular's lenses to tell her that he gave a flying fig about deserting her.

Fine for him. She tried to harden her heart, but it was no use. He was wrestling with demons from his past and she could only hope that he won, and returned to her a whole man. She'd keep him, somehow she'd keep him, even if she had to feed him a truffle every day and two at night to ensure that he was too aroused to spend time worrying.

LATE THE NEXT DAY, Alex buzzed at Karina's door. It was an hour before the party, and she'd been back and forth between the shop and apartment a dozen times throughout the day, finalizing preparations and seeing to business. Each time, she'd checked his window. If he was watching, he was well hidden. She'd wondered if he'd backed out of his plan to catch a thief.

"Karina." Alex's voice on the intercom was hushed and distant, as if he spoke into a seashell. Appropriate, she thought. "We, uh, need to talk."

She swallowed. At least he hadn't said *discuss.*

"Talk?"

"And make our arrangements."

"Stay there. I'm coming down." She grabbed her keys and ran out the door, brushing by Mr. Alonzo coming up the stairs. They exchanged good cheer.

She tempered hers as she approached the lobby. Sure, Alex was back…this time. But what about tomorrow, or next week? She liked stability, consistency. She couldn't make a relationship with a man who was so unpredictable. So stubborn, so unknowable.

So mystifyingly right.

The vestibule door was open today. Alex was waiting inside when she reached the ground floor. He looked apologetic and her immediate response was to offer him a hug. She was weak.

"I only have a minute," she said, trying to be brisk. "My party supplier was late dropping off the extra chairs and tables, and the caterer is upstairs, getting the buffet ready to go—"

Alex interrupted. "Karina, look at me."

He knew he was asking for too much from her, between his disappearing act and his reluctance to answer any questions, but that was how it had to be.

"Karina," he said again, coaxing her. Finally she brought her face around and stared at him with big solemn eyes. Her mouth quivered at the corners before firming up.

"I'm sorry about yesterday," he said.

The apology got a nod. She was back to being the untouchable princess—hair braided into a tight knot, the serene countenance betraying very little emotion, her posture perfect in a ruby-red party dress that made her bare shoulders and arms look like they'd been carved out of alabaster. But he knew the warmth of her, inside....

"It was the photographer," he blurted, ashamed of himself for letting the old instinct for self-preservation take over. "And the reporter. If they had taken my picture—" The same old worries had come back, as strong as ever. He shook his head, disgusted with himself. "I can't chance being exposed."

She let out a small sigh. "Yes, I thought that might be it."

He steeled himself, but she asked for no more explanation and simply turned away, saying, "Let's do this quickly, shall we?"

He followed her through the small vestibule to a narrow space behind the stairs, ducking his head beneath the slanted ceiling.

"You see why I don't use this door." She sorted through the keys in her hand, unlocked the rough-hewn door and pushed back a rusty bolt. "It also locks from the other side. I had one of my employees clear out the supplies blocking the way so I could get to it."

"You've opened this door for previous parties?"

"Only at Christmastime."

"So it's no secret to your employees and the tenants in the building."

"Not among those who've been here more than a year. But you can see for yourself that the door hasn't been used lately." She gave it a shove.

"Let me help," he said, pushing with her when the door stuck.

It creaked as it opened, and they stepped through to the dimly lit storage corridor running between the kitchen and the office area of the shop.

Karina moved along, speaking crisply. "The children, especially, love entering the chocolate shop through this door. It gives them the feeling of sneaking in, I suppose, and getting to roam through areas they never see. The shop is set up for the visit, of course. Stocked with goodies. The guests are free to wander throughout, choosing as many treats as they like. Some are eaten on the spot, but the remainder go into the goody bags I provide. Otherwise they'd all be sick, going home."

Throughout this, she had given Alex a quick tour of the industrial kitchen, where the workers had departed but left behind the worktable strewn with a variety of chocolates. The candies were lined up on waxed-paper sheets, as if freshly made and not put away.

They wound up in her office, where the desk light had been left on. "Show me the safe," he said.

She went to a particular panel in the wainscoting and pushed her fingertips against the molding. The hidden door sprang open, revealing the heavy steel facing of the safe.

"What do you keep there?"

"It's fireproof, so I store business records, tax and insurance documents, a few computer disks. Nothing of particular value." She shut the panel. "I do have to go. The guests will be arriving soon."

"What's the agenda?"

"We have drinks and music, then the gift opening. I've booked a Santa Claus who arrives with a bag full of presents to distribute. Afterward, we eat, and sometime after that when the party starts to wind down, we come here for the desserts."

"All at once? Everyone?"

"A few of the adults might linger upstairs…." She gestured to the grate in the ceiling. "You'll hear us when that point comes, I'm sure."

"It's not me I'm concerned about."

Karina's hands clenched nervously. "I don't like you doing this. Please promise that you'll be careful."

"Nothing to worry about." He opened the small coat closet that he'd previously identified as his best hiding spot. "I don't even have to confront them, if you prefer. Identifying who's double-crossing you is what matters, especially as there's nothing for them to steal."

"But—"

He took a couple of swift steps and stroked his hand across her furrowed brow. "Nothing to worry about."

"Say it once more and maybe I'll start to believe you."

"Nothing…" He pressed his lips to her forehead. "To worry about."

She threw her arms around his neck in a tight hug. "Oh, Alex."

His eyes closed. *Nothing to worry about.*

"Come to the party instead." Her small hot kisses peppered his jawline. "Please."

"Too many people."

She inhaled. Stiffened. Stepped out of his arms. "Yes, of course." One palm stroked over the smooth satiny sheen of her hair. She pinched her nose. "Yes. Do what you want, then. I have to go."

Before, he would have believed she was back in control.

Before, he would have believed he was on his own.

TWO HOURS LATER, the party was in full swing. The somewhat disappointing Santa—too short and nasal to be convincing—had finished distributing the gifts. The guests had moved on to enjoy the elaborate buffet stocked with turkey, beef and a huge glazed ham, along with a dozen side dishes. Karina had told the Santa to help himself before leaving, then escaped to the kitchen on the pretense of getting more wine. What she wanted was a moment to think.

As far as she knew, Alex was still hiding in her office, waiting for the mole or his accomplice to return. She'd tried to keep track of anyone who might have disappeared from the party, but that was proving impossible. There were at least fifty people out there, the noise and activity astounding.

Karina gnawed her lip. Should she race downstairs to check on Alex? Or would that be one of those ditzy-heroine moves that she'd sworn not to do?

She peeked around the refrigerator into the party. Debby and Kyle stood nearby. He was chomping his way through a plate loaded with goodies, while she stood by his side, looking distracted. And not eating.

Karina waved to catch Debby's eye, then motioned her into the kitchen.

"Great party," Debby said when she arrived. "What are you doing in here all alone? Where's Alex?"

Karina waved off the question. "You're not eating."

"I'm on a diet."

"Oh, Deb. I thought Kyle likes you the way you are. You know—cuddly."

"Yeah, that's what he *said,* but…"

Karina's tone sharpened. "Has he given you a reason not to believe him?"

Debby let out a huge sigh. "As a matter of fact, yes. For the past few days, I've been trying to figure out if I should tell you."

Karina nodded reassuringly, even though she was stricken with apprehension. "Of course you should tell me. We're best friends. I'll understand. *Whatever* it is."

"Mmm, well, this is about you too."

Oh, God. Karina licked her lips. "The chocolate recipe?"

Debby's nose crinkled. "Sort of, I guess. Do you remember when I told you that Kyle wanted to talk? It turns out that he had a confession to make. He felt guilty because…"

Debby stopped to pluck a piece of tinsel off her black cashmere sweater. Karina grabbed the contoured lip of the granite countertop to stop herself from shaking the story out of her friend. What was wrong with her? Where was her usual cool head and practicality? This urgency was out of character.

Debby blinked at Karina. "I told him about the chocolate, about the sexual side effect."

"I see."

"I went on and on, blathering about how happy I was that he was attracted to me even without the chocolate.

It's not that I'm above using it, you know that, but it was just really nice not to have to. I didn't get it right away, but that's when he started acting funny."

Karina nodded energetically. *Get on with it.*

"So…he finally confessed. That day when I fell off the ladder into his arms? He'd just eaten one of the Black Magic truffles. And the thing is—" Debby pushed the fringe of curls off her forehead and looked at Karina with concern. "The thing is, he got the truffle from Alex. A whole box of them, minus one."

Karina was so taken aback she pulled her head in like a turtle. Alex had given away the truffles, right at the beginning? And she'd wasted her time, back when she'd worried that his feelings were chemically induced…?

She blinked. "I don't get it."

"It was the day after you went over there. Kyle happened to run into Alex on the street, and Alex gave him the truffles as a friendly gesture. Said he was allergic. Kyle didn't realize it was *your* Alex until I started blabbing. Maybe I shouldn't have done that, huh? I'm sorry."

"But…" Karina's mind spun, flipping through all the times she'd mentioned the truffles to Alex. Had he actually said he'd eaten them, or had she only assumed that he had? No, he'd claimed they were delicious at least once. After that, he'd been noncommittal. Now she knew why. "All right. So what if Alex didn't eat the truffles?"

"Don't you see? That means your affair is legit." Debby's shoulders slumped. "And mine isn't."

"That's all?" A wild laugh erupted from Karina. She threw her arms around Debby. "Oh, honey, don't worry about it! Here I thought you had something really serious to tell me, and this was all just about the truffles. I am so relieved, you wouldn't believe."

"Well, yeah. Alex has the serious hots for you. Me and Kyle, we're just—" Debby shrugged. "I know I always said that I wouldn't mind keeping a man in truffles as long as he made me happy in bed, but I was wrong. I don't want a cocoa-bean love affair. With Kyle, anyway, I want the real thing."

"That's not a difficult problem to solve. You cut him off from the chocolate and see what happens."

"Nah. Easier said than done. Kyle's already addicted. He keeps asking me for more of the stuff, and he has very effective means of persuasion. So far, I've been weak." Debby giggled, getting a little of her *oomph* back. "I'm not a drug dealer," she said with a wail. "I'm a chocolate dealer!"

"What's happening here? A little girl talk?" Nikki Silk entered the kitchen and with a natural ease, jumped up to plop her behind on the kitchen countertop. She swung her legs. "What're we gabbing about?"

"Chocolate," Karina said, too elated to care about what Nikki would make of them. Her gut had told her all along that what she had with Alex went beyond aphrodisiac, but now she was certain that Debby and Kyle were innocent. There was still the break-in to deal with, but that was minor to her, in the scheme of things. Love always took precedence.

"Chocolate," Debby echoed. She grinned. "And sex."

Nikki flashed them a toothy smile. "Ooh, my favorite combination. Like I always say, the only thing better than a naked man is a naked man covered in chocolate."

13

THE MECHANICAL FEMALE VOICE drifted down from above: "Give me your hand. I will tell your fortune."

Leaning inside the closet, Alex gritted his teeth. For the past two hours he'd listened to Esmeralda the Gypsy Queen and her plinkety-plonk music play over and over again. Karina would make back the cost of the party on quarters alone.

The Santa Claus's refrains of *ho-ho-ho, Merry Christmas* had trailed off, which meant the guests were moving on to the buffet. Alex had begun to think that he'd guessed wrong and there would be no attempts on the safe tonight. But he wasn't giving up. Not on any of it.

The closet door was open a few inches for air. He put his ear to the crack for the hundredth time, listening for sounds from the reception area. This time, he heard what he'd been waiting for.

Murmuring. A conversation.

Two men? Surprised, Alex pulled the door shut, leaving himself the narrowest crack for spying. Adrenaline raced through his bloodstream. The instincts he'd honed in the year since he'd left California were as sharp as ever. He battled the urge to run, or to leap out and fight, telling himself that there was no reason to believe that these men were after him.

He was here to defend Karina, no matter what terrible images and stark terror the situation made him relive.

The push-button knob on the office door was locked, but anyone with a paper clip could open it with a little effort. Alex stopped breathing when the knob rattled. On the other side, there came more murmuring, then the metallic *snick* of the potential thieves springing the lock.

Alex used the intruders' entrance to cover the small muffled sounds of moving himself deeper into the closet. In case they would think to check the closet, he'd hung up his long coat for camouflage and had positioned himself behind it. Good enough to fool a cursory glance.

"Quickly," said a man.

"Should be right here." Soft thumps and pats came from the office. Alex didn't want to risk peeking yet, but he could tell they were looking for the safe.

"Aha. Here we go." The second man had a cold, humorless chuckle. "Do you have the combination?"

"I thought you memorized it. Be my guest."

"Shh. No talking."

Alex heard the quiet clicks of the lock being turned. He put one hand on the coat hanger nearest him so it wouldn't screech and leaned toward the door. Two figures were huddled at the safe opposite Karina's desk.

The light in the inner office was too dim for him to make out the hunched man working the dial. But the other was…

Santa Claus?

Nice move, Alex thought, remembering that Janine had handled the booking.

"It's not opening," the safecracker hissed.

"Let me try," Santa said. He spun the dial, worked the combination, then pounded on the heavy door when it refused to open.

Inside the closet, Alex smiled. Apparently Karina's ploy had worked.

"It was your girl who got us the combination," the second man said. "What now?"

"I'll try the computer. You keep working on the lock." Santa went to sit behind the desk, barely three feet away from the coat closet. A bald head with a fringe of iron-gray hair was revealed when he swept off the fur-trimmed hat. He rubbed the sweat from his brow, then slipped on a pair of glasses and limbered his fingers. "Heh. Now you'll see what I can do."

Alex pulled back a couple of inches. He'd instantly recognized the man in the Santa suit. It was the same guy who'd been lurking in the store, the customer he'd suspected might be after *him* instead of the chocolate.

Still a faint possibility. But remote, Alex reassured himself. He flexed his fingers before reaching around for his gun. Just in case.

The computer keys clicked rapidly. "Okay, I'm at the protected files. What was that password?"

"Look for yourself. Under the blotter."

"Thought you memorized it, Freddy."

A fist rapped on the wood paneling. "Quit the nit-picking and get on with it, will you? We don't have much time."

Santa moved a couple of items off the blotter and tilted it up. "KJSTRSTALEX," he read. "Or is that A-*one*-E-X?"

"Read it to *yourself*."

A robotic female voice interrupted. "Give me your

hand." Giggles accompanied the carnival music drifting down through the grate. "I will read your fortune."

Santa jumped. "What the hell was that?"

"Keep your voice down." The other guy pointed at the grate. "It's from upstairs. Remember, I told you. They thought that was why you got away last time. They didn't figure I might have called to warn you."

"Scared me out of my boots," Santa muttered.

"Is the password working?"

Santa typed, then cursed. "No."

The other guy came toward the desk and in the light of the computer screen, Alex finally identified him.

Karina's mild-mannered neighbor, Mr. Alonzo.

"We've been tricked. Dammit." Alonzo flipped up the desk blotter, then tossed it to the floor in anger. "I knew that was too convenient. Both the combination and the password, in one place, so easy to find when they weren't before? And your foolish daughter fell for it."

"So did you."

"Shut the computer down. We're getting out of here."

"Give me ten minutes. I can crack this code and get into the files."

"What good will that do us? The recipe's got to be in the safe."

"You don't know for sure. At least let me try. We may never get back in here again. Tonight's our best shot. My contact is waiting for that recipe. I need it *now*."

"Go it on your own, then," Alonzo said. "I'd rather live to try another day." His gaze scanned around the office, traveling from the safe to the grate to the computer…but lingering on the closet.

Alex, his eye to the thread line of the crack, did not

move. Even in darkness, the slightest shift might be apparent.

"Guard the door," Santa said. "If you leave and I find the recipe on my own, I'm keeping it for myself."

"Bullshit you are. I was the one who found out about the aphrodisiac effect of the chocolate in the first place."

Alex blinked. *Aphrodisiac?*

"So what? The recipe wouldn't be worth squat if I couldn't sell it for a bundle. Those greedy corporate bastards will pay this time." Santa tapped the keys. The screen flashed: *Password Denied.* "Remember, putting Janine on the inside with that fake résumé was my idea."

"I wouldn't be bragging about that if I were you. If she had any smarts she would have been able to get into the safe on her own instead of wasting weeks looking for the damn thing." While Alonzo talked, he walked slowly around the desk until he was standing behind Santa's shoulder. His rabbitlike eyes stared straight ahead.

Alex's instincts prickled. He clicked the safety off on the gun.

He was ready when Alonzo made a sudden grab for the knob. With all his weight, he shoved the door open, knocking Alonzo into the desk chair, which skidded forward, mashing both men up against the computer in a tangle of arms and legs.

Before the yelling pair could sort themselves out, Alex was out of the closet, gun raised. "Hey, guys. I've been waiting for you. Put your hands up in the air and don't move."

Santa said, "What the hell?"

Alonzo's chin jutted. "Are you a cop?"

"No, I'm not a cop," he said. "So there's nothing

holding me back from shooting you for trespassing and attempted burglary." He waggled the gun. "Hands up."

They both complied, though Santa's knees gave out and he collapsed into the swivel desk chair. It thunked against the desk. "Goddamn. This can't be happening. We were so close. Wanda was counting on the recipe bringing us a big payday."

"My sister never should have married a loser like you in the first place," Alonzo hissed. "I told her that at the wedding."

The other man's face twisted with bitterness. "The layoffs at my company weren't my fault."

"Quit the squabbling," Alex said.

The two of them were so hapless, he felt safe in letting his guard down, after he'd done a quick pat down to be sure they had no weapons. He tucked his gun away and picked up the phone.

"Not the cops," Santa whined. "I've got one of the top guys at Royal Foods sweating bullets for this secret recipe. I'll cut you in on the cash."

Alex didn't bother responding. After a couple of rings, a voice he didn't know answered in the apartment above. He asked for Karina. "It's safe to come down now," he said. "Bring Janine. And Kyle."

Alonzo's eyes shifted toward the door. Alex put down the phone and positioned himself to block the way.

Santa stood. "We can take him, Freddy."

Alex shrugged. "Go ahead. Try it."

But Alonzo was thinking it through. "Keep cool, Sam. We haven't done anything illegal."

"Except breaking and entering," Alex said.

"We're guests at this party. We wandered downstairs. The door was open, so who can fault us?"

"The office door was locked."

Alonzo's mouth twisted into an ugly grin. "Got proof?"

Alex had to concede, if only to himself, that there would be very little to charge the pair with.

Karina rushed into the office. Kyle was right behind her, escorting a reluctant Janine. An excited Debby pushed in behind them, pressing Janine forward into the room.

The office assistant gasped. "Dad! Uncle Freddy! What are you doing here? And, uh, why are you wearing a Santa suit?" Janine Gardner was not a good actress.

"Mr. Alonzo?" Karina gaped in shock. "Why are you here?" She looked at Alex. "What the hell—"

He tried to explain. "From what I can figure, Alonzo and this man are brothers-in-law. They picked your lock and entered the office. Tried to break into the safe and the computer—unsuccessfully, thanks to the fake codes you planted."

"Those were fake?" Janine said, genuinely surprised this time.

"Keep your mouth shut!" the bald man, Sam Gardner, said. He ripped off the red jacket of his Santa suit; underneath was a pillow strapped to a rather sunken chest. He aimed a sickly smile at Karina. "You're a nice lady. Why don't you just let us out of here and we won't be any more trouble to you?"

"I know you," she said. "You've been in the store."

Janine frowned. "I *told* you that you didn't need to keep an eye on me, Dad."

Karina had put together the pieces, but her expression remained puzzled. "Why did you want Kyle?" she asked Alex. "If you think he's involved, you're wrong. Debby and I talked—"

Alex cut her off. "Kyle's here as muscle, that's all. I didn't want these two trying to make a break for it."

Kyle nodded and set himself in the doorway, arms crossed over his chest, bulkier than ever in a red sweater knitted with a snowflake design.

"Okay," Karina said softly. She seemed relieved, until her gaze returned to her neighbor. "Mr. Alonzo! How could you?"

"Sorry," he said in a plaintive voice, making his mouth go droopy. "I only did it because of this jerk, my brother-in-law, Sam. He worked in the computer division at Royal Foods for twenty-seven years, but they laid him off with only a measly pension."

Cue the violins, Alex thought.

"He came to me and said that if he could just bring in a big idea like the aphrodisiac chocolates you sell, the company would rehire him. What could I do? I had to help, to keep my sister and niece off the street." Alonzo gave a heaving sigh. "I didn't intend you any harm. I swear it. All we wanted was to find out the secret to your recipe."

The meek-and-contrite act was ruined by his brother-in-law's snarl. "You weasel! Blaming this on *me* when it was your idea all along. Janine will back me up. You came to me!"

Santa Sam reared back to take a swing. Alex stepped in, grabbing the man's arm. He forced it down, then looked at Karina for further instruction. She seemed to be taking everything in stride. Perhaps too calmly. "Listen, Karina, don't be fooled by their excuses."

"You don't have to tell me that. I can see for myself." But she looked sadly at Alonzo. "Janine's betrayal is bad enough, but I'm shocked at you especially, Mr. Alonzo.

My neighbor. How dare you try to rob me—and then have the gall to lie about it right to my face?"

Color flared in the tenant's face. "Go ahead and call the cops then. You don't have anything on us."

"I'm afraid he's right," Alex said. "An attempted burglary is about it."

Debby chimed in. "How about the one who masqueraded as Santa Claus?"

"I hired him," Janine said. "Fair and square."

"Just shut up, Janine," Karina snapped. "You could have had a legitimate job here, a good one."

"You want me to call the police?" Debby asked.

Karina put her hands over her face, took a deep breath, then obviously came to her decision. "All right. Here's what we're going to do. Janine, clean out your desk. You're fired. You—Santa, whatever your name is, you can go with her. I don't want to see either of you ever again, and you can consider yourselves *extremely* lucky that I'm not pressing charges. Mr. Alonzo—your lease is officially broken. I want you out immediately. Tonight."

"But it's the holidays! Where will I go?"

She gave him a grim smile at the absurdity of his statement. "I'm sure your loving family will take you in."

Karina turned to go, but then stopped to make one more pronouncement. "And just so you all know, the chocolate recipe was never here. It's in a safety deposit box. At the bank. Right, Debby?"

Debby nodded vehemently. "Abso-frickin-lutely."

Karina linked arms with her chef. "Come on, let's go serve up some chocolate. I hear the guests arriving." She glanced at Alex, then Kyle. "Can you two clean up the garbage in here?"

"Sure thing," Kyle said. "As long as my girlfriend saves me one of those extraspecial truffles."

Debby stopped short. "What if I can't? Will I still be your girlfriend?"

"Hell, yeah. You're plenty sweet enough for me."

"Oh, huggy bear. I hope you mean that." Debby launched herself at Kyle and the two locked lips.

Karina hovered in the doorway, seemingly only slightly ruffled from the confrontation with the trio of crooks. She smoothed her dress, gave Alex a long look that he wasn't able to decipher, then hurried away to divert the converging guests. If she'd wanted him to stay, she'd given no overt sign of it. Not even a nose pinch.

His initial relief at learning that he was still safe, identity intact, had turned sour. The situation hadn't improved. He remained stuck between the proverbial rock and hard place, knowing that there could be no sweet freedom without Karina at his side.

KARINA WOKE UP ALONE on Christmas morning. She stretched, scratched her head, mumbled to herself. Delaying getting out of bed. There was nothing waiting for her.

Not Alex, anyway.

With a groan, she buried her head under the pillow. She'd wanted a fling, and she'd had a really fabulous one. Nothing to be sad over.

Several days had gone by since the employee party and the discovery of the trio of crooks. Frederick Alonzo had moved out that night as directed, and Karina felt fairly confident that the incident was over. Alex had grumbled at her later about giving them a free pass, but in her estimation, all's well that ended well. The recipe had never been in danger, although she'd learned a valuable lesson about keeping the most important component—the contact information of the supplier of the special cocoa beans—equally safe. Mr. Alonzo and the Gardners would never know how close they'd actually come to the secret ingredient.

A ringing phone finally got Karina out of bed. She exchanged holiday greetings first with her parents calling from Switzerland and an hour later with her brother and his family in California. She then put a pot of coffee on and went to the bathroom.

She washed her hands and brushed her teeth at the pedestal sink. The mirror revealed a sorry sight. Bedhead and pillow creases, rumpled pajamas. Bloodshot eyes. She'd been to a wild office party at *Hard Candy* with Nikki and Whitney, and they'd overindulged in vodka chocolates while taking turns spying on Whitney's alleged "Strangler" and his latest conquest. The man was a Lothario, not a murderer.

She tried to flatten her hair, then gave up with a shrug. What did it matter? Alex had given no indication that he wanted to join her, despite the earlier promise.

He'd wigged out on trimming the tree, too, she remembered. The man was simply not a stayer. Not a keeper. And she had no business feeling so empty inside. They'd had a good time while it lasted.

Karina slumped into the living area and plugged in her Christmas tree. Later, she'd have to put on a happy face. Debby and Kyle were coming over for dinner and drinks. How ironic that they were the couple who were going to last, when they'd been the ones who'd actually founded their relationship on a chocolate-based attraction.

Technically, so had she. Never would she have gone

over to Alex's that first time on her own. But after that, when she'd been so willing to blame their actions on the chocolate…

Her face flushed as she admitted the truth to herself.

The lust had been real.

Whether any of it had turned to love remained to be seen.

She looked across the street to Alex's place. The binoculars were long gone, and so was he. Since the staff party, she'd seen him a couple of times. Briefly. He'd seemed apologetic, but distant. Her pride kept her from begging for another chance when they both knew that it was he who had to make a decision.

Gaily wrapped gifts awaited her under the tree, but she had no enthusiasm for opening them. There was only one present she wanted to unwrap—Alex. That evening in Central Park, he'd loosened up and she'd gotten a tantalizing glimpse at who he really was.

Karina pinched her nose. *Get a grip, girl. He's a Chinese puzzle box. You'll never know—*

The door buzzed.

She froze, not daring to hope.

It went off again. *Bzzzz.*

She ran to the door, slipping on her socks, and stabbed at the button. "Alex?"

"Yes," he said.

She dropped her head forward, praying that he was here for the right reasons. "Are you coming to say goodbye?"

Six seconds passed like an hour before his voice crackled through the intercom speaker. "I'm coming to say hello."

With a shaking finger, she buzzed him in. *Please, please, please…*

She had the door open before he arrived. No need for acting cool when she was as jumpy and expectant as a kid on Christmas morning. Alex appeared, looking so good her heart began beating like crazy.

He nodded down the hall. "Alonzo?"

"No sign of him, and the locks have been changed."

"And me?"

She stepped aside to let him in. "You're always welcome."

He looked closely at her flushed face. "Have you been eating chocolate already?"

"Not even a sniff." They hadn't talked about the aphrodisiac, or how she'd attempted to seduce him under the influence, but from a couple of comments he'd made, she knew he'd figured it out.

"In fact, I haven't had any of the special stuff for days." The vodka chocolates from the night before hadn't been from her shop, though Debby had started talking about developing a few recipes to inspire their customers to new heights.

"Maybe you should go eat one of the truffles," Alex suggested. "Make this easier on me."

"No way. I need a clear head when I'm dealing with you."

He opened a hand. "But I was hoping to trade you." A chocolate kiss sat on his palm. "Even up."

She melted. "Oh, Alex…"

He kissed her, and as always she lost herself to the sweetest pleasure she'd ever known. Chocolate be damned. Alex was the aphrodisiac for her.

"I have to tell you." She made herself step away. "That first day, when I came to your apartment with the truffles—"

"Later," he said, skimming off his coat.

"This is important."

"Gifts first." He put a hand on Esmeralda's booth for balance and started taking off his boots.

Karina didn't care. She grabbed him for a hug, laughing at her sudden sense of elation. In the blink of an eye, her world had been wonderfully transformed. "You bought me a gift?"

"Of course I did." Standing on one leg with a boot hanging off his toes, he teetered and grabbed again for Esmeralda, jarring the booth. The light flickered, red, purple, gold. The mechanism whirred.

"Give me your hand," Esmeralda said. Alex kicked a boot at her. "I will tell your fortune."

"Don't be so skeptical." Karina grabbed the card as it emerged from the slot. She stuck it in her pajama pocket without looking. "Esmeralda's always right. On the day that we met, she told me a dark stranger would enter my life."

"Sam Gardner?" Alex teased.

"Uh-huh. Sure." She led him to the sparkling Christmas tree. "Perhaps I fed truffles to the wrong man. Or rather *didn't* feed them…."

"Trust me. You got the right man." He took her hand. "The truffles don't matter a bit when it comes to how much I want you."

"You know, then?"

"Aphrodisiac chocolates? I suppose if people believe in them, they work."

"It's true, I promise you." She stared at Alex, unblinking, her fingers tightening where they laced with his. "I'm going to trust you with my biggest secret. Mr. Alonzo and his brother—they went after the recipe, when all they really needed was to buy out my Brazilian supplier of the bulk chocolate made from some very unique cocoa beans. That's where the magic is, not in a recipe."

Alex shook his head. "There's no recipe?"

"Oh, yes. There is. And it really is in a bank—in Switzerland. It just also happens to be on a card in a recipe box in the kitchen at Sutter Chocolat. Debby doesn't really need it, she knows the instructions and ingredients by heart. It's a good recipe, too, but any other recipe would do nearly as well. The aphrodisiac is in the cocoa beans."

"I can't tell if you're kidding me."

She gave him an enigmatic smile, then stepped closer to smooth a hand over his lopsided collar. "So you're allergic to chocolate, huh?"

His eyes narrowed. "Who told you?"

"Debby, via Kyle. You gave him the truffles."

"Oh, yeah. That's right." He lifted their linked hands and kissed her knuckles. "Forgive me for misleading you?"

She tilted her head. Their eyes connected. The current was as strong and hot as ever. "Forgive me for trying to seduce you with inappropriate measures?"

"That's not something that's necessary to forgive. I prize the day you showed up on my doorstep with your funny hat and fevered face. I thought you were crazy, of course—"

She closed her eyes, expecting to be mortified all over again, but her feelings had changed. Maybe she wasn't as in control, but that meant she was open to a lot of wonderful experiences she would have missed otherwise.

"—but you've never been out of my mind since. As hard as I've tried to get away."

Her eyes welled as soon as she opened them, spangling her lashes so his face was a blur. "How hard did you try?" she asked, but what she really wanted to know was *why.*

He only squeezed her hand, using it to draw her down to the furry white throw she'd placed near the tree. Gifts from her friends and family were piled nearby, but the only one that she cared for at the moment was the small package that Alex pulled from his back pocket.

He sat beside her, offering it without a word.

The gift was wrapped in wrinkled tissue paper and tied with a bit of colored string. No tape. When she scraped off the knotted string, the wrappings fell away. Alex had given her a rough wooden box with painted decorations. Swoops and swirls of once-bright color were now faded by wear. A decal in the center, half-rubbed away, bore the image of a Ferris wheel and the words Orange County Fair.

"It's not new," he said. "Obviously. It's mine, from when I was a kid. I won it at a fair. A carnival."

"Ahh."

"Look inside."

She lifted the lid. Empty.

Alex's eyes glinted at her, and suddenly she understood. She ran her fingertips over the small box, soon discovering a hidden panel that tilted up to reveal a second compartment, flat and narrow. Reverently, she lifted out the small pile of photos it held. Old pictures, slightly discolored. She went through them. A laughing boy romping in the surf. The same boy with what must be his parents, standing on the deck of a sailboat. The father looked like an older Alex, tall and dark, one arm around his wife, the other around the child.

Alex. The next photo was clearly him. A teenager with sun-bleached hair and a big white smile, holding a surfboard and a trophy.

Karina's heart was beating so hard she could feel it. Two more photos. The first was a candid of an adult version of Alex, amid a group of friends, both men and women, most of them with a beer bottle in hand. He was laughing again, his eyes as bright as a sunny sky. He was more subdued in the final picture, posed standing on the steps of what appeared to be a courthouse, wearing a suit and tie. She looked closer. The tie sported a hand-painted hula girl.

So this was Alex. She was meeting him at last.

"That's me, Mark Lexmond," he said.

"What?" She flinched. "Your name is Mark? Not Alex?"

"Now it is. Alex, I mean. I'm going to stay Alex Anderson. It feels right to me. Because—" his hand slid along her arm and she leaned into the reassuring touch "—I like how it sounds, coming from you."

She tested the other name. "Mark Lexmond."

"My nickname was Lex."

"Lex?"

"Not as in Luthor. But I did have a Superman complex, until I learned without a doubt that I was no man of steel."

She spoke through numb lips. "What do you mean?" There was something horribly sad in his eyes now and she almost didn't want to know, but this was important. Life-and-death important, she could tell.

"I've lied to you about a lot of things. I was never a writer—I was a lawyer. A defense attorney. I'd had a friend, in high school, just eighteen. He got in trouble, but he didn't belong in prison...." Alex shook his head. "Long story short—I was out to protect the poor and downtrodden, only it didn't take too long before I realized that ninety-five percent of them were guilty as sin. It was the other five percent who kept me going."

She put her hand on his. "And what happened?"

"A couple of years ago, I took on a murder case. The defendant was guilty. I knew it, the prosecutors knew it, the judge knew it. But halfway through the trial, I helped broker a deal between my client and the federal authorities and the charge was knocked down from second-degree murder to manslaughter."

Alex stopped. "I shouldn't be telling you this."

"Why?"

"It's dangerous for you to even know me."

She looked at the photo of the laughing boy on the beach. "Finish the story." Hearing the wrenching pain in his voice hurt her, but he needed to tell all of it. The best she could do for him now was to listen.

"Let me skim some of the details. They don't matter to you." He pulled loose from her to rake his hands through his hair. "What happened was...the father of the young man who'd been killed by the defendant in the case wasn't pleased with the outcome. To put it mildly. He was a powerful man, a kingpin in the drug trafficking trade. He swore that my client would pay, and that I would, too, for brokering the deal. A few months later, the defendant was found dead."

Alex lifted his shoulders, then let them fall, defeated. "The Feds who'd been after the kingpin wanted me to go into protective custody, for a few months at least. I refused. Stubborn, partly, but I also couldn't believe what was happening." He glanced at Karina, with a ghostly smile on his lips. "Even with the uglier aspects of my job, my life up to then had been easygoing—surfing, partying, sports cars and beautiful women. The death threat didn't seem real."

"But it was."

He nodded. "Someone invaded my house one night, but I heard them breaking in and I got away in time. After that, I was convinced. So…"

"No more Mark Lexmond," she guessed.

He nodded. "I said goodbye to my friends and father, still hoping I'd be back before too long, and went into the Witness Protection Program. For a while I was in limbo while the authorities tried to put together a case against Nor—the man who threatened me. They weren't successful.

"So I was given a new identity and sent to Florida. For a time I retained my paranoia. The threat hung over me, making me suspicious of everyone I saw. But eventually I began to believe that I was safe."

His voice was hoarse now. The strain in his face tugged at Karina's heart. She wanted to hold him, love him, tell him that it would be all right. But what did she know?

"I began to relax," he continued. "I had a new name, was working as a bartender. Living the good life in the southern sun. I almost felt like my old self. Then one weekend morning, out of nowhere, a tourist was shot by a sniper. One foot away from me. I'd bent down to pick up a few coins the guy had dropped after buying an Italian ice from a street vendor."

An anguished cry flew from Karina's mouth before she could clap her hand over it to keep her distress inside. She didn't want to add her emotions to Alex's burden.

He went on. "They shouldn't have been able to find me. All I could think was that there'd been a mole in the system who'd leaked information about my whereabouts, so when I left Florida I did it on my own—no more contact with the U.S. Marshals. Completely alone. I figured that's how it'd be for the rest of my life until—" His voice, fissured with cracks, finally broke. "Until you."

It all made sense now. The surreptitious use of the binoculars, the suspicion masquerading as rudeness, his inner struggle. The vivid chapter he'd written. The extreme reaction to Nikki Silk and the photographer. Even his dedication to finding *her* mole.

"I'm trying to…" She waved a hand, at a loss for words. His story was too much to take in. Far more devastating than her silly guesses. "W-what happens now?"

"I've been asking myself that question for the past several weeks."

"Do you think you're safe?"

"So far, yes. I had a few suspicions about your lurker, but clearly I was way off."

"You told me that you might have to leave at any time…."

"Yes. Just pick up and go."

"But that's no way to live!"

He sighed. "I know. If I stay, though, I put you in danger, too."

She placed the photos in his childhood keepsake and closed the lid. "Then this should be *my* choice." Hugging the box to her chest, she raised her eyes to his.

One look and he knew. "Karina, I can't let you sacrifice—"

"What sacrifice? We'll go on as if you're safe, and if ever there's reason to suspect…well, then I'll go with you." Determination surged through her. "Don't bother trying to change my mind. You forget that I served time as an ambassador's daughter. I'm familiar with tight security and emergency plans, and even moving from one place to another. I can handle it."

"No. If you had to give up everything just for me—" Alex's voice broke off. He couldn't stop shaking his head.

Until she pushed the box under the tree and clasped his face between her hands. "That might not happen, right? But if it does—I'd rather be with you, anywhere in the world, than here, alone."

"You're not alone. You have friends and family. I know what it's like to leave people behind and I wouldn't wish that on my worst enemy, let alone…" He turned his face to kiss her palm. "The woman I love."

"Ah." She touched her nose to his. "That's no way to deter me." Her lips pooched out to plant a tiny peck on his mouth. "Tell me, without being a noble martyr, do you *want* to stay?"

She swore she pulled the word out of him by her own strength of will, but finally his resistance crumbled and his body relaxed and he said, with a longing that matched her own, "*Yes.*"

"Then you'll stay. As Alex. And we'll be vigilant. You can write, I'll run the shop and we'll live happy, full lives without any fanfare."

"It won't be that easy."

"Nothing ever is." She kissed him again. "Except seduction by chocolate."

His mouth twitched. "I really am allergic, you know."

"That's okay. We'll leave the truffles to Debby and Kyle."

He looped his arms around her waist, pulling her

closer. "Tell me, if there's an aphrodisiac in the chocolates, how did you dare let your party guests consume so many at once? Children too."

"Oh. Well, the thing is—we get a limited supply of the special chocolate. So the majority of our candies are—" She held up two fingers. "Just a *teensy* bit potent. It's amazing what the power of suggestion will do."

"Don't I know it." He gave a dry laugh, the haunted look lingering in his eyes. She supposed that might never change.

They must always live for the moment, she realized. And that meant no holding back. No keeping tight control.

"Alex…" She wanted to kiss him again, but even more, she wanted to say this while looking deep into his eyes. She would drive out the past and replace it with the here and now. "Alex, I love you, with all my heart. And you'd better get used to it, because I'm no fling. There won't be any leaving me behind." To combat the urge to pinch her nose, she took his hand and threaded their fingers together into a knot. "We're bound by a secret now, you and I. I'm pretty good at keeping secrets."

"So I found out." He smiled, before leaning in to kiss behind her ear. "About your password…"

"I don't give out my password."

"The fake one. KJSTRSTALEX."

"Just a little message to you." She smiled. "My initials are KJS. TRST—trust. I trust you, Alex, no matter what name you use."

She sensed that he wanted to debate, threaten, scold, anything at all to get her to see reason, but she wasn't having it. Not on Christmas morning, when she'd been given the gift of a lifetime. Alex, Lex, Mark, it didn't matter. The man was hers.

Their kisses were sweet, soft, sacred. After awhile they began to laugh for no reason, except relief, perhaps, and then Alex's hands were inside her pajama top. She tilted her head back, lost in the glimmer and spicy musk and the pleasure moving through her, so good even without the chocolate rush.

Alex stopped. "What's this?" He felt Esmeralda's card in her breast pocket. "Ah, the fortune."

"We don't need that," she said, finally understanding that the future was unknowable.

"Just this once." Alex put his fingers into the pocket, wickedly stroking across her breast before he fished out the card. He looked so serious when he read it that she expected the worst, a dire prediction of doom and gloom.

"Huh," he said. "What do you think of that?"

She read the card he held up. Machine Out Of Fortunes. Buy More At Sanders Carnival Supply Co. 1000 Cards For $10.00.

Humor plucked at Alex's mouth. "What do you think that means? We're out of luck?"

"No." Karina took his hand and returned it her breast. "It means that from now on, our fortune is our own to create. And I think we will do just fine."

"Remarkable, even."

"Spectacular."

"Stellar."

"Stellar," she agreed. "Merry Christmas…*Alex.*"

He stroked her hair. "Merry Christmas, Karina." Kissed the tip of her nose. "And, finally…hello."